BRETT EDWARDS

Sacred Land

BANDIDOS YANQUIS
incorporated

First published by Bandidos Yanquis, Inc. 2020

This novel is entirely a work of fiction. The names, characters and incidents portrayed in it are the work of the author's imagination. Any resemblance to actual persons, living or dead, events or localities is entirely coincidental.

First edition

ISBN: 978-1-7348226-0-1

Editing by Jackson Palmer
Agent: Alison Marckstadt
Cover art by Jonathan Sainsbury

This book was professionally typeset on Reedsy.
Find out more at reedsy.com

1

PAPPY CUSTER could see the casino through the window, above the ponderosas, its gold trim glinting in the sun. The longer he stared the closer it seemed to get, like a mast, expanding, consuming everything in its path.

At the base of the mountain was a good chunk of the Flying-C—at least where some of the action was. The segundo and a few other hands had run about three hundred head into the corral and were now separating the calves from the cows. The days were long gone since Pappy was in the mix, though he didn't miss it like he thought. Times were different and changing faster than he cared to keep up.

Out in the pasture he could see his grandson riding this way astride a red roan, a small plume of dust kicking against the slanted rays of the rising sun. And there, trailing maybe ten paces, was a smaller plume skipping and bumping over the rolling terrain.

As the roan drew closer, Pappy could see a calf across his grandson's lap, what looked like entrails coming out of its midriff. And that small plume of dust trailing? Pappy could now see it was a grey wolf being dragged by a rope. He watched Cody dismount then pull the calf from the saddle as two ranch hands and the segundo rushed to help. They hauled the calf away, but not before exchanging a few words. Cody said something and everyone nodded except the short, barrel-chested one. He seemed to laugh, or maybe it was a scoff, before saying something back which made Cody turn and say something else, this time more assertive, pointing a finger at the calf, then at shorty.

"Just initial here, here, sign and date here," the attorney said, snapping Pappy's attention back to the fold-out tray before him.

Pappy glanced at the document and pretended to skim it. "And that's it, right? 'Cause the last one come in wouldn't do what I asked."

"You seem perfectly coherent to me. Once you sign, it's stone."

Pappy lifted the cheap pen. His hand shook. He wondered why this guy hovering in his fancy suit couldn't use something with a little more weight to it. He scratched his initials on a few pages, but couldn't remember where he was supposed to sign so he looked up, hesitating when he saw the guy fixed on the bookshelf.

"That flag is quite unique," the attorney said. "Looks very old."

Pappy sighed. He kept forgetting to get rid of that damn thing. Have Cody put in storage or something, but goddamn was he tired of looking at it. Tired of people like this guy asking questions about it.

He told the attorney it was a parting gift from Uncle Sam after his great-grandaddy was slaughtered by Crazy Horse at Little Bighorn.

The attorney swiveled back, looking down now over the gold rim of his glasses. "Your great grandfather was *the*

Colonel Custer?"

"Unfortunately."

"What do you mean, *unfortunately?*" the attorney said, bouncing from the flag and back to Pappy again.

"Ain't exactly a legacy I'm proud of. Man was an egotistical sumbitch. And the papers, they kept feeding it. Made up a load of shit and built him into this war hero he never was. Sure, maybe he was a fine officer a point in time, but he bought into his own press and that was beginning of the end. And how you think that served me—a last name that comes locked and loaded with a shitass reputation?"

The attorney looked uncomfortable, his eyes drifting to a corner of the ceiling. He started to speak but Pappy told him it was rhetorical. Tired now of looking at this guy, his narrow frame, his soft hands. Guy like this, a little pissant, he wouldn't last a day on this ranch.

The attorney said, "Yes sir, of course." He wiped the sweat beading over his lip, then grabbed the document and tucked it under an armpit. "If you need anything—"

"I didn't sign it yet."

"Sorry?"

"The last page. I's tryin to figure out where I'm supposed to sign when you started on Old Glory over there."

"Oh, right," the attorney said, flattening the document on the fold-out again. He flipped to the last page, pointed near the bottom and held the edge as Pappy signed. "Now if you need anything, anything at all, my card is next to the lamp."

That's when Pappy heard the boy coming up the porch steps, his boots popping over the wooden slats.

* * *

Cody Custer entered the ranch house thinking about the noises that heifer made when he found her. The high-pitched whines, the congested, gargled breaths.

It had taken most the morning to round up the stock. Another hour and a half to run them down to the corral. He remembered having the roan at a nice lope, running ramrod, when the segundo cycled back on his paint mare saying, "Three-forty-nine, *y tu?*"

"Shit, I thought my count was off." Cody eased the contact against the roan's mouth and looked at the tree line. "Keep 'em movin. I'll double back, see if any scattered."

He rode across an arroyo and breached the first row of trees. His world became a few shades darker, a few degrees cooler and it wasn't long before Cody heard the cow mooing yonder, its drawl strained and weak. He halted the roan, feeling dwarfed by the ponderosas—like a bunch of oil derricks erecting from the earth. Their tips narrowing, disappearing into the fog.

There it was again, another moo at nine, maybe ten o'clock.

He put a heel into the roan and it wasn't long before he came upon the calf, her tongue slack against a bank of ponderosa roots, half-chewed entrails staining a small patch of snow.

Cody scanned the forest and saw nothing which made the hairs on his neck rise. Something was out there, he was sure of it.

He dismounted. Knelt before the calf. Tears and grime matted the hide beneath her ducts. Her breath was shallow, it seemed to crawl from the wells in her snout. He dug his fingers under her flank and started to lift when he heard it, the intermittent crunch over half-frozen snow...

Tha-chunk, tha-chunk, tha-chunk.

4

Twenty yards at his six, closing fast.

Cody swiveled, drew a Colt 1911, shoved the front-sight at the grey wolf and squeezed the trigger thrice.

And now, as he rounded the corner into Pappy's room, he shoulder-checked a little man in pin stripes. Cody stared at him, thought about saying sorry or my bad, but didn't.

The man said, "Pardon me, sir," but refused to make eye contact as he went out the door.

Cody entered the room, saw the old man kicked back in the recliner, the whir of the oxygen machine filling the room. "Who the hell was that?"

"Just worry about the goddamn cattle, let me worry about the bidness. Wanna make yerself useful, load me up another," Pappy said, lifting an open-nosed syringe.

"Doc said two mL's ever four hours...I done gave ya a shot but two hours ago."

Pappy looked at him. "Way I feel might not make it another two. So shut up'n do what I tell ya."

Cody grabbed the syringe, crossed to the bedside table, jammed the tip into a bottle of morphine sulfate and watched the blue liquid fill the chamber. Looking past the syringe, he saw what looked like a business card. Plain white with block letters.

JIM MOFFAT, ATTORNEY AT LAW
Real Estate. Taxes. Estate and Family Planning.

Cody glanced at the old man to make sure he wasn't looking, then shoved the card in his pocket.

"Saw you with that calf," Pappy said. "She gonna make it?"

"I don't know."

"What was all that shit with the one guy...the hell's his problem?"

"That sawed-off sumbitch?"

"Yeah, whatshisname?"

"Randy-somethin," Cody said, crossing to Pappy.

"He any good?"

"He's aright. Hard worker, stronger'n shit, but talks too damn much. And truth be told, I ain't real fond of most a his opinions. Better learn his place or I'm a give him the boot."

"What'd he say about the calf?"

"Didn't think it worth the cost for Murdoch to come out, try'n salvage her."

Pappy said, "Whaddayou think?" and opened wide as Cody thumbed the plunger. He licked his lips and sunk into the chair, sucking air past the cannula plugging his nostrils.

"It was a bull I'd say he's right, but..." and Cody left it at that, the old man nodding in agreement until his eyes fell shut and he seemed to be off somewhere for a while. Mumbling, nodding, having a conversation with someone. Telling whoever he was talking to how much he loved that blue shit, how good it made him feel.

Cody hated seeing him like this. Used to be such a tough geezer, too. Even into his seventies, Pappy could still punch cows and haul bales like a man of forty. Then one day, blink of an eye, he was dying. And Cody found himself awake most nights, scared of waking up one day in the same capacity, old and worthless. Beholden to someone. He glanced out the window, saw the segundo heel a calf and drag it to the center of the arena. When he heard the old man begin to snore he moved for the door, walking soft on the balls of his feet to prevent the hardwood from creaking.

"How many's that make?" It was loud and clear. The old man was awake again. "Where the hell'd you go... Cody?"

"I'm here."

"Well get back here where I can see ya." Cody did and the old man said, "How many's that make?"

"If the calf…"

"Yeah."

Cody took a deep breath. "Five calves, six cows. Three of 'em heifers."

"Lotta beef. How many you figure in the pack?"

"Three, four the most."

The old man's eyes, a translucent blue, shifted this way.

"They ain't eatin all of 'em," Cody said. "Get their fill on the calves and kill the cows. Like they're doing it for sport. I'm tellin ya Pappy, these fuckers're actin erratic, brazen like I never seen."

"They rabid?"

"My guess, yeah. You ever heard of a wolf chargin a man?"

"Not this part of the country, no. But back when I's a boy, maybe seven or eight, this town was plagued with a lone wolf killing stock left and right. Horses, cows, didn't make a lick. He'd castrate 'em, mutilate 'em. Course the papers, you know what they did…"

"Made up a load of shit."

"Crazy talk. Sayin it's some kinda mountain lion wolf hybrid. Calling it this *outlaw wolf*, hell-bent on vengeance 'cause its mate and pups were killed or whatever—you know the crazy stories them folks concoct."

Cody nodded.

"And, uh—shit, I'm blanking," Pappy said. "What's that guy's name? East side of town…?"

"Mueller."

"Yeah. His daddy tracked the wolf for five years, didn't get squat. Never even saw the damn thing. Then the feds send in this guy named Williams, ordering him to stay in state till the wolf's dead. And when he first sees that wolf—you'll never believe this, but two coyotes had teamed up with it—"

"Bullshit."

"Honest to God. What they were doin, they'd flank the wolf, traveling ahead to warn him of any danger."

"What'd the coyotes get out of it?"

"All the scraps they could eat. And Williams, he shot both of 'em pretty quick, which spooked the wolf and the only thing he saw for the next few months was a little hair caught up in a triggered trap. Then another month goes by, attacks on the stock continue. And not but a few weeks before winter does that wolf step on a trap. But he don't stop there. No, that wolf ran about a hunnert fifty yards till he got caught up in a tree and broke the swivel off the trap. Three more miles," Pappy said, holding up three fingers, his pincers making a circle, "Williams tracked him till he shot that wolf dead. And guess what? All that shit about it being a monster, this cougar half-breed? It's just a reg'lar wolf. Hunnert pounds soakin wet."

"I'll be goddamned." Cody rubbed his chin and realized he had forgotten to shave.

"All told, that sumbitch killed over five hunnert head."

"Five hunnert?"

"Damn right. Now *we* got rabid wolves. As if it wasn't hard enough already making a buck, this cowboy shit." Pappy shook his head, looked out the window. "Should keep you busy."

"Better'n bein bored, I guess."

"Ever think what you'd do if you didn't grow up with all this?"

Cody just looked at him. The thought never crossed his mind.

"There's a whole world out there. You gonna look in the mirror one a these days, be an old fart like me, and realize ya ain't never left this goddamn place. And yer gonna regret it."

"Aright, I think that's enough morphine," Cody said, moving for the door. "Holler if you need anything."

"Maybe that's what happened to yer daddy..."

Cody stopped.

"...Saw 'at casino going up'n got out when the gettin was good."

"He's gone 'cause he was weak. Ain't have what it took to run this outfit."

"Then I don't need to tell you the importance of not losing another goddamn cow. Or you'll find out what that's like real fucking quick."

Before Cody could respond, he heard a voice behind him say, "You can tell him..." He turned to see his sister in the doorway, a pink box in her duke. "But has that ever worked?" She lifted her shades and grinned to insinuate she was joking, but Cody knew she was just being a bitch. Regretting now that he didn't walk out when Pappy had dozed.

Cody watched Shea Custer approach the old man—he was chuckling at the dig—and ask if he was feeling as good as he looked. Which was ridiculous because he looked and smelled like shit. But what Cody couldn't stand most was the softness in her voice, the touch of matron like she actually cared. *You feeling as good as you look?*

Shove it.

"Better now that yer here," Pappy said, his eyes dropping to the pink box. "What's this?"

"Your favorite." She opened it revealing six maple Long Johns.

Pappy told her how kind, how thoughtful she was.

"How about something to wash them down?" Shea said.

Cody thought he should be out there waiting for Murdoch. Or in the arena helping the guys. Or even on the pot taking a shit. Anywhere but here listening to them go back and forth, playing nice. It wasn't until the old man asked for something whiskey-based that Cody intervened.

"What's it, gonna kill me?" Pappy said, turning now to look at Shea. "You'd think after eighty-eight years there'd be a point when people stop telling me what to do."

"Had ya listened to 'em the first place, wouldn't be in this perdicament."

"It's *pre*-dicament, you idiot," Shea said.

"Like I give a shit."

"Shut it, Cody," Pappy said. "Why're you still standing there anyway, ain't you got work to do?"

He waited in the hall for Shea to deliver the whiskey. When she closed the door to Pappy's room, he said, "Don't think I don't know what you're doin."

"And what is that exactly?"

"You can blame it on a shitty childhood, fucked-up parents, whatever, but you deserted this family and this ranch. And now that Pappy's dying, yer trying to weasel yer way back in. Kiss his ass enough, hope he cuts you in on the will."

She snickered. "The last thing I care about is the miniscule amount of money he has."

"Not the money. The land. And I don't know why yet, but I

know it's got somethin to do with that…whatshisname…that Injun you seem so fond of."

"Go ahead, say it."

"What?"

"What you *wanted* to call him."

"I was not."

"Please. You think I don't know how you and Pappy talk when I'm not around? Well let me tell you something, Kenny's done more for this town—"

"Yeah, I know, he's a fuckin saint."

"Jealous, are we?"

Cody squinted, used his tongue to shove the plug of dip to the other side of his mouth. "Guy's a fuckin lotto winner, Shea. He's no good for this town and he's no good for you."

"In all honesty, what would you know? You're a mediocre cattle rancher who's leveraged to his ears in debt." She pushed past him, opened the storm door, saying, "I were you, I'd get on my knees and thank Kenny for all the revenue he brings this shit town."

"What is it with you? You get some kinda sick pleasure from all this?"

She threw the door and turned back, letting it slam shut. "Oh no more than I did from Daddy all those nights in the pasture."

"That's why then…payback."

"Oh don't you dare judge me. You were never there when I needed you. Like many other things in this life you failed at being a brother."

Cody glared at her, a mass forming in his throat. He thought about everything he had done. Things she'd never know. Things he swore he'd take to the grave. He stepped closer, kept his voice low and said, "Let's get one thing clear: this is *my* ranch. I've sweat for it. I've bled for it. I've earned it."

She bit her bottom lip, showing some teeth—a stupid little grin. "Life doesn't yield what you think you've earned. The only thing it yields is what you're willing to take."

After she left, Cody found himself looking at a painting of *Custer's Last Stand*. The colonel valiant, standing over his wounded, fighting to the death. Saber in his left, smoking revolver in his right, trained on a charging Crazy Horse. Beneath the painting Cody read a quote he had read a thousand times...

"There are not enough Indians in the world to defeat the Seventh Cavalry."
—Colonel George Armstrong Custer

He went into the kitchen, stopping dead when he saw the bottle on the counter, the cap lying adjacent. He thought about how it would taste, what it might feel like moving down into his stomach. The instant buzz. He contemplated a whiff, curious if he still enjoyed the notes of sour mash and oak. But he remembered the men that came before him. The inheritance. The poison in his blood.

He fastened the cap and returned it to the cupboard, feeling more like he had lost a battle over emerging victorious.

2

THE DUSTY RANCHER across from Kenny "Black Elk" Shepard was easy pickings. He sat hunched under a straw hat so big Kenny mistook it for a sombrero when the guy had entered. The rancher pretending to admire the art, the relics, the big-game mounts on the wall. And Kenny, he was ready with an answer if the guy asked about any of them. Oh, the elk? Two years ago in the Rockies. One arrow straight through the heart. And that pronghorn over there? Northern Cali with my .338 Lapua. Yeah, it's a beast.

But the rancher didn't ask.

He just talked about his land, how it's been in the family over a hundred years—which was why he had a great many qualms about being here. That's how he put it. *A great many qualms.*

Kenny said, "I get that, but I also know you wouldn't be coming to me if the bank extended you that half-million-dollar loan."

The rancher leaned back. "How the hell'd you know about that?"

"I'm on the board." Kenny pulled a smile, trying to show the white man he could be friendly. "But don't be ashamed. You're part of the majority in this town. And I feel for you guys, I really do. I mean, you've been in the cattle business most your life, am I right?"

"All my life."

"And when's the last time you made money?"

The rancher didn't answer. He went back to hunching, looking down at his knees.

Shit, all that talk about cowboys looking you in the eye and meaning what they say? Not this one. Not today.

"Right," Kenny said. "So all due respect, I can't offer you any kind of loan."

"Look, Mr. Shepard…"

That felt good, the cowboy calling him mister.

"…I know the beef bidness ain't what it used to be—"

"Unless you have a quarter million acres, several thousand head, and two dozen wetbacks under the table, it'll never be what it used to be. The way of the cowboy is dead."

"Not sure I like your tone."

"No? Then how's this… Instead of a loan, I want to buy you out. The land, the business, everything."

The rancher laughed. "It's worth over three million dollars."

"And you're in debt at least half a mill. So how about I cut you a check for three-seven-five and you can retire on a beach somewhere."

There he was, alive again, sporting a grin. The rancher spoke out of the side of his mouth. "You got that kinda cash?"

"I got a lot more than that."

"What's the catch?"

"The land goes Fee to Trust," Kenny said, using a finger to draw an imaginary line across his desk.

"Making it official tribal land…"

"That's right."

14

The rancher shook his head. "I don't know. Some a the guys would have my head they heard I sold out to you."

"Yeah, but you already thought of that didn't you? And the fact you're here means you've come to terms with it. So any fallout that may result from the straw hat brigade is nothing but noise. Because if I were paying you what it's worth, they might have a leg to stand on. But the fact I'm willing to give you over asking *and* wash your debt, means they're just pissed they don't have a seat at the table."

"Why don't they?"

"Have a seat at the table?"

"Yessir."

"Because I don't want their land right now. It's out of the way, not worth my time, nor is it worth whatever they think it's worth. No, all I want is yours, and one other."

"Whose?"

"That's none of your business."

"Well if it's the Flying-C yer wasting time. They ain't never gonna sell. No shot in hell. Them boys'll go down swinging over selling out to someone like you."

Kenny furrowed his brow.

"I mean that with all due respect of course."

"I'm sure you do. But what's it gonna be? Right here, right now. Take it or leave it. Three million, eight hundred thousand—"

"Thought you said three-seven-five?"

"I'm feeling generous. And to be honest, I like you. Think you're a good guy, salt of the earth." Kenny pulled a smile, then said the number again to let it sink in.

"You'll write the check today?"

Kenny fingered the intercom button on the landline. "Bring

it in."

The automated double-doors parted. Hector Vargas entered and handed a Manila folder to the rancher.

Kenny watched him open it, saw his eyes light up, the years of fatigue vanish as he read his name in bold at the top of the check.

The rancher whistled. "What if I agreed to three-seven-five?"

Kenny shrugged, stretched his lips.

The rancher looked down at the folder again. "Mr. Shepard, you got yerself a deal."

Before Kenny could respond, his phone buzzed. He saw the screen light up, his girlfriend's name written across.

Kenny watched the rolling numbers on the little screen as he rode the elevator, thinking about the only time he had met Pappy Custer. Christ, he didn't even know his real name. Everyone always called him Pappy. Shea had set it up a year ago over at Ruth's on Third—what she called neutral ground. Kenny remembered walking in, all the cowboys staring. The looks on their faces were clear: *this stupid Injun must be lost.* They would turn and look at Hector—the man stone-cold in his Hugo Boss suit, a pair of shades on—decide they didn't want none, then turn back to glare at Kenny. The meeting lasted three minutes and Kenny didn't say a word except for his name at the beginning and the amount he was willing to pay at the end. Offering a hand, the old senile fuck not reaching out to meet it. Shea said something, referenced the ranch and Pappy cut her off, said he wasn't selling—and even if he was, he sure as shit wouldn't to the goddamn Injun trying to ruin the town. Still, Kenny offered his price thinking that might force him to reconsider. But the old man asked if Kenny was stupid. No means no. Then he proceeded to bitch at Shea, giving her an earful all the way out the door as Kenny and Hector sat there alone, the whole restaurant staring, no waiter coming by asking if they wanted a coffee or even some fucking water. Kenny remembered sitting in his office, getting the call from Shea sometime later saying Pappy had been diagnosed with stage four small cell lung cancer. He was only supposed to last another four to eight weeks, yet here we are, over a year later, the man subsisting like asbestos.

The doors parted and Kenny walked over to Wagyu, a chic steakhouse across from the nickel slots. It was empty save a few bowties moving about, prepping for the looming dinner rush. And Shea Custer was at the bar bent over an empty lowball. He approached her, asked what in the hell was so urgent.

"I don't want to wait for him to die," Shea said, gesturing the bartender for another drink. "I want it, and I want it now."

"I offered three times what it was worth, he won't sell."

"Then we make him."

Kenny waited as the bartender poured, catching the "25" on the label. Drinking the good stuff. Living it up on his dime. "You really think this is the best thing right now with you halfway down the campaign trail?"

She stood up straight, shifted her glossy eyes. "Is the big tribal boss-man getting cold feet?"

"I just closed on the Cooper ranch, okay? Now there's a right way to do things and a wrong way—"

"And the only way to get it done is the wrong way. I told you from the start he wouldn't sell."

"And yet you want to force him. So how do you suggest we do that?"

"You being a wiseass?"

"Just trying to see where your head's at…how far you're willing to take this."

She took half the scotch in a gulp. Kenny figured it was worth twenty-one and a half retail, maybe seven and a quarter wholesale. He watched her roll it around in her mouth, really enjoying the notes.

He'd be lying if he said it didn't piss him off.

"Run him out of business," Shea said. "Kill off the stock, make it look like an act of God."

Not a bad idea, Kenny thought.

"We'll send Blackfoot in—"

"No, find someone else."

"Come on, he's a drug addict and a disgrace to the Yawakhan."

"He's the only family I've got…" Kenny stopped. He didn't like the way the bartender was pretending to cut limes, half-turned this way. Kenny said, "Hey," and when the guy looked up, Kenny told him to take a fucking hike, then texted Hector to fire the nosy brat. He looked back at Shea now. "He's all I got, all right? I'm not throwing him in the gutter to do our dirty work."

"Oh, don't start on that blood is thicker than water crap, you'll make me throw up. Kid's never had a job and he owns two six-figure cars. You gave him the good life and he's shitting on you. He owes you."

That was true. And Kenny had fantasized about a hostile takeover of the Flying-C on more than one occasion—never mind the rancher's words stuck in the back of his mind about how they'll go down swinging.

Kenny didn't care.

He wanted it. Bad. More than any other parcel in the county. He figured, if he was going to get it, he'd have to be willing to do anything. So Kenny Shepard asked her to lay out what she had in mind.

When the phone rang, Cody was headed north on County Road 75. Tanya Tucker coming through the speakers, singing about Laredo. He tossed Jim Moffat's card on the dash and flipped open his phone, said, "Yeah?" and waited as the segundo told him they lost the calf.

He saw that coming. Prepared himself for it. But somewhere in the back of his mind, an ounce of hope.

He ground his teeth, spat tobacco into an empty bottle as he made his way past the Yawakhan Reservation. And there, turning out of the main entrance was Bobby Cooper heading south. Could tell it was him too by that stupid ten-gallon hat. The man looked jovial, chatting it up on the phone like he'd just hit it big in Blackjack.

The segundo asked if he was still there.

Cody said, "Yeah. Hit the rack early, we're going wolf hunting tomorrow." He pinched the phone shut and watched Bobby Cooper's truck get smaller in the side-mirror. He drove another two miles, then made a right into town.

A few minutes later he was standing in front of Jim Moffat, a cluttered desk separating them. A heavyset, middle-aged blonde was behind Cody raising hell about him not having an appointment, saying he needed to wait in the lobby.

Cody didn't speak. Just stood there staring at the squirt in the pinstripes.

Jim Moffat lifted a hand, said, "It's all right, Janice," and waited for her to close the door. "What is it I can do for you, Mr. Custer?"

Cody noticed the guy had a different air about him. A little pompous now that he was in his element. "Wanna know what you was doin at my ranch."

"Well that's between me and your grandfather."

"Come on, don't give me that shit. Man's pumped with so much goddamn morphine you can't take anything he says at face value."

"Unfortunately, that's not for you to decide."

"Then at least tell me if it pertains to the Flying-C."

"No."

"Or if he signed anything…"

"No."

"Come on, you gotta give me something."

Moffat eased back into his chair. "Okay, maybe you don't understand how this works. I don't have to tell you anything. In fact, I am prohibited from doing so per rule one point six of the American Bar Association which states…"

Cody didn't understand any of the bullshit coming out of Moffat's mouth—something about confidentiality between the attorney and the client. Cody's mind drifted as the guy talked a mile a minute. He thought about the calf, the money wasted on a house call from the vet. All for nothing.

"…So unless you are privileged personnel, which you are not—"

"Yer aware I'm foreman, right?" Cody said.

"Giving oneself a title does not an officer make, Mr. Custer."

"The hell's that supposed to mean?"

"It's a sole proprietorship. You can call yourself foreman all you want, but on paper, and to the estate, you hold no more value than that Mexican segundo."

Cody wanted to drag the jerkoff across the desk, give him a good licking.

"We can do this all day if you want," Moffat said, "but I am very expensive and know you don't have the cash to accommodate. So unless you want to explain to your grandfather the surge on his next bill, I suggest you leave. Or, if you like, I can have Janice call the police."

If Cody thought a few punches sounded good a moment ago, it was nothing compared to what he was thinking now.

On his way out the door, he heard Moffat say, "I think it's just great what she is doing, by the way."

Cody turned to face him. "Who?"

"Your sister. Working in unison with the Yawakhans to build Spearfish into one of the greatest towns the Midwest has ever seen. She certainly has my vote."

"Not mine."

3

BODAWAY BLACKFOOT heated the spoon until he saw the crystals liquefy and begin to boil. His heart pounded as he syphoned the skag with a hypodermic—this one still in decent shape, having been used only a handful of times with the last batch.

Wouldn't be long now.

An hour ago, withdrawal had set in so he took the G-Wagon over to the Vagabond, a trailer park bunched with meth-labs and wife-beaters. They always had a steady flow of the good shit, none of that brown-brown made by the wetbacks. The dealers knew he was Yawakhan, knew he had money, so they charged an arm and a leg but Blackfoot didn't care because man, did he need it.

He was getting excited. The weight of the world about to evaporate, all of his problems would be gone in the blink of an eye.

He managed to poke a vein on the fourth try, thumbing the plunger, feeling a warmth climb his arm and saturate his brain, morphing it into a tool of limitless power, the universe his oyster, anything was poss—

DUNT-DUNT-DUNT.

A knock at the door. Heavy. Like a cop knock.

Blackfoot froze thinking they'd go away if he didn't move. Them motherfuckers can't get in without a warrant anyway, he told himself. So be cool.

DUNT-DUNT-DUNT.

But his mind raced.

And now he was thinking what if they saw him score the shit earlier. Maybe they followed him back to the rez, cut a deal with the feather patrol to come in and bust him. Maybe they had a search warrant—

DUNT-DUNT-DUNT.

Fuck.

He looked to the window, thought if he could slide out, make a run for it...

DUNT-DUNT-DUNT.

...And go see Uncle Kenny, have him cover—

DUNT-DUNT-DUNT.

"I know you're in there Bodaway, open up."

Blackfoot leapt to his feet. Only two people ever called him Bodaway. One of them, he was pretty sure, was dead. He pulled the needle from his arm and sucked the oozing blood. He hustled to the kitchenette, opened a cabinet beneath the sink and threw the syringe in the trash, rustling the top layer until the needle dropped from sight. He unhitched the tourniquet, threw it in a cabinet next to the fridge, behind cereal boxes.

DUNT. DUNT. DUNT. "Let's go!"

Blackfoot moved to the door, catching his reflection in the mirror. He primped. Fluffed his long, stringy mane. Then he cracked the door and saw his uncle and Hector Vargas on the stoop.

"Sup Nephew. We interrupting something?"

"Nah, it's cool. What's goin on?"

Both of them lingering, staring. Seemed like forever until someone spoke again.

"...You gonna invite us in?" Kenny said.

Blackfoot hesitated, then opened the door and stepped aside. Kenny entered first. When Hector came in, Blackfoot tried to play it cool, holding up a fist for the bump, saying, "Sup, Hector," but the douche didn't even look or say nothing. He just walked in, kept his shades low and scanned the place, running a finger across the coffee table, holding it up to the light coming through the window.

Blackfoot wanted to tell his dumbass to take them glasses off, might find what he's looking for, but decided it was best to stay quiet. His pits were sweating, staining the threads of his tank. And he couldn't stop himself from blinking, so he squeezed his eyes shut until his uncle said, "Being full-bred Yawakhan, what's Bodaway's annual share of the profits?"

"About four hundred twenty-eight thou," Hector said, disappearing into the kitchen.

"And you've defaulted on two separate car payments, a speed boat, and you live like a fucking animal!" Kenny flipped the card table, sending pizza boxes and half-empty beer cans to the floor.

Blackfoot looked at Kenny but didn't know what to say. What could he say? Shit was expensive. He could hear Hector opening things now—cabinets, the refrigerator—and got that sinking feeling in his stomach, the same one when you're getting pulled over.

"You know what you are?" Kenny said. "The epitome of what everyone in town thinks when they hear the word native. Nothing but a casino-rich timber nigger who pisses away his welfare check on drugs and alcohol."

"Why you give a fuck what they think? We don't need them."

"Look at this place. You're in the top ten percent, but you live in a FEMA trailer and can't even drink the water coming out of the tap. Like it or not, we do need them because they have all the land, which means they have all the power."

Blackfoot went back to the couch, way too lit to be dealing with the chief and all his bullshit right now. The dude rolling up in here with a bone to pick.

Kenny said, "It could take me weeks, months to close a deal, but the second they see someone like you, they get it in their head that you and I are no different. And everything I have worked for, the advancement, the integration and reputation of our people in the community would be gone."

Blackfoot laughed. He didn't mean to it just came out. The chief stomping around, huffing and puffing, all high and mighty. Before this, Uncle Kenny was no different. Partied all the time. Dabbled in a little dro, though he preferred uppers. Now look at him: pony greased back, expensive clothes that looked like he jumped off the page of a men's lifestyle mag. Hector always around, shadowing him like he's the president or some shit.

"Man, you know who you sound like?" Blackfoot said. "That white bitch you been bringing around."

Blackfoot was yanked off the couch onto his back. His uncle was yelling through clenched teeth but he couldn't make out nothing the man was saying. Couldn't feel anything either, save the warmth of Kenny's soft hands gripping his neck. He saw contours of vibrant colors. Reds, blues, and purples flowing in the windows, funneling into Kenny's ears. Steam hissed and spewed from Kenny's tear ducts. Blackfoot felt the rug swallowing him, pulling him into its depths. Then the room started going black, a mass swelling from his peripherals, consuming everything in sight...

"Boss," Hector said, standing in the doorway. He was holding something, showing it to Kenny. Blackfoot couldn't make out what it was.

Kenny turned back, his black eyes filled with disgust. "You're high right now, aren't you?"

"Nah, man. I'm cool."

"Don't lie to me. After everything I've done for you."

Blackfoot felt it coming. He swallowed, flexed his jaw, did everything he could to bite it back. He saw quick snippets from his past. The time Kenny was there when he got picked on by the white kids, the little turds calling him a spic. Kenny swinging, taking more punches than he gave but standing his ground. Or the time when Kenny put a hand on Blackfoot's shoulder after his mother OD'd on the very same couch. Making the funeral arrangements. Selling the jalopy to pay for a proper burial. Kenny pulling him in, standing in the snow during the ritual, telling him they would get through this. Kenny promising to take care of him, becoming the father figure he never knew. Bailing him out. Only seeing the good, the potential...

Blackfoot broke down and sobbed, overwhelmed by guilt. He nuzzled his face in Kenny's shoulder and pleaded for mercy.

"You're better than this, you know that?" Kenny said.

"I know man. I'm fucked up. I need help."

"You're leaving me no choice. I have to cut you off—"

"No bro, come on—"

"I'm not doing this anymore. I can't—"

"Please Uncle Kenny, please. I'll do anything man, I swear."

Kenny pulled back so they were face to face. He thumbed away a tear. "Yeah?"

"Anything, Unc. Name it."

Blackfoot saw his uncle glance at Hector then back again, like he already had something in mind.

4

"**I'VE SAID IT BEFORE, I'LL SAY IT AGAIN...**" Shea Custer said, standing at the altar before the township. City hall wasn't big enough, so at the last second her campaign manager had the venue switched to Jesus Is The Light Church, the little white one with the bell tower over on Saddlebow.

When Shea had asked why the hell it had to be a church, Toni told her because it was a win-win. They could accommodate a bigger crowd *and* show 'em Shea Custer's a woman of faith without ever having to say it.

Shea said whatever.

She didn't believe Toni until right now, looking out at two hundred faces watching her, hanging on her every word. Shea continued, "This town was built, and will continue to thrive on the sweat and hard work of ranchers. The economic stability of the beef market will be my number one priority should you elect me mayor of this great city..."

She paused, waited for the claps.

"And I know your feelings about the ever-increasing expansion of the Yawakhan reservation, and I'm here to tell you, it's not a bad thing."

A hollow-cheeked man in coveralls booed. A few others joined him and a small group of Hispanics watched, their arms crossed, their faces apathetic.

Shea held up both hands. "Now hear me out…it can and will be *mutually* beneficial, because I vow to use the success of the Mingan Tribal Casino to our benefit…"

The Hispanics rotated back, curious.

"…If they want to infringe on our community—our schools, our businesses, our churches—they will be taxed for it. And not only will the increase in tourism bring more revenue to you small business owners out there, but the ranchers will see a significant improvement in the market value of your livestock across the board…"

Someone shouted, "Hell yeah!"

Shea lifted her pitch over the applause, really getting into it. She made eye contact with a weathered man—a brass star on his shirt, a thick mustache over his lip. "And I've heard your cries and your pleas and when I'm mayor, I'm putting my foot down on this pipeline situation. So you can take solace in the fact that you'll never have to worry about the Dakota Access Pipeline infringing on *your* land."

She pointed right at him, trying to get a reaction, but he just shifted his weight from one foot to the other.

"I'm Shea Custer for Mayor, and I have your back, working for the blue-collar people of Spearfish. This is our new beginning."

She left stage with them cheering, moving through a back door into the priest's chambers. She wasn't in the mood for shaking hands or answering stupid questions from stupid people about how she was going to change the town or make it better. She moved into a long corridor that led to the grammar school. Every several feet, a numerated relief depicted the Stations of the Cross. This one here, Jesus just wiped his face on the towel of that whore. Or was it the mother? Or was the whore the mother? Shea could never remember.

Toni came up quick, jazzed, talking about the crowd, how they were gushing and fawning. "You nailed it. Totally nailed it."

They went through a bank of doors into the parking lot. Shea felt the air bite at her face and couldn't remember how the town felt when it was warm.

Toni was buried in her phone, still yapping—something about the itinerary—as they approached an idling town car. The one that came stock with the suicide doors and the 20-inch rims. When Toni mentioned where the car was going, Shea said, "Do I really have to?"

"It's the Local 49 dinner."

"Local 49?"

"One of the unions. Operating Engineers, I think."

"What does that even mean? Operating… Is there a union for engineers who don't operate?"

"I don't know, but you're speaking. So yes, you have to go."

"I just gave a speech."

"Yeah but this one you can be yourself. You know, off the cuff."

Shea cocked a thumb over her shoulder. "Who was I back there?"

"It was you, only a different version—tailored for the lower class. People that *need* someone to rally behind. Someone that gives them hope."

"False hope."

"Like there's another kind in this climate."

Shea could see the masses flowing from the church under sodium-vapors, their elongated shadows careening the tarmac.

"You could tell by their faces… Didn't matter what I said, it's as if those idiots are programmed to clap at anything sounding halfway decent."

"Even if most of it is improbable."

"Put a little umph into it, they start yipping like a pack of coyotes."

"Well not all of them…" Toni said through her teeth, looking off.

Shea followed her gaze. The group of Hispanics were piling into a minivan. She counted ten of them. "Who cares, this isn't Texas. There's not enough to decide it one way or the other. So until that's an option, we target the base."

"Absolutely. Why I suggested putting the L after your name instead of a D."

"It was a good move." Shea saw the man with the mustache leaving, the brass star covered by a canvas jacket. He looked this way, but didn't linger or stop to talk to anyone. "What's the deal with him?"

"Who, the Sheriff?"

Shea nodded.

"He didn't look too impressed. Just stood there with his arms crossed majority of the speech."

"You saw I pointed at him, talking about the pipeline?"

"Didn't seem to faze him one way or the other…couldn't tell you where he stands on it."

Shea watched him get into a boxy two-door SUV, a lone gumball stuck to the roof. The exhaust pumped a cloud of smoke. "What do you know about him?"

"Retired military. Green Beret, I think."

Shea waited.

"Like special forces or something. He's an import, too.

Keeps to himself. Doesn't seem to have very many friends unless you count that deputy with the dreadful haircut—shoot, I'm blanking on her name right now. You know, I can't imagine what the stylist looks like, charging money, letting her walk out the door with all those greasy curls—"

"You want to digress Toni, do it on your own time to that faggy little boyfriend of yours. But spare me the bullshit and just provide the bullet points, would you?"

Toni stood there, her back arched, her eyes agape.

Shea could tell she was insulted but knew the peon wouldn't say anything. A slave to her job. Stars in her eyes. Dreams of one day running and gunning on Capitol Hill—the trusted confidant to a major player. So Shea waited for the priss to collect herself.

Toni said, "Yes ma'am, sorry about that. One moment please…" She swiped and tapped her phone. "Sheriff Weston Harris. His parents moved here from Alabama shortly after he shipped overseas on his first deployment."

"Why?"

"I believe his father was relocated here for work, I can double-check that if you want."

Shea shook her head. "No, it's fine. Go ahead."

"The next several years is just his service record. Yadda-yadda-yadda. Afghanistan. Iraq. North Africa. Southeast Asia. He was busy. Oh, here we go. Some years later, when his father died, he was coming up for re-enlistment and, word has it, he opted out to come here and care for his mother until about three years ago when she died. Dementia, I think." Toni stopped and looked up from her phone. "That reminds me…"

"Let me guess, you found her?"

"Actually wasn't that difficult, which is a little concerning to say the least. Any journalist, shoot, your opponent finds out, there will undoubtedly be a spread of you two on the front page."

"You run the numbers?"

"Yes ma'am. Worst case? It'll cost us the election. And if that happens, you can kiss any future Senate run goodbye. This is the kind of baggage that won't go away, not in this day and age."

Shea looked at the idling town car. She couldn't see through the tint but figured Kenny was in there jiving on the cell phone, spinning her speech to David and the rest of the pipeline investors. Shea looked back at Toni and asked where she parked.

"Over there," Toni said, pointing past the roof of the town car. "Wait, why?"

"Just give me your keys."

"What about the dinner?"

"I'm going to be late."

Kenny Shepard was looking through the back window when the campaign manager handed Shea a set of keys. He wanted to get out, ask where the hell she was going, but the guy coming through the phone wouldn't shut up about her speech, about the pipeline. When the guy finally stopped to catch his breath, Shea was pulling out in a Honda sedan. Kenny hawking her until she turned a corner, saying into the phone now, "Then you weren't listening David—she said *your* land. Because by the time I'm through with this town, that pipeline'll be running through *my* land, you understand? Two years, I'll have it looking like a goddamn theme park."

David said he had to get up there and see the operation. He asked would Wednesday work.

"No, I've got that TV thing," Kenny said. "Apparently it's going to take most of the day."

"Which network?"

"Whichever one plays *42 On The Hour*. They're doing a whole spread about the Mingan being the fastest growing casino in the nation."

David said, "Shit, that's legit, bro. How about Friday? Could we do Friday?"

"Let's lock it in. But listen, I got a proposition for ya. As you know, I got a lot of things shaking over here. So when this thing goes through, I'll need a lead, someone who can spearhead the operation. You interested?"

"Fuckin-A, are you for real?"

Jesus. Could anyone just answer with a yes or no anymore? "I'm serious man, this is no bullshit."

"Then I'm your guy, Mr. O-T-O-B. You just tell me where to fucking sign."

"Mister what?"

"That's our nickname for you back here at the Exchange. Mister On Time, On Budget."

"Which one of you idiots came up with that?" Kenny said, grinning a little, liking the way it sounded.

"You're talking to him. Come on, you know how I do. Me and a few of the other junked-up suits were shooting the shit, talking about you, and I'm thinking, why can't everyone do business like Kenny motherfucking Shepard, know what I'm saying?"

Kenny chuckled. "I do, I do. Listen, I'll send the jet Friday morning that way we can finalize everything."

"I'm on it, bro."

The campaign manager knocked on the window.

Kenny finished the call with David the Douche—a nickname he just came up with—before rolling the window down. The campaign manager popped her head in and said she needed a ride. It was clear she was freezing her tits off and a little ticked that Shea had taken her car.

"I'll let you in if you tell me where she's going," Kenny said.

"I couldn't even if I wanted to. Miss Custer had some personal matters to attend to. But she told me to tell you she would call when she was through."

"That's what *she* said, personal matters?"

"She didn't elaborate."

Kenny sighed. He wanted the campaign manager to know this was all a pain in the ass. But he said okay, threw his head back and told her to get in. Then he caught Hector's eyes in the rearview. "Let's go, I guess."

The car eased out of the parking lot. No one spoke for a few blocks. They passed Hamilton, made a left on Grant when Kenny's phone buzzed. It was a text from Bodaway telling him the operation was about to get underway.

So Kenny called him and said, "Stop putting that shit in writing you dumbass. Do the job, keep your mouth shut, and meet me at your place, noon tomorrow."

Toni was looking, an eyebrow cocked.

"Millennials. They don't want to fucking work no matter what you pay them."

Toni's phone was buzzing now. Kenny watched in his peripherals as she answered and did more listening than talking. He could tell it was Shea, but that was about it.

When Toni hung up, he asked for details.

"Miss Custer wants me to look at the sheriff a little closer, find out if he has any patterns. I think she's hoping to *drop in* on him. See if she can get his endorsement, know what I mean?"

Kenny forced a smile. He looked out the window, saw telephone poles and silhouettes of trees whipping past. He thought about Bodaway, if he had it in him to succeed. About Shea, and just what in the hell she was headed to do.

5

THE STATION hadn't been painted in years. The faded, yellow drab walls were tinged from cigarette smoke. A vent near the ceiling had been replaced, but no one bothered to repaint the stain crawling from it where the air conditioner had leaked. There was a faux-wooden desk off the entry outfitted with a computer, the tower blinking, ticking, taking up half the leg room underneath. Two holding cells were catty corner from that, on the same parallel as the sheriff's desk—also faux-wood—which was barren save a legal pad for notes and a handheld spittoon wrapped in bison hide.

Sheriff Weston Harris liked his desk that way because he hated computers. On rare occasion, he'd use the desk to eat lunch—if for some reason he couldn't make it to Ruth's on Third, sit in his regular booth. Or, he'd have a victim come in, tell their side of the story. But if he was being honest, he'd rather be in the field. Only thing that ever happened in the station was administrative stuff and that shit was for the birds.

But there he was, boots propped on the desk, thinking about that Custer gal. Not what she said so much as the *way* she said it. It seemed theatrical, manipulative. He didn't like her. Not for mayor, or any other public office. And the way she pointed at him, talking about the pipeline—what was that about? He could see her steel blues under that thick blonde hair pulled into a neat top knot.

Man, was she something to look at. He had to give her that.

But Sheriff Weston Harris couldn't shake the feeling that she was the kind always after something more. Those sharp, evil-looking eyes. The kind of eyes that could cut a man to his knees. They'd suck you in, make you do things you normally wouldn't just to keep her—only to realize she was always half-a-step out the door to begin with.

The deputy at the entry desk asked what he thought about the speech.

Harris leaned forward, cleared his mouth in the spittoon. "I don't know, something about her just don't sit right."

"Think she's fulla shit, don't ya?"

"Well—"

"'Cause I think she's fulla shit, acting like she gives a damn about ranchers." The deputy sat slouched, a cloud of Jheri curls backlit by a computer screen that consumed most of her attention.

Harris figured it was Solitaire by the way she was moving the mouse. Click and hold, slide and release. He said, "She comes from a big ranching family, apparently."

"Like I don't know that. But tell me, when's the last time she shoveled shit or weaned a calf? Want my opinion—"

"I don't actually, Thelma."

She swiveled around, stared right at him. "Well I'ma tell ya anyway. She's after two things: money and power. And the problem is she might win 'cause them old farts down the township're more interested in watching her walk away'n they are what she says."

Harris thought on that a moment. "Whaddayou know about

her?"

"Family owns that spread offa 75. Got ol' Bobby Cooper on one side, the reservation on the other."

"I said whaddayou know about *her*..."

"Well I's gettin to that. But if you wanna be an ass about it, I'll just email ya the Cliff Notes."

"Please, God no."

"Well from what I been hearing..." Thelma paused to lift a cigarette from the ashtray and take a drag. "She's kinda the black sheep a the family. Went away to college..."

"Where at?"

"Upstate New York. One near the Catscales."

"You mean Catskills."

"However you say it. Look, don't interrupt. You'll make me lose my train a thought." Thelma paused again. "Shit, where was I?"

"College."

"That's right," Thelma said, snapping her fingers. "Custer gets herself a good education, learns how to walk amongst all them whackjob liberals they got out there. And you gotta understand this was all after her family imploded. One day, everthang's hunky-dory, cattle prices booming, the Flying-C's a top outfit. The next? Mom runs off with some guy and the dad could only take it for so long 'fore he disappeared too, leaving the two kids, the youngest not even a teenager at that point..."

"Disappeared how?"

"No one knows exactly. But word has it he lit out to track the wife down, the man that took her. Then Shea goes to college, migrates to the city and works there for about a decade—some venture capital firm—and now she's back all a sudden, running for mayor. A little convenient you ask me. And you know what? I heard she even tried to broker the sale of the ranch not too long ago. Course that went nowhere."

"Where you hear all this stuff?"

"The salon, where else? See these ringlets? This ain't no ten-minute job. Shit takes time."

Harris thought on that—the bit about Shea, not Thelma's hair. No, he was quite sure that wasn't a ten-minute job. He put the spittoon to his lips and spat. "So I take it she don't have yer vote."

"Ain't no politician this earth ever had my vote. Call it a right, but comes down to it, feels more like a bribe."

"How you figure?"

"Well say you wanna go down the polls and cast a ballot. And yer gonna do it right, and what I mean by that is you ain't just gonna find the one with an "R" after his name—"

"Or *her* name," Harris said, grinning, tipping the spittoon at her.

Thelma threw her hands up. "Oh for the love of God."

"World's done changed, Thelma. Gotta get with the times."

"Are you serious? Yer schoolin *me* on the times? I don't think so. Not with that ugly-ass mustache yer not. You wanna talk about modernism, shave that shit off yer face first."

"Come on, I'm just pullin yer leg."

"And I'm just trying to make a point here. So do you, or don't you, wanna hear it?"

"I'm all ears."

She sighed and dropped her head. "What I'm trying to say is, you do yer research and you really like some of the things they stand for, but then you go see 'em speak and can smell the bullshit a mile away. So you leave thinking, if I vote for this *guy*..." She paused to look at him.

Harris smiled, just a little.

"...Is *he* gonna get *me* what I want? See what I'm saying?"

"I don't. Who's bribing who?"

"Both. It's a two-way street. It's like, yeah, I'll help put'cha in office, but are you gonna get me what I want? And what I'm sayin is, it shouldn't be that personal."

Harris was lost. And he couldn't figure out how they got from the Custer gal to here. He wanted to look at the clock because it felt late, but Thelma was holding his gaze, awaiting an answer. When he took too long, she asked if he understood where she was coming from.

The only thing he could muster was, "I think ya hit the nail on the head. Couldn't of said it better myself."

Thelma nodded, said, "Knew you'd see it my way," and turned back to the computer, gripping the mouse, dragging it across the pad. "And let's be serious here...ain't no mystery she in cahoots with that Indin."

"Who, Custer?"

"That's the one."

"What difference it make? You got something against them now?"

"Only thing it does is prove my point. She's shacking with the guy—who only cares about money by the way—and she sits up there the altar saying she gonna tax 'em for this and that? Give me a break, man. This county ain't never finished in the black till that Indin built his casino. So if anyone's callin the shots it's bound to be the slick with the ponytail. And what chaps my ass is all them dumbshits hooting and hollering after ever-thing she says like they believe her. So no, I ain't particularly got nothin against some Indin wants to make a buck. But what I do got something against is any one enterprise in a city a eighteen hunnert making too much dang money. Politicians, big-business, I don't like 'em. Breeds corruption. Ol' blue eyes wins this election, I suggest keeping yer head on a swivel. Or you'll wake up one day and realize you don't recognize this place."

6

MORGAN TAYLOR liked the way he ran his fingers down the center of her chest. He was sweet, delicate, and nothing like her husband. She could lay in bed all day with him, feeling his body pressed against her. That feeling when you can't seem to get close enough or hold each other tight enough.

Ooh, she just wanted to eat him up. Nibble on his ear or tell him things she thought about doing to him when they were apart. He'd say, "Yeah baby, whatever jou want, I'm jour guy." That sexy little accent. The language of love.

She liked that he was the docile type, the way he'd take ten minutes to catch a bee buzzing around the double-wide and set it free instead of swatting it with a newspaper. You could spend a lifetime with this guy and never get bored because he was always talking about interesting things in exotic places. Places with beautiful beaches, amazing food.

Morgan giggled as he fluttered those long lashes against her navel, inching the plaid sheets down a little further to kickstart round two.

Yeah, she liked that part about him too.

She saw the chiseled angles of his body against the pale drywall, the veins running down his lean biceps. Her heart scuttled. She closed her legs, pulled him up to her face, trying to make it last. "Wait, wait. Just do it one more time. Please?"

He flashed a crooked smile, alabaster teeth stark against that mocha skin. "Okay. *Eres…*"

"Air-ez."

"*Mi persona.*"

"Me. Person-ya."

"*Favorita.*"

"Pablo-rita."

He chuckled. "*Eso, cariña.* Jou are getting better."

"What's it mean?"

"Jou are my most favorite person."

Morgan smiled, getting lost in those eyes, those two perfect drops of molasses. She'd look deep into them, see the little dark flakes scattered around the iris and imagine a life they had yet to lead. She could see the sun, big and bright against a cloudless sky. Her toes curling, digging into the soft white sand. Palm trees torquing in the wind. The crash of the surf.

What stood out most every time she did this was that she always seemed to be happy. She said, "I love you Gustavo Florez Portill-yo."

"And I love jou, Morgan soon-to-be *Portillo.*"

She kissed him. Hard. Felt his wet lips envelop hers, his tongue swimming back and forth. She ran her fingers through his coarse hair, saying between breaths, "Playa…Tunco…it's a beach town, right?"

"*Si*, baby…*es muy bonita.*"

"And we gonna…have…lotsa babies…"

"*Si…mucho cariña…mucho…*"

She grabbed his hand and shoved it down there. Relaxing into it, letting him work his magic. This hot hunk of man meat making all the right moves until the headlights came through the window—parallel streaks moving up the wall, swelling.

"Shit. He's early," Morgan said and could hear the brakes squeaking. She crawled to the foot of the bed, split the venetians just in time to catch the headlights cutting off, revealing the man's thick frame behind the wheel. All shoulders, no neck.

She rolled to her feet, her sweaty heinie catching the window unit's warm breeze as she rushed into the kitchen, opened the freezer and pulled out a microwavable—the chicken-fried-chicken one with the sweet corn and taters. She slipped it from the box, started nuking it. She cracked a beer, set it on the card table.

By the time she made it back to the room, Gustavo already had pants on and was snapping his shirt together. She pouted her bottom lip, said, "I hate this," picking at the loose thread dangling from his shirt patch—not the one with his name, the one that read LEUDERS, *MORE FOR YOUR DOLLAR*.

"I know. But soon, we be forever together, *amor*." He used a finger to lift her chin. "*Beso*."

She kissed him until she heard the lock at the front door clicking. She told Gussy he better scat and watched him climb through the window, blowing a kiss before he dropped out of sight.

She stepped into a pair of sweats, moved out of the bedroom as Buck Taylor entered the trailer. Splotches of crude pocked the legs of his coveralls. His beard was matted on one side and Morgan wasn't surprised when she caught the whiff of cheap whiskey wafting from his clothes.

Gussy never drank. Never had that irritable hangover. The one where it doesn't matter what you do, your presence alone pisses the person off.

Morgan felt uncomfortable standing there as he removed his toboggan, his jacket. She noticed the place was a wreck. She'd forgotten to clean but couldn't start now because then he'd for sure notice and it would light a fuse. So she just stood there smoothing her pant legs, saying, "Evenin hon. How was work?"

"Been a long day, woman. Ain't in the mood for small talk."

She anticipated his move to the card table and beat him to it, pulling a chair out as he sat. Buck was saying how sick he was of having to unlock the goddamn door. From now on, he wanted her to be prepared. That when he was approaching the house he had better hear the damn thing unlock.

Morgan said okay, clocking the handle of the Colt Cobra peeking over his waistband. She wondered if it was loaded. If there was a safety button, or something she had to do to make it work. Just how easy would it be to snatch the piece and start shooting? Catch the fucker blind as he was sitting down for one final TV dinner. A beautiful end to a miserable life. She thought about the weight of the trigger. How easy was it to pull? She decided it didn't matter. She'd just keep pulling with all her might until there was nothing left. The bastard would never know what hit him—

Ding!

The microwave snapped her out of it. Buck was staring at her, an angry look across his face. "Hey, you deaf? I said where's my goddamn dinner?"

"I'm grabbing it right now," she said, crossing to the counter.

"Jesus Christ. Break my back all day to put a roof over yer head…you'd think, at the *very least*, it ain't too much to ask for the fucking thing be ready when I get home. I mean, I'm home the same goddamn time ever day. Take some initiative why don't ya? Start being the wife, the woman of the house, or I swear to God I'm a find a replacement."

Morgan popped the microwave open and smoke billowed out. "Damn," she said to herself, fanning it. She rushed it to the table, the plastic tray burning the pads of her fingers. "Sorry Buck, here ya go." She turned to shake the pain away, sucking air through gritted teeth. When she looked back, she saw Buck just looking at the food, not eating.

"The fuck's this?"

Morgan looked at it for the first time. The shriveled, dehydrated chicken-fried-chicken looked more like sun-dried horse shit; a brown-black ring of burnt plastic had bled around the upper half of the sweet corn and the taters had been reduced to a few granules floating in a puddle of steaming water, a bubble surfacing here and there.

Morgan took a step back. "I think I overdone it."

"Don't take a genius figure that out."

"Sorry, I can make another, or go pick something up—"

He swatted the tray off the table. "And waste more a my goddamn money!?" He sprung to his feet, shoved Morgan into the wall and moved up on her. "One job and you can't even do that right, you lazy, good-for-nothin bitch. I come home this place a fuckin pigsty. Whaddayou do all day, huh?"

"Buck, please... I had a rough day, okay?"

His eyes were bulging from their sockets, a vein wriggled across his forehead. Beads of spittle clung to his beard. "Bout to get a whole lot rougher, woman."

"No, come on. Let me run to Leuder's—it won't cost nothin, I'll fuckin jack whatever we need. Please—"

"Shut up," Buck said, holding a finger to her face. "Get yer ass in that bedroom...show me yer worthy of bein in my house."

She was already a little sore from Gustavo and knew it would be too painful taking Buck right now, the way he did it. "Please. Not tonight."

The force of the backhand sent her to the ground.

Her head ached, her cheekbone throbbed. She looked up at him, her vision blurry from the tears.

"Ain't gonna tell you again and I sure as shit ain't gonna take no lip."

Morgan stood. Tried to picture Gustavo, his boyish grin, his handsome face. She treaded to the bedroom and removed her sweats.

7

SHEA said, "Hang on, I can't...you're breaking up, what'd you say?"

"It can't be me," David said. "I've got four bars."

"No, it's me. I'm in the middle of nowhere right now."

And she was, somewhere between Tilford and Piedmont going south on I-90 in Toni's Honda. The Black Hills on the right, a few speckled lights from Nowhereville, USA to the left. The car was okay, but it drove nothing like her Benz. The fabric seat cushion was too short to support her legs and the turning radius sucked.

"Shit, I musta lost you again. You there?" David said.

"Yeah, can you hear me?"

"Yeah, there we go. Where were we?"

Shea was already irritated that she had to hold the phone because it wouldn't sync to Bluetooth. And now this? Christ. "I was asking what you said. I heard something 'Spearfish', but that was it."

"Oh yeah. I was saying, guess who's coming all the way to butt-fuck Spearfish to see you?"

"Get out."

"For real, it worked. I don't know what you did or what you said, but your little Native boy-toy's sending the jet Friday morning, gonna let me run point on the entire thing."

"God, don't call him that," Shea said. "Bad enough I have to sleep next to the guy."

"Harder than you imagined?"

"It's not just that. He reeks, and I don't mean B-O. He walks around in a vat of cologne all the time."

"It's called a wetback shower. All the fuckin janitors do it around here."

"Well it's overwhelming, like a full-on assault to my face. And the pomade, or whatever it's called that he uses to slick his hair? They can't wash it out of the pillowcases, David, they're permanently stained."

She was passing a Taco John's billboard but saw a Taco Bell off the exit, the silhouette of a heavyset guy in the window by himself. The Taco John's billboard was stilted with repurposed telephone poles and painted in two different shades of yellow. A caption read EXIT 62 – WE'RE MILES AHEAD! The potato olé's with the cup of cheese sauce and the hard shell tacos looked so damn good it made Shea hungry.

Maybe on the way back.

"I don't know how you do it," David said. "I cringe when I think about you lying next to him, the two of you doing it."

"And then you think about your future bank account and praise me for the sacrifice I'm making."

"Oh, I do baby. I do. The things I'm gonna do when I get there."

"God, I can't wait. Haven't had a good lay in months."

"Don't tell me," David said, chuckling. "Mister On Time On Budget doesn't satisfy you?"

"Please, he can't even get it up unless you tell him how great he is. 'Master of the deal.' 'Top Negotiator.'"

"What a weirdo. You shoulda heard me on the phone, talking it up, kissing his ass. Shit worked like a charm."

"I told you."

The back and forth made Shea miss the city. The constant buzz. The energy. Everyone in these parts moved so doggone slow. Shea would smile, say hello. And they would stop, try to have an entire conversation about nothing because they didn't have anything better to do. It's not that she wouldn't love to talk all day about how it's been so cold and dry out, but she has shit to do, okay? Small town people, their simple minds, just wanting to get by. No thank you.

David said, "Have you told him you love him?"

"Why would you ask that?"

"Because the answer is yes or because it's a stupid question?"

"Consider it reversed. Would you bring me—a white girl, the enemy—into any deal that would affect your entire Nation? A deal that'll undoubtedly change the course of history. Would you really trust someone like that if you weren't head over heels in love with them?"

"That doesn't answer my question."

"David, there cannot be a morsel of doubt for this thing to work. And the moment he even thinks I'm not in as deep as he is, is the moment he starts to realize he doesn't need me."

"Like hell he doesn't. The whole thing doesn't work without you or your family's ranch. And it's abundantly clear he's not able to get it."

"It would work, though. Because he's patient. And what'll happen is he'll start buying all the land in town and when Pappy's gone and Cody's left there—the only white fucker in the valley trying to make a living off beef—he's gonna wake up one day and realize it's not worth it anymore. And he's going to sell, doesn't matter for how much. And Kenny will have the whole fucking city to himself. He'll still get what he wants. Maybe you'll still get what you want, but I'll be out. And the only reason I'm telling you this, thinking you won't turn around and call him soon as we hang up, is because it's bigger than just Spearfish and you know it. We've talked about it. When this thing goes through, we can go to the next tribe and the next tribe, say, 'Look how good we did for the Yawakhans up in Dakota. Look at how they've flourished.' And the country will crave that kind of leadership because the media will run it until everyone knows our face. It'll be on every network multiple times a day for months. I'm talking CNN, MSNBC, and you know what they'll be saying? That we are the shepherds for progressivism and social justice. That we are the future of this country."

"And I'm on board for all that. But where does it end?"

"It doesn't, until I reach the top."

"Hang on, you talking Washington?"

"A much smaller parcel than that," Shea said, glancing at herself in the rearview. She could see it now: the reflecting pool, that penile implant of a monument. Giving the speech. Thousands of people groveling, holding their babies out for a peck.

"Shit, I fuckin knew it," David said. "You're talking about the White House, aren't you?"

"Damn right I am." She eased the Honda into the left lane and passed a slow-moving tractor-trailer, a banner with OVERSIZED LOAD plastered across the back.

"Well, it's clear you've said it to Kenny, but what about me? You love me?"

Pssh. Men. So predictable. So needy.

Shea didn't even have to think about it. "David…"

"Yeah?"

"…David? You there?"

"Yeah, I can hear you. Can you hear me?"

"David, I can't…I'm losing you… Hello… Hello…"

The little prick kept talking until she hung up, calling back twice before sending a follow-up text. Shea didn't respond. She would text him on the way back to keep his ass on a short leash. Make up something a little poetic: *Of course she loved him. He was her world. That every time she laid in bed next to Kenny, she was thinking of him.*

It took her another twenty minutes to reach Rapid City, another hour after that trying to locate the woman. She went to O'Malley's and the Oasis, asked the bartenders and the bouncers and all of them said the broad looked familiar when Shea flashed a picture, but no one had seen her.

She drove past the man camps at the oil fields, asked the tricks on the corner. One of them asked did she check the Brass Rail or the trap house on Van Buren?

When Shea pulled up in front of the dilapidated Victorian, two spooks blocked her route to the front door and inquired if she was looking for work—the fat one saying they could have a good run with a ho fine as her. Said they'd make her rich, too. Get her out of that piece of shit Jap car, put her in a fly Beemer or a Caddy if she turned out.

Shea kneed him in the ballsack and got a real kick out of it when he started bitching about the stomach pain. Shea asked if he was stupid, if he thought she looked like a prostitute.

The plump turd wasn't listening—in the fetal position on

wet concrete, yelling about all the shit he was going to do when he could see straight again.

Shea held up the picture—a washed out Polaroid—in front of the other one, a skinny dude with a du-rag. He glanced at it, then said, "Wha'chu want wit her?"

"Just to have a talk."

"You a cop?"

"No."

"Her lawyer?"

"No."

"Then the fuck y'all gonna talk about? Matter fact, tell *me*, I'll give her the message."

"Come on, I know how this works. How much you want?"

"Oh, you seasoned at the game, huh?"

"That's right," Shea said, getting annoyed.

He looked past her, rubbing his chin, thinking. "Aight then. Throw me a bill, I'll tell you where she at."

Shea slipped a hand in her back pocket.

"Throw me three bills though, I'll tell you where she at, *and* give you some shit make her sing like a bird."

He was right.

When Shea found her, she was bent at the hips, leaning in the window of a late model Impala. Shea waited until she got in, then followed them three blocks, continuing straight as the Impala made a left on Lindbergh.

Shea drove to the next block and doubled back. Now thirty yards away behind the Loaf N' Jug, she could see the back of the john's head. It was tilted back, a hand gripping the headrest stilt. He lurched forward, convulsed, then seemed to slump in his seat.

That's when Shea saw the woman's head emerge from his lap, wiping at her mouth, not wasting any time getting the money then getting out, lighting a smoke on the sidewalk as the john drove off.

Shea felt queasy, the taste of stomach acid beneath her tongue. She watched the hooker sling a purse over a shoulder and make her way back toward Haines, letting her get a block before pulling up alongside and whistling.

The hooker stopped, drawing on her cigarette, the cherry glowing orange. She strutted this way, leaned her head in the passenger window and the sapphire light coming off the dash painted a face closer to the grave than its prime. Her eyes glided up and down before she clucked her tongue. "Sorry, honey. Don't eat pussy."

The hooker turned to leave when Shea held up a baggy of black tar. "But you do like skag?"

The hooker snapped back. Seemed to gravitate toward the baggy, mesmerized, wiping her tongue across that top row of stained teeth. "You a cop?"

This again.

"No."

"Hafta tell me if ya are."

"No, I don't. That's a myth."

The hooker hesitated. "What's in it fer you?"

"I'm making a documentary and want to hear your side. Like a day in the life kind of thing."

"Aright, but if I'ma be outta commission—"

"I'll pay your rate," Shea said, just trying to get the bitch in the car.

The hooker held out an open palm. "One-twenty an hour,

up front."

"It's sixty-five, you really trying to bullshit me?"

"How the fuck would you know?"

"I worked it out with J-Slide," Shea said, picturing the skinny one. "Believe you're sporting his brand." She watched the hooker glance at the hash marks etched on the inside of her arm. "He said I could have you for the night and you keep the full freight. What do you say?"

"How much you pay *him* for that?"

"Enough." Shea clocked a pair of headlights cruising past, checking the side mirror now to make sure they kept going.

"Show me the cash." The hooker was closer to the car now, unblinking.

Shea came up with a folded stack of hundreds and moved her clutch to the backseat when the hooker pulled the door open.

Shea cut across Haines and accelerated onto the 44. Ten minutes later she took the exit for Hisega and began carving her way up into the Black Hills. The car's high beams stretched up the road, catching guardrails, yellow signs, the occasional turn off. Shea could feel the hooker's eyes on her, sizing her up.

"We met before?"

"No."

"Hm...feel like I seent you somewhere." The hooker shrugged, pulling a glass-pipe from her purse. "Cool if I freebase?"

"Be my guest."

The hooker plucked a few pinches of black tar and sprinkled them into the nose of the pipe. "So where we goin?"

Shea kept her eyes on the road, the double yellows snaking

into the void. "Back to my hotel. Got a camera crew waiting."

"You mean motel."

"What's the difference?"

"Hotels is nicer. Most of 'em got a real shower, no tub. Normally got a place to set'n watch TV, maybe a desk with a phone on it you can make local calls or dial nine-one-one shit hits the fan. Motels, though…" The hooker snickered. "Motels got but one thing, and that's a bed for fuckin. And I know they ain't no hotel in this janky-ass part a town. So you mean motel, which means that cammer crew you got waitin must be all huddled around the king size, holding each other's dicks waiting for the star to arrive."

Shea rolled her eyes. "It actually has two double beds, so…"

"Well look at you. Miss fancy pants."

"It's the best the production could afford on our limited budget."

"So I take it this ain't no Hollywood pitcher."

"If you're concern is whether or not people will see it, rest assured, all the majors are interested." Shea thought it was a nice touch, saying *majors* like she was in the game.

The hooker shrugged again, not a care in the world. "Well in that case…" She sparked the Bic, touched the bowl with fire and inhaled deep, saying through bated breath, "I guess…I best…get ready…for my close up." She exhaled a cloud of white smoke, wriggled in her seat and her eyes rolled to the back of her head. Then she turned to look at Shea, squinting. "You sure we ain't met?"

"Positive."

"Somethin so goddamn familiar…just cain't peg it."

She hit the pipe again, but this time coughed and started hacking up.

About time, Shea thought, slowing the Honda.

The hooker smacked her chest. Her lower jaw started seizing. She eyed the bowl, confused, a stream of smoke floating up, curving around her face. "Shit, stuff's no joke. Thought you said it was skag?"

Shea looked at her, coming to a stop now. "Laced with Fentanyl."

The hooker's eyes widened. Her hands tremored, her body convulsed. She coughed heavy, mucus-laden coughs and Shea saw the impact spatter of blood against the dash in the glow of ambient light. The hooker started choking, her chin stretching skyward.

A phone buzzed.

Shea pulled it from the cup holder, saw KENNETH SHEPARD on the screen and said, "You've got to be kidding me," but answered, saying, "Hi, baby," in a playful tone, covering the receiver now as the hooker slipped deeper into an overdose.

God, was she loud. The gargling, the hacking, all of it annoying.

"What the hell are you doing?" Kenny said. "For fuck's sake, you're supposed to go on in fifteen."

Shea didn't know how to answer that. He was saying, Hello, you there? but with all the commotion Shea had trouble focusing. She told him she was tying up some loose ends, then hung up.

"The fuck…" the hooker said. "Why'd you do this to me?"

Shea reached over, opened the passenger door. "Because you don't even recognize your own daughter anymore." Then she leaned back, jammed a heel into the hooker's rib cage and thrusted her to the curb.

Shea made it a quarter mile when she saw the glass pipe and

the bitch's purse on the floorboard. She flipped a U-turn and tossed the pipe at the corpse but kept the purse, thinking it would make for a nice keepsake. It felt good seeing the hooker flush against the asphalt, a puddle of vomit and blood around her face.

Shea rolled the window up, aimed the car for Spearfish and hoped she might see that Taco John's along the way.

8

THE EARS gave it away, standing erect when it saw the cavorting calves. And even from a hundred sixty or seventy yards, Cody could see its coal-black nose twitching. When two more flanked the alpha—the glare of the rising sun at their backs—Cody whistled for his segundo.

As the wolves descended into the arroyo, Cody pulled a repeater from the scabbard, clucked his tongue and put a spur into the roan's flank.

The wolves came out of the arroyo at full gallop and flushed a calf from the herd. It stumbled and the alpha snipped a chunk from its shank. The calf crow-hopped, kicked the wolf in the jaw, creating some distance.

Cody gave the roan its head and shouldered the repeater. Past the iron sights he could see a smudge of charcoal, a little darker than the fog, juking this way and that. He kept his elbows tucked, waiting for the sights to hover center-mass. He squeezed the trigger, saw a jolt of pink mist leap from the alpha's flank. When he lowered the rifle, Cody saw two of the wolves collapse—the third darting back the way it came.

Cody looked at the segundo, saw him grinning, the barrel of his rifle smoking.

"*Vamanos, cabron! No dejes que ese chingada se escape!*" the segundo said. Don't let that fucker get away!

Cody grinned, spurring his horse, levering another round into the chamber. "Twenty bucks whoever gets him."

The segundo belted a *grito*, told Cody game on.

As the wolf climbed the ridge, Cody fired. The bullet splashed dirt a few yards short. Now the segundo's rifle belched, but the wolf kept moving.

Cody chambered another round, led the wolf a full-length and fired.

The wolf stumbled, disappeared into the fog.

"*Hijo de puta*," the segundo said, reining in the paint.

"Better fetch yer wallet, *compadré*."

"*Tiro suerte. Suertudo*."

"Lucky my ass. That was a damn good shot and you know it."

They rode to the ridge, found a trail of blood but no wolf. They followed it, pushing deeper into the fog and could hear wheezing, labored breathing.

"Don't sound like no wolf, *cabron*," the segundo said.

Cody drew the 1911, kept his horse at a walk and could make out a dark shape on the ground. He cocked the hammer, slid a finger inside the trigger guard when the fog parted and they came upon a rawboned Indian on his back, both hands gripping his stomach, a head of long, stringy hair framing his face.

"Shit," Cody said. He dismounted, rushed to the Indian who seemed to be in shock. "The fuck's he doing here?"

"Probly some junkie from the rez, out here tweaking." The segundo nodded at the knapsack laying adjacent.

Cody put pressure over the wound, told the kid it would be okay. Saying now to the segundo, "Come on, help me get him mounted."

The segundo sat his horse, cocked his head in disbelief. "You gonna try'n save this kid?"

"We can't just leave him here."

"I say throw him in the woods, let the wolf get him. Shouldn't of been here to begin with."

Cody stood to face the segundo. "The hell's wrong with you?"

"Think about it. What happens he lives? You send him back to the rez, say please don't tell nobody? Come on..."

"It was an accident."

"Like anyone's gonna believe that. The headline'll read *White Man Shoots Unarmed Native*. And you can guaran-damn-tee them motherfuckers on the hill will own your ass when it gets out."

Cody knew he was right.

"Put him out his misery and be done with it."

Cody turned to look at the Indian—his eyes were full of fear, bouncing from the 1911 to the segundo and back. Cody weighed his options, the consequences that were bound to follow. He approached the segundo. "This is *my* outfit. Either help me, or get the fuck back home and I'll deal with you when I'm done."

The segundo stared a moment, his lips pursed. Then, he slid off the horse. "I'll get his legs."

They lifted the Indian into the roan's saddle and fashioned a lariat around his waist, anchoring it to the saddle horn. Cody mounted, told the segundo to fetch the knapsack and they headed home.

It took almost an hour to reach the shop barn. A few times the Indian went limp and Cody would pinch him in the ribs to wake him up. It felt weird, but what the hell else could he do?

"*Que vas a hacer?*" the segundo said.

Cody looked up at him. "Gotta get the bullet out, right?"

"No, no, call Murdoch, someone knows what they're doing."

"We don't got that kinda time."

"Oh, you an expert now?"

"I don't fucking know, it looks like he's dying. Go to the kit, get me gauze and alcohol."

The segundo said, "Shit," and took off running.

Cody pulled a Kershaw from his pocket, flipped it open and felt the Indian tense as he slipped the blade under the kid's shirt and sliced up through the collar. When he peeled the shirt back, Cody saw a leaking hole just above the navel.

The Indian said he was cold, asked if he was going to die.

Cody looked at him but didn't respond.

The segundo came back, a box of gauze in one hand, a bottle of whiskey in the other. "This the only thing I could find."

"Yeah, I know. Ran outta the clear stuff. Clean it."

The segundo unspooled half the gauze and started mopping blood.

"The hell're you doin?"

"*Mande?*"

"How'm I gonna patch him up you mow through all that?"

"What you expect me to use, *cabron?*"

"Grab a goddamn grease rag off the tractor, I don't know."

The segundo made a face. "You know how dirty those are?"

"This ain't the fucking Mayo Clinic, Manuel. Just do what I tell you, aright?"

Manuel backpedaled toward the tractor, staring, pointing with pronged fingers at his own eyes then flicking them at

Cody.

After Manuel cleaned the wound, Cody poured whiskey in the hole, pinning the Indian down with a forearm as the kid writhed in pain. He soaked the blade of the Kershaw, then offered some to the Indian who drank several times.

"Tie 'im down," Cody said.

"Tie him down?"

"Yeah."

"With what? You can't just keep shouting demands like I done this a thousand times."

"Whaddayou mean with what? A fucking lariat. You take the loop, rope 'em around the work bench—you know what, forget it, I'll do it myself."

Cody stormed off. He exited the shop barn to where the horses were hitched, grabbed a rope from his mount. "What does he mean with what? You'd think it's self-explanatory. What else on this ranch could he possibly tie a human being down with?" He looked at the roan. "You know what I'm saying? Shit."

Cody went back inside.

He fed a loop around the Indian and the workbench. "Now lift it up so I can get'er past the legs."

Manuel did.

"There we go." Cody pulled the slack, welding the Indian to the workbench. He handed the rope to Manuel. "Aright, now hold this shit tight."

Cody drew the Kershaw again, held it over the wound and locked eyes with the wide-eyed, terrified Indian. He said, "This gonna hurt," and waited for the Indian to nod before easing the tip of the knife into the hole, the blade grooving flesh as he worked it deeper into the pit. The Indian screamed and bucked, but the lariat did its job and the kid's midriff remained static.

Cody had half the Kershaw in when he felt something solid, not knowing if it was lead or bone till he got the blade underneath and felt it budge. He said, "I got it. I got it," working the bullet up against the wall of flesh, prying it to the surface. With a swift flick of the knife, it came out. The Indian fell slack against the workbench and the barn became silent.

"*Tu lo mataste*," Manuel said. You killed him.

Cody cut his eyes at the segundo. "Check his breathing."

Manuel bent over, put an ear to the Indian's mouth. He looked up, started to shake his head when the kid jolted awake, screaming, sending a frightened Manuel stumbling onto his rump.

It spooked Cody, too. Acting on instinct, Cody smoked the Indian with a left hook, knocking him out cold.

The barn was silent again.

Cody sighed. "Fuckin shit…"

Manuel stood and approached, fixed on something. He brushed away the Indian's hair. "*Mira, mira*."

Cody leaned in, saw a tattoo of two feathers that appeared to dangle behind the Indian's ear, then drape over his collarbone. The tip of the lowest feather formed an arrow, stopping in the space just above the Indian's heart, the letters YWK etched within the arrowhead.

"He's full-blood Yawakhan," Manuel said.

"So he's got money."

"*Si-si…*"

"Well, what the fuck's he doing here?"

Manuel shook his head, started rummaging through the

knapsack as Cody patched the wound. Manuel pulled out a wallet, went through it. "Some cash…few credit cards."

"He got ID?"

"*Si*, his *nombre es…*" Manuel said, flipping the wallet over. "Something Blackfoot." He reached in the knapsack again, but froze this time, said, "Oh shit. We got a problem," and came up with a Glock.

All black with smooth, well-defined edges. No chatter or dings in the metal. 23GEN4 was embossed along the slide and Cody figured it had never been used. "See if it's loaded."

Manuel dropped the clip, yanked the slide back and Cody clocked the spinning brass before it disappeared beneath the workbench.

"What else he got in there?"

Manuel reached in, came out with a cell phone, a bovine needle, and a vial filled with pink fluid.

"The fuck is that?" Cody said, pointing at the vial.

Manuel scrunched his nose trying to read the label. Said, "*Yo no se*," and handed it over.

Cody didn't know either.

Two words he had never seen. It gave him a bad feeling. This fucking no-good tweaker out here pumping his stock full of something. "Cull the cows. Start running inspections."

"What about him?"

"Give 'im a shot of bute. Then take him out to the shed…tie him up."

9

"APHTHAE EPIZOOTICAE," Murdoch said, handing the medical journal to Cody. "More commonly known as Foot and Mouth Disease, or Hoof and Mouth Disease."

Cody thumbed through the journal which contained several close-ups of infected cows. Painful, puss-filled scabs pocking cow hoofs, their gums, the inside of their cheeks.

Oh, and look here—ain't that nice: a bull on its side with globs of phlegm stretching from its nostrils down to the grass, bleeding from the gaping wounds in its hoofs. This invisible speck—however you say it—capable of bringing a two-thousand-pounder to its knees.

That goddamn sumbitch, Cody thought.

Murdoch lifted the vial off his desk. "Where'd you get this?"

Cody hesitated. "Found it in the pasture. Why?"

"Well it obviously came from a lab, which tells me it's more than likely a synthetic strain."

"Meaning what?"

"It's ten times more potent than the natural virus."

Cody wheeled his hand around, annoyed. "I meant what's it mean for me?"

"Right. Well, for starters, it's stronger against the elements when it's without a host. So it spreads faster, the cattle progress through the symptoms quicker, making them harder to cull."

"Well ain't that fuckin dandy." Cody flipped to the next page. The word VESICLE was at the top with a definition that didn't sound all that different than a blister. So Cody asked Murdoch about the symptoms, or what he should be on the lookout for.

"Usually they'll stop eating. The blisters in their mouth make it too painful, so what happens is they end up losing all the good weight. And another problem is the calves…something about the virus shuts down the mother's milk production."

Cody pinched his eyelids. He had a headache and could use a cup of a coffee. This goddamn day, just full of surprises.

"Here, check this out—might give ya a frame of reference," Murdoch said, waving Cody behind the desk.

Cody went around to look at the computer streaming video of a backhoe shoveling hundreds, maybe thousands of cows into a massive grave. The camera cut to a tight angle on a fire raging, and, through the flames, Cody saw the empty stare of cow eyes. The camera then panned to a rancher standing off to the side, crying, while an Englishman could be heard doing a voiceover. "This, ladies and gentleman, is mother nature at her worst. Truly, an *epidemic* of *catastrophic* proportions…" It cut to a soaring bird's-eye view. The fire engulfing what Cody was now certain to be at least a thousand head underneath a blanket of black smoke. The camera cut again, this time a medium shot, to the Englishman pacing toward the lens—that stupid, slow walk reporters always do. "Ranch owners forced to terminate and *stamp* out the virus to keep their cows from suffering. I'm here now with Frank Hatton,"—the Englishman draped an arm over the rancher's shoulder, this poor bastard also with an accent—"What have you got to say, Frank?" The rancher named Frank wiped tears, kept looking back at the flames. "It's over. It's all over. I...I don't know what we'll do now." He turned away, apologized to someone out of frame and asked would they turn off the camera. But it kept rolling, closing in on him in this slow, dramatic fashion as he wept.

"Turn this shit off, would ya?" Cody said.

"Sorry, pard. Just wanted you to know how serious *it* is."

"Kinda asshole video tapes somethin like 'at? I can't stand it. It's like the shit you see on the news after a tornader come through'n wipe out someone's house. And they're interviewing 'em, right, and in the background's just this pile of rubble where their house a fifty years used to stand. Then, middle a the interview, you hear this whining, and it's the owner's dog barking. So they run to it, find it buried beneath half the house. And they're so old they can't even lift a rock, but they're crying, trying to dig through these two by fours and brick and sheet rock—and whatever the fuck else the tornader dumped on 'em—to rescue their only friend. And what's the cameraman and the asshole with the microphone do? Jam it in their face, ask what they wanna say'n how they're feeling, 'stead a putting the damn thing down and helping."

"Jesus Cody, relax, I's just trying to show you—"

"The man lost his livelihood, Doch. Don't nobody give a rat's ass about that?"

"It wasn't just him. That's the point I'm trying to make. How many other ranches in the vicinity got livestock?"

Cody thought about it, seeing the fence-lines in his mind. "Ever one of 'em, 'cept the reservation to the north."

"Right." Murdoch pointed at the monitor. "This one happened in the UK back in '99 and saw two thousand cases inside a month. And I'm not talkin two thousand head, no...

Two thousand ranches across several hundred miles. This is some nasty shit, pard. It clings to your clothes, your tractors, it can get airborne, hell, even the cattle pass it back and forth to one another. I'm talkin bad."

"What about horses?"

"Only cloven-hoof animals," Murdoch said, shaking his head. "Cows, sheep, goats, pigs, bison…"

Cody became lightheaded and thought he might faint. Right here, just let it all go, knock himself out. Maybe he'd wake up tomorrow, find out it was all a dream. He stumbled, caught himself on Murdoch's desk and decided no, this was real. It was happening.

"You all right, bud?"

Cody nodded, said he was fine.

"How long ago did you find this?"

"Just this morning."

"And when did they get infected?"

"That I don't know. And I ain't even positive they *are* infected, I just didn't know who else I could go to."

"Well, hate to break it to ya, but, see this here?" Murdoch was pointing at the top of the vial where a tiny hole had punctured the black cap. "While that don't necessarily mean they were injected, what it does mean is that serum was pulled. You by chance find a bovine syringe in the same vicinity you found this?"

Cody nodded.

"Any residue in the chamber or was it dry?"

"Didn't even look."

"Well shit. Safe to say you're no detective." Murdoch pointed at the medical journal. "Pass me that." He slipped on his reading glasses, flipped a few pages one way, then the other, using a finger to skim the columns, tapping the finger now, saying, "Here we go. This says incubation is twenty-four hours. What that means is—"

"I'll know by then if they're infected."

"I guess you're not as dumb as you look. So assuming you culled 'em, the virus can be contained."

"But what happens it gets airborne?"

"That's a whole different conversation with a lot of science and math I don't think you need to worry about right now. And look, it's not like they cough or sneeze and a crapload of viruses float on the wind shitting on anything with hoofs. It may affect some that are downwind, it may not. You got enough acreage where you put plenty a distance between 'em, they might be alright. And humidity's low, so the shelf-life of the virus once it's airborne ain't as good as if it were, say, August. But I'll tell you this, and you're not gonna like it. Assuming they are infected and you culled 'em right, there isn't nothing you can do till they start showing symptoms. And if and when that happens—to keep it from spreading and to keep the cows from suffering—better *prepare* yourself 'cause you may have to terminate a few."

Cody took the vial and thanked Murdoch for the wonderful news. He started out of the office, but stopped at the doorway. "One more question…"

"Shoot…"

"What's it do to humans?"

10

SHERIFF HARRIS bit into his cold cut and thought they put too much goddamn mayo on it again. He wiped his mustache, removed the top piece of bread, shaved a layer off, took another bite and thought the hell with it, he'd just have it without the bread today.

He heard the jingle bells bounce off the door, but didn't look up to see who it was. He had a nice view of Third and Main. The post office was across the street to the left, the station over to the right, and that new coffee shop run by some hipsters from California was directly across the street.

Harris glanced at the TV mounted in the corner. The local news was showing a headshot of the Custer gal—it wasn't as flattering as he remembered her in person. She was tracking two points over her opponent, but they still had some time before the election, so Harris didn't think much of it until he heard someone say, "Sheriff Harris?" and looked over and saw the woman from the photo, smiling, her hand extended. She had bags under her eyes, like she hadn't slept. She said, "I don't know if you remember me—"

"I know who ya are," Harris said, cordial, no smile. He noticed the haggard purse on her shoulder and thought it didn't match the rest of her professional, well-tailored ensemble.

"Mind if I have a seat?"

She was already sliding in the booth and Harris got the feeling he was being cornered and thought it was a bad look. The two of them hanging out, shooting the shit for the whole town to see. "Yeah, I do actually."

She cocked her head, said, "Seriously?" but didn't get up.

"Yep." He shoved a palm skyward, gesturing for her to stand. And she did.

Harris could tell it made her feel awkward. He thanked her, his tone a little more serious than smartass. He took a bite of salami and waited for her next move.

"I'm sorry, did I do something wrong?"

"Well yeah, you interrupted my lunch. And I know it ain't 'cause yer concerned about how I'm doing or how my day's going. It's 'cause you want something."

"What makes you say that?"

"Only thing a politician knows how to do."

"Well I'm not a politician yet, so…"

"Yeah, ya are. It's just a matter now of whether or not these people want you to be theirs. And correct me if I'm wrong, but you coming in here, it ain't just by happenstance. You knew you could find me here."

"Hate to break it to you, Sheriff, but you're not that high on my agenda. I just stopped in for a cup of coffee, saw you sitting here and thought it'd be nice to officially meet."

"All due respect, Miss Custer, but that's a crock of shit. Don't no one come here for the coffee. It's got a air a diesel fuel about it, they don't do lattés, and if you asked Ruth over there for a cold brew, she'd probably just throw something at ya."

Shea brushed a golden lock from of her face—wearing her

hair down today, a little wave to it. "I'm impressed you know what that is."

"What, cold brew?"

She nodded.

"Oh, I'm cultured as shit. And forgive me for passin judgement, but a gal like you more'n likely fuels up on that frothy shit them kids're cooking up 'cross the street. So let me ask ya again, and if ya ain't figured it out yet, honesty's kind of a big deal with me..." He grabbed the lemon hugging the rim of his sweet tea and took it all in one bite. "It wasn't just happenstance. You knew you'd find me here, why?"

"Because you eat here every day."

"Right. And I never seen *you* in here before, so how'd you figure that out?"

"Apparently a few guys from the Local 49 are quite fond of this place."

"The Local 49?"

"It's not important. Look, I just wanted to introduce myself and have a nice, casual conversation—"

"Because you want something," Harris said.

"Who doesn't?"

He could appreciate that. "Then do us both a favor'n just get to it."

"I think we can work together."

"Ya do, huh?"

"Six months after I'm elected, you're up for re-election..."

"Little over-confident for someone only up two points."

"Be that as it may, it's going to happen. Then it's your brass on the chopping block. And look, I like you, think you're doing a great job as sheriff."

Harris let it slide, her being a smartass.

"But to win that next election, you'll need votes from people like me and those I'm affiliated with."

"Those yer affiliated with... You talkin about the Indians?"

She nodded. "And before you shrug it off, because we all know their ballots typically end up in the trash—"

"It ain't that I'm for the way it is now. But the law says what it says. No physical address, no vote."

"And the ones that do, but don't speak the language?"

"You wanna put some obscure translator in the budget for a language ain't even written, be my guest."

"It's a bill my team is already drafting. And let's be honest, the legislature is a bunch of politically correct pushovers, so there's no way they'll deny or even stall it. Which means by the time you're up for re-election, those one hundred sixty-eight Yawakhan votes are going to be quite substantial in a town of this size."

Harris leaned back, wondered how everyone could be so stupid. Two points up in the polls, are you kidding? The broad's saying one thing and doing the complete opposite. But her cards were on the table now, and Harris wanted to see how far she was willing to go, so he said, "Whaddayou want from me?"

"You seem to be well liked. The lower-class, blue-collar types, they relate to a guy like you."

"You want me to come out the rallies, show my support. I scratch yer back, you scratch mine kinda thing?"

"Exactly."

He acted like he was thinking about it. Looked out the window, saw Thelma pulling up in her Ranger. "What's in it for me?"

"Other than re-election?"

Harris nodded.

"You want an incentive, I can appreciate that. Your salary is shit, I'm assuming?"

He showed some teeth. "It's nice we're on the same page."

"Well I have no doubt we'd be open to the discussion."

The bells clinked against the door as Thelma entered. She had a surprised look and beelined for the booth, but was intercepted by Ruth.

"I'd need something concrete. Give me a number 'fore my deputy gets here and ruins it for both of us."

Shea glanced back. "Not a fan, huh?"

"That'd be an understatement. So what's it gonna be?"

"A hundred grand a year."

"Cash, I'm assuming?"

Shea nodded. "Most likely from our friends on the reservation."

"Well that sounds aright to me. Cain't even begin to think of all the shit I could do with an extra hunnert kay…" He waited for her to grin before saying, "But I'ma have to pass."

All she could muster was, "Huh?" like it just fell out of her mouth.

Harris stood, threw a twenty on the table. "Yeah, ironically enough, I ain't in this job for the paycheck. But now I know a *whole* lot more about you. So I'm gonna say thanks, but no thanks on the showing support bit."

He smiled, hiked his Wrangler's. At five-ten his eyes were dead even with hers. He said, "Have a good rest'yer day," and moved past her, approaching Thelma but stopping when Shea asked if he liked what he did for a living, an edge to her voice.

Harris turned back, grinning. "Yes ma'am."

"And I heard you were in the Army before this, is that right?"

76

Harris nodded.

"So law enforcement seemed liked the obvious route, but did you ever think of doing anything else?"

He shook his head, still grinning.

"You might want to start."

Harris felt the grin evaporate. Shea brushed past him, past Thelma and Ruth, and Harris heard the jingle bells clink against the door.

Thelma came up quick. "You gonna tell me the hell that was about?"

"It's nothin."

"Bullshit it's nothin. I know when yer lying, Weston."

"Really, how?"

"That mustache lifts ever so slightly in the corners, like yer tryin yer damndest not to smile."

"It does not."

"Then how'd I know? I'm tellin ya, get rid of it, you could be the next big poker stud. I can see it now: Weston 'The Alabama Black Mamba' Harris."

"The Black Mamba?"

"Yeah, you know, the snake…"

"Christ, ain't no black mambas in Alabama, Thelma. That's a damn African snake, ain't it?"

Thelma looked up at the ceiling. "I don't know. I'll look it up the computer later."

"I'm sure you will."

"Whatever, you get what I'm sayin. You got a tell and it's that damn mustache. So instead a lying, tell *me* what the hell that was all about."

Harris sighed. "She offered me a bribe. A good one."

"I knew it," Thelma said, watching Shea cross the street

toward the hipster coffee shop. "I damn knew it. That good for nothin, low-down, piece of—"

"Hunnert kay a year. Cash."

"Well what'd ya say? You'd at least think about it?"

"Wow, yer a brick wall. Seriously, a hunnert kay, that's all it'd take? What was all that shit about keeping my head on a swivel?"

"You have any idea what I could do with all that moolah?"

"Six months, you'd funnel it right down a slot machine."

Thelma turned, put her hands on her hips. "Really, you take me for some old bag, a cuppa quarters, sitting the damn slots? I'm insulted, really."

"My bad. Yer a craps gal." It felt good to be joking with her, easing the tension, the bad feeling in his gut.

"I wouldn't piss it away gambling, Weston."

"Then what would you spend it on?"

"I'd pay ya to shave that damn mustache off yer face. Would you do it for that, a hundred-thou?"

Harris rubbed the edges of his mustache, trying to remember how he looked without it. Then he eyed Thelma and told her, No, not for a million bucks.

11

PAPPY was looking at a dead man in a shallow grave when he heard her voice. The man reminded Pappy of himself, some thirty-five, forty years ago. Cracks spiderwebbed across a dehydrated earth littered with dead bluefin tuna. The woman's voice was beckoning from beyond the ashen horizon and Pappy turned his horse as a black swell flooded the surface, enveloping the horse. He saw the dead man smiling, mumbling what sounded like, "See you soon." The surface of the black mass continued rising, swallowing the dead man and the horse. Pappy tried swimming, fighting to keep his chin above the surface. As it inched up his neck, he could no longer move his arms or his legs, so he accepted fate and allowed himself to be consumed.

When he opened his eyes, he saw hers and nothing else. Those steel blues full of concern.

She asked if he was okay.

He didn't nod right away. He could hear the tube, commentators gabbing about a senior in the on-deck circle. One of them saying, "I mean, look at the size of those shoulders." The other one saying, "How many bats is she...is that three? Is she swinging three bats to warm up?" Pappy turned, saw the sheets rustled on the bed and figured at some point he must have moved from the bed to the chair, but didn't know if Shea had helped him. He remembered a brief conversation, though he couldn't recall details or even when it was. Could have been yesterday or a few minutes ago. It was all hazy.

"Fell asleep, huh?"

She straightened. "Yeah. Whew. Scared me for a minute."

"Sorry honey. All these drugs're screwin me up." He glanced at the tube, saw a gal built like a brick shithouse in the on-deck circle with three bats in her duke, loosening her shoulder. He looked back at Shea and said he had the strangest dream.

"About what?"

"Yer daddy." He wiped at the cannula irritating his nose. "Been looking all over for him last twenty-seven years of my life. And…and…"

"You found him?"

Pappy nodded. "Out in Californy. Buried in the dirt up to his neck, surrounded by a buncha beached tuna. Big suckers. I'm talkin thousand pounders. His teeth were rotted, mouth fulla sand. But he said he didn't need no help. Said he was at peace. Then I heard you. Yer voice echoed from across the sky like you was God or something. And then the tide come in, this black shit, like crude, it come in and he was gone."

Shea was looking off, perhaps trying to visualize it.

When she didn't speak, Pappy said, "What were we talkin about…'fore I fell asleep?"

"I was trying to figure out why in the hell you're watching softball."

"Can't find the damn remote."

"And what's Cody doing? He doesn't help?"

"Really? I tell him I lost the remote, he says, 'It's probly in the chair or some shit,' and walks out."

"That figures. Any idea where it might be?"

"Only other place…" Pappy stopped to cough up phlegm. The salty, soft chunks idling on his palate. He looked for something to spit in and saw an empty bottle across the room. He pointed at it, mumbled, and waited for her to pass it over before clearing his mouth. He could tell it grossed her out. "Only other place I go is the bed or the can."

Shea went to the bed, rustled the sheets, looked under the pillows. Then she came back to the recliner, said, "Can you pull the leg rest?" and stepped back as Pappy cranked the lever. She swiped at her phone, a cool white light beamed from it.

"The hell is that?"

"What?" She was on her stomach now, searching under the leg rest.

"That damn thing's brighter'n a Maglite."

"Yeah, but you can't drop it a thousand times or bash a window in and expect it to work."

Pappy shrugged, impressed just the same. The girl at the plate smacked a pop-fly. The shortstop moved under it, snatched the ball then whipped it around the horn. The camera cut to the brick shithouse as she spat. Crimson streaks under shadowy eyes fixed on the pitcher. The half-pint on the mound staring right back. A cute little thing with a nice figure.

"Got it," Shea said, getting to a knee, the remote in hand.

"Thank God. Put it on 205, would ya?"

"Long as you tell me why it's on softball in the first place."

"Bullshit. Ain't copping to that."

"Come on, just admit it. You were flipping channels, had every intention of moving on until it showed one of those co-eds bent over, ready to steal second, and you liked the way her tush looked in those pants. So you thought, maybe I'll watch for a minute, see what happens. One at-bat turns into an entire game, at which point you lost the remote."

Pappy grinned. He told her she was more or less correct about the snug pants and all. That he was a guy, it was only natural. Then he asked would she put it on 205 because he just wanted to move on from the subject.

Shea changed the channel. "I should've figured. You ever watch anything else?"

"Let me tell you something... When the other guys start talking the truth, I'l take a gander, cross-reference it with what these guys're saying."

"I meant other than news, but whatever."

"I got something like a thousand channels on this thing, and there ain't never anything to watch. I stick to what I know."

Shea's phone buzzed. She looked at it, the screen lighting her face. "I get it. Nothing but bad reality shows these days." The screen went dark and she slipped it in her purse. "What I need to do is put some Velcro here"—running a finger over the back of the remote—"and put a strip on the fold-out, maybe another near the bed so you don't lose it again." She sat on the chair arm. "How's your breathing? You sound congested."

"Could use another shot of that blue stuff, I guess."

"Where is it?"

"On the dresser."

Loading the syringe, she said, "You know, the more I'm here, the more I think about how much this place means to me."

"Really?"

"Mm-hmm." Shea stepped in front of the tube, bent at the hips and Pappy tasted the sweet nectar as she thumbed the plunger. He licked his lips, felt the tension in his chest subside.

"All the history, the memories from my childhood…" She paused to look out the window. "It's hard to fathom what'll happen if it's left in the hands of incompetence."

"He's a good rancher, Shea."

"Well, he's a good workhorse."

"What is it with the two a you? Y'all can't agree on shit. Been that way ever since you was kids. It's like God put something fundamentally different in each of ya so you could drive me up a fucking wall till the day I die."

"Oh, come on…"

"It's true. You really think I can leave a piece of this place to both of you and not expect anything but all out warfare when I'm gone?"

"You know what'll happen if he takes over? I give it six months before the entire operation's in the ground. And it would be a shame and a disgrace having the Custer name knowing I allowed it to happen. Knowing I didn't do everything in my power to keep it alive. This ranch, it's a staple—"

"Then why'd you leave it?"

She lowered her brow, flared her nostrils. "You really want to discuss that right now?"

Pappy knew the look. Knew she'd start on that shit about her daddy again, everything she *claimed* he did to her. "Why're you doing this? I'm here today, gone tomorrow, and all you wanna do is argue about what kinda deal yer getting. I ain't doin it. If you wanna sit here, watch some goddamn news with me, then pull up a chair. But I ain't talking about the ranch. It goes to Cody. Was always going to Cody. That's the end of it."

"Fine," Shea said, grabbing her purse, moving for the door.

Big surprise, Pappy thought. The hubris of this girl. "I mean, how stupid you think I was?"

"Excuse me?"

"Get back here." He waited for her to block the tube again. "You know, I put up with it—you acting like you give a damn about me. And I'll admit, it was nice having you around. Having a woman back in the house. Even though I knew the whole time it was all a ruse. You always wanted something."

"How dare you."

"Yeah, how dare me. What an asshole I am. A year ago you tried to get me to sell. Now yer standing there talking about the name, the legacy, how sentimental it is."

"Because I want to see it thrive," Shea said. "I don't want to see it wilt away—and I know if you give it to Cody that's exactly what'll happen."

"Then that's what'll happen and I'm fucking fine with it. He's earned it."

Shea moved close, squatting down until her eyes were level with his—a look Pappy had never seen. The concern had been replaced with a smoldering rage and it seemed the Shea he had known forever wasn't the one operating those eyes. Someone evil, someone darker was lurking in the backs of them.

"You're sure that's what you want to do?" she said.

"You damn right."

"Then so be it." She kissed him on the mouth. "When you're good and dead, I'll sit high up on that hill and watch this place *burn*. And any legacy you think you or Cody could've left behind will vanish with the Custer name."

She left. And Pappy figured that'd be the last time he'd ever see Shea Custer.

12

KENNY couldn't stand the heat coming off the studio lights. He was beginning to sweat and worried his makeup would run. The first broad they gave him—some emo-chick with tattoo sleeves and a nose ring—said she did *all* the makeup for *all* the talent on the James Cordon show.

Kenny had no idea who that was.

When she spun him to face the mirror, saying, "Check it out, tell me what you think, babe," Kenny had said, "Are you fucking serious?" unable to take his eyes off the alabaster face looking back at him. Kenny thought the bitch did it on purpose, because no way could a professional be this bad at her job. So he grabbed a producer, told the son of a bitch to fire her ass for whitewashing. Then he had Hector scramble to find someone at the Mingan who knew what they were doing. Someone who could accentuate the natural caramel in his skin.

He wondered why so many people were standing around doing nothing. Or why only one guy could plug in the lights, but another had to set them up. Seemed like a waste of money when he could hire a few wetbacks at seven an hour, have everything done in half the time.

"Are you ready?" the reporter said. He was in a snug khaki

suit. No socks, a pair of hairy ankles showing beneath his pant legs.

Kenny stretched a smile. "Let's do it."

A guy swept in, pulled tissues from Kenny's collar and someone else started counting down from ten as red lights illuminated atop the cameras.

"It's going to be great," the reporter said. "Just act like they're not even here."

Kenny looked at him. "The cameras or the people?"

The reporter didn't answer. A female voice called action and the reporter looked past Kenny, right at one of the cameras. "A descendent of the legendary Crazy Horse, before thirty he accumulated more wealth than many working Americans will see in a lifetime, and at thirty-nine, became the tribe's youngest ever chief. But it wasn't—"

Kenny snickered. "We use chairman now. But yes, that's correct."

The reporter paused. He looked at someone behind the camera. "We're going to take that back, yeah?"

Kenny could see figures moving behind the lights. A man with graying hair stepped in between them with a whiteboard, yelled it was take two, then clapped the fucking thing so loud it made Kenny's ear ring.

When he could see the reporter again, Kenny said, "I'm sorry. It felt weird with all the cameras on me. And the term chief is—I don't know where you got that by the way, but it's antiquated. Gives the impression I run around the office in a headdress with a fucking bow and arrow."

"It's fine. I'll change it to chairman. We'll take it from the top, but wait for me to finish the lead in, at which point I'll turn to you, ask a question—you remember the question, yeah?"

"You say, 'It wasn't always like that,' or something around there…"

"That's correct. From there, the scene will move into a dialogue between us, but it's very important I get the lead-in first. It's kind of what I'm known for."

Kenny rolled his eyes. "I get it. Let's get the ball rolling, uh?"

The reporter gave himself a countdown, then started the lead in. Kenny waited until the guy said, "But it wasn't always like that?" before he shook his head, saying, "I remember as a kid standing in line with my mother for brick cheese and powdered milk and all the other awful government surplus options."

It still felt weird. The energy in the room had changed. Kenny found it hard to speak at first, could sense the tension in his cheeks and thought maybe he was smiling too much. He remembered one of the producers telling him, "Don't sweat it. Do whatever you want. The camera loves you." But the reporter—this dick named Dwyer—would say things like, "Do nothing." Or, "Less is more," right before someone yelled action.

"And now the Mingan," Dwyer said, "which you founded, is *the* fastest growing tribal casino in the nation."

"It's the fastest growing casino, period. Most *tribal* casinos are a joke."

"Alright, let's cut it." He looked at Kenny. "Does it really matter?"

"Yeah, it fucking matters. I don't know who did your research, but if I were you, I'd show 'em the door."

The reporter hesitated, looking past the camera again, beyond the lights. He turned back to Kenny. "Fine, whatever. We'll do it your way…"

God damn right you will.

"...but just give me one clean take all the way through. Then we can go bit by bit and tweak things however you want. That work?"

Kenny looked at his watch. He'd been under these damn lights for two hours and it seemed like they hadn't accomplished a thing. His ass cheeks were numb. His foot was asleep. "One take and that's it. I've got money to make. You want to start the countdown, or should I?"

Dwyer glared, but started the countdown. As they went through the questions, Kenny liked the edge in his voice. It no longer felt like a TV interview where he wanted to please the millions watching on the other end. It seemed more like a negotiation, a business deal.

Dwyer was back to the part about the Mingan being the fastest growing *casino* in the nation...

"That's right. And I'm proud to say, since its inception four years ago, we've paid each of our hundred and sixty-eight members nearly two million dollars."

That got the guy's attention, made him perk in his seat. "Each?"

"Every single one. That's the beauty of our system and the Yawakhan Nation. If one of us advances, the entire tribe reaps the benefits."

"How does that make you feel? Before the casino, many in your tribe had assimilated into the Hispanic communities, ashamed of their Native roots."

Kenny shook his head, a slight grin. "Not anymore. Now they golf at country clubs and vacation in Paris."

"Instead of working."

"Excuse me?"

"Well it's no mystery unemployment rates on the reservation are at an all-time high—ninety-seven percent."

"Because they no longer need those thankless, underpaid jobs."

"Do you feel it's deserved? Because so much was taken from your people, it's a sense of poetic justice?"

"I don't care how many casinos we build," Kenny said. "We'll never overcome what was taken from our ancestors."

"Sounds like you're referring to the Black Hills."

Kenny nodded. "Imagine if Italy decided it no longer cared for Catholicism, so they overtook the Vatican and forced the Cardinals onto a piece of land so small they're living on top of one another in poverty with no running water or electricity. And then decided to turn the Basilica into a night club."

Dwyer scoffed. "Well that's a little different."

"How so?"

"Because Saint Peter's is sacred to Christians all over the world, some one billion people."

"It was a cemetery before it was a church, and it's only a church because Constantine was Christian."

Dwyer looked off, placed two fingers over his earpiece. "There are many out there that believe the only reason you want the Black Hills is for Mingan expansion—"

"Not true."

"Well I'm getting an earful from my producer right now saying our field team has interviewed several ranchers, and many of them believe the reason you're buying the land back and putting it in trust is an effort to essentially work the system. It becomes tribal land you can do whatever you want with it—avoid taxes, build another casino, shopping malls, what have you—and the government would have zero control or the ability to regulate."

"A little ironic Americans would be up in arms about something like that," Kenny said.

"But what do you say to that? These are things you'll have to make a case for, because some will say you're doing it for the money. The gold, the timber and the other lucrative resources—and you're using the *welfare* of your people as a scapegoat."

"That's laughable."

"Yeah, I get that from you, sitting there grinning like it's a joke. But the proof is in the pudding, and I'm telling you these are pressing issues bound to be on everyone's mind after seeing this. Sure, they'll see the glitz, the glam of the casino, but they're also going to see the trailer park, the ghetto that most of your tribe lives in. I mean, you're rolling around town in luxury—"

"As are they."

"Fine," Dwyer said, getting irritated. "But they're living in shanties."

"You know I bought an entire subdivision two hours from here in which every home is now owned by a member of the tribe. My thinking was it's a way for them to venture off the reservation, try to integrate and grow with the general population. But ninety-nine percent of the time those homes are vacant, and you know why? Because ever since John O'Sullivan coined the term Manifest Destiny, you fucking people thought it was incumbent upon yourselves to shove democracy down the throat of anyone you came across that didn't operate like you. And if they rebelled, you either slaughtered them, enslaved them, or shoved them onto a reservation. So now it's become engrained—whether you're willing to admit it or not—that when you see brown skin or a feather, you turn a cold shoulder."

"That's race-baiting and you know it."

"I don't think with that pale face you're in a position to tell me or my people how we're supposed to feel in public. Because the fact of the matter is simple: when people like me start going to *your* grocery stores and *your* banks they get shunned and made to feel not welcome—like we're the assholes, that we did this to ourselves. And I'm not talking about a Native here or a Native there, because let's be honest, all you people love a good token so you can feel good about yourself, like you're this beacon of tolerance and inclusion. But the attitude changes when it becomes five, ten, hell, twenty percent. And all of a sudden, people put their hands up, say 'Woah, I don't know about this. Things are changing a little quick.' So guess what? I've talked with my people and found they'd rather live in the *shanties*—your words, not mine. And the reason their homes are the way they are, is because there is zero room left for us to build. To start anew. So yeah, I'm buying it all back—the Black Hills, Spearfish, everything—and I'm doing it at an incredible rate. And when I'm done, my people will have enough room to flourish—shit, to walk out on their porch and catch a breath of fresh air for once. That's our American dream. So you can say I'm doing it for gold or timber, whatever, but the Black Hills—or in my language, *Paha Sapa*—means, 'the heart of everything that is.' It's more than sentiment. It's all that's ever mattered to my people. And if it takes an asinine amount of money to get it, so be it, because I won't stop at anything, *anything* to get it back."

* * *

"Fucking wannabe Dan Rather," Kenny said. They were moving down the hallway, Hector lagging behind. "Can you believe the generalizations from that racist prick?"

"You're handling it well," Shea said.

The bitch and her snide comments. Kenny let it go, picking his battles. "He basically compared me to Kim Jong Un."

"I wouldn't go that far."

"That's exactly what he did. Maybe he didn't come right out and say it, but to tell me I'm using the tribe as a scapegoat to advance my own agenda? I should've knocked his fucking teeth in."

"And risk getting blood on your Brioni? I can't picture it."

Kenny stopped. He hated when she put on this front, giving him a hard time, talking to him like one of the boys. "Really? You're giving me shit right now?"

"He's a reporter, okay? The only time he *cares* about the facts are when they support his agenda. You knew that going in."

"Yeah, well I dealt with it, put him in his place. That's all the matters."

Shea scoffed.

"You think I didn't?"

"Oh you put him in his place all right, but in doing so, talked shit to the majority of your clientelé. Maybe you haven't realized all the rednecks downstairs shooting craps, but they don't come to Spearfish just to see what the Mingan's all about. They're in the region for Mount Rushmore, Sturgis, or to snap a few photos of the Black Hills. And, quite frankly, the only thing you *had* going for you was its proximity to those hotspots."

"Fuck the hotspots."

"The point is you may have just ruined a good thing because you allowed the priss in the tight suit to get under your skin."

"It doesn't matter. The casino's done its job. We close on the Flying-C, I'll have everything I need to license a spread the size of Rhode Island for that fucking pipeline. So by the time this bullshit interview airs, crude'll be pumping money into Yawakhan pockets so fast they won't have enough places to put it."

"Yawakhan pockets," Shea said, biting her lip. "You know, the more I hear you talk about it, the less I feel like I'll have a seat at the table when it's all said and done."

"No, that's not what I meant."

"But it's what you always say. And it makes me wonder if you really do love me, or if you're just stringing me along to get what you want."

Well...maybe he loved her, maybe he didn't. But one thing was certain: he could never love her as much as his majority stake in the transportation system for American crude. "Baby. This does not work without you. And there's no point to any of it unless I have someone to share it with. Okay?"

Before she could answer, Kenny's phone buzzed.

"Who is it?" she said.

He showed her the screen with Bodaway's name written across.

13

BLACKFOOT couldn't feel his arms when he woke. They were secured above his head at the wrists and his feet were tied at the ankles. The right side of his jaw ached, though nothing compared to his gut or the inside of his mouth. His tongue was swollen and he could feel it pressing against the inside of his teeth. He remembered he had been shot, but that's about it.

Wait. Cowboy hats. That's right. Two of them, both dirty. One dark brown, the other tan or khaki; silverbelly he thought it was called.

He felt something move over his foot. Looked down, saw a rat—a big fat one—licking at a pool of blood. The blood, he realized, had been dripping from the soaked gauze taped to his stomach.

He spooked. Kicked at the rat until it scurried into the corner and disappeared. He spat. Cursed. Then, he eyed the taut ropes hitched to a support beam overhead and yanked on them, but had no strength, no feeling, and they didn't budge. He became nauseous, felt a cold sweat breaking, his body revolting from the lack of opiates.

He vomited, mainly stomach acid.

When he looked up at the rusted door straight ahead, two

shadowed columns appeared in the streak of light across the bottom. The handle shook. Voices could be heard. A white man's and maybe a wetback's—Latin for sure. Keys jingled.

When Blackfoot heard the door unlock, he panicked. Let his knees drop and winced from the pain in his shoulders as he hung there, pretending to be asleep.

The door opened. Heavy footsteps fast approaching. A sharp pain struck his leg and he thought he'd been shot again. He screamed.

When he opened his eyes he saw the big-ass fucking bovine needle sticking out of his thigh. Christ, the chamber filled with that pink diseased shit from the vial. A tall cracker stood over him and the wetback was behind, off to the side.

"There's enough in there to kill fifteen hunnert pounds," the cowboy said. "Any idea what'll happen to a little shit like you?"

"Pleathze...don't." Blackfoot was confused by his newfound lisp but chalked it up to the cottonmouth.

"Then tell me who sent you."

"Come on man, I can't thell you that."

The cowboy gripped the syringe, shoved it deeper and Blackfoot wailed through clenched teeth.

"That a bone I'm hitting?"

"Motha...Ah! Mothafucka! You know I can't thay nothin, they'll kill me I thsnitch on 'em."

"I'll fuckin kill you right now, I don't give a shit. You decide how you want this to end."

Blackfoot looked at the cowboy underneath a felt hat—the brim funneled low over a pair of deep-set eyes. He said, "Fuck you, white boy," and hocked a loogie in the dude's face.

The cowboy recoiled and Blackfoot caught a glimpse of the wetback's pocket knife before it was jammed into his good leg then ripped out.

He screamed again.

The wetback, inches from his face now, muttered something in wetback.

"Gothamnit," Blackfoot said. "Kenny Black Elk, man."

"Why'd he send you?" the cowboy said.

"I thell you, you promise not tha pump that thit into me?"

"I'll think about it."

Blackfoot saw the cold stare in the man's eyes and thought spitting in his face was a stupid fucking idea. He wished he could have that one back. He said, "Fuck, this is thum bull-thit," then proceeded to tell them why he was there.

The cowboy cocked his head and turned to look at the wetback. "I can't understand a damn thing he's sayin. You?"

The guy shook his head, said something else in wetback and motioned this way.

The cowboy approached. "I'm a look in yer mouth. You even think about biting me or spitting on me again, I got a lot cooler shit to cut you with than a needle and some pocket knives. And I'll let you guess which appendage goes first. *Comprendé?*"

Blackfoot's eyes widened. His peter shriveled. He nodded.

The cowboy told him to open.

His fingers were rough, thick with callouses. Blackfoot tasted dirt as the cowboy held his jaw open, the dude's eyes gliding back and forth, a small clump of mucus stuck in his eyebrow. What it was, too. One thick eyebrow. Thinner in the middle, sure, but a single eyebrow nonetheless.

"Can't see shit," the cowboy said. "You got a light, Manuel?"

The wetback pulled a mini Maglite out and beamed it over the man's shoulder.

"Say ah."

Blackfoot did.

"Well I'll be goddamn," the cowboy said. "Look at this." He stepped aside, and it was the one named Manuel's turn.

"*Chinga tu madré*, Cody. You hit him so hard he bit off his tongue."

"Not all of it."

"A pretty good chunk, *cabron*. So swollen it takes up his whole mouth."

"The hell'd you expect me to do? One minute yer sayin he's dead, the next he's sitting up like a damn Injun possessed."

"*Dios mio*. Kinda feel bad about stabbing him."

"Don't even."

"Well shit, Cody, he been shot, stabbed—with a knife *and* a big-ass fucking bovine needle—and now this?"

"Coming from the guy wanted to kill him."

"I feel like he woulda preferred that."

"Shut it, would ya?" the cowboy said, turning now to face Blackfoot. "Tell me again why you're here. And don't leave nothin out."

Blackfoot sighed, then told them everything. It took a while with his tongue. They'd stop, ask him to clarify, or blurt out random words trying to figure it out to help finish his sentences.

What a shit show. Blackfoot was tired of talking by the time he finished.

And now they were the ones looking possessed, rage filling their eyes.

It reminded Blackfoot of an ancient Yawakhan proverb: *The spider and the fly cannot make a bargain.* Which, in modern times, meant that Kenny and these fuckers would never make a truce. No doubt about it. The only way he would make it out alive is if both of these dudes were dead. And the only way that would happen is if he struck first. So Blackfoot decided to keep his cool, to be patient. They would leave, and when they came back, he'd be ready. He was the spider. The shed was his web.

Manuel said, "Why's he buying all the ranches? And don't give us that Uncle Sam stole our sacred land bullshit."

"Think he thold me? I'm thust onna thob, man, thrying thoo make a buck. Thraight up."

Cody stepped closer. "How many my cows you get?"

Blackfoot shook his head. "I thidn't."

Cody gripped the syringe again, the needle jabbing the inside of Blackfoot's thigh.

"I ain't fucking around."

"I thwear thoo God—"

"How many."

"I thidn't—"

"How many!"

Blackfoot tasted metal on his teeth. His heart thumped in his chest. "I thidn't thouch none. I thwear thoo fucking God, man. Pleathze thon't thoo this. Pleathze…"

The syringe hurt almost as bad getting ripped out as it did going in.

Cody reached into his back pocket, pulled out a phone Blackfoot recognized as his—the protective cover made to look like an old cassette tape. The cowboy kept pushing the button at the bottom, giving the phone a baffled look.

"The hell's the goddamn passcode?"

Blackfoot sighed, gave him the six numbers, and Cody dialed.

After a moment, he said, "Oh you bet yer ass it's done," then listened some before saying, "I think ya already know who it is. Got somethin belongs to you."

Cody held the phone out, told Blackfoot to speak.

"Thsup…" Blackfoot said, then heard his Uncle Kenny coming through the speaker, asking if he was okay.

"Yeah, Unc. I'm awight."

"You're all white?" Kenny said. "What'd you say?"

"I thed, I'm aw-wight."

"Speak louder, I can't understand you…"

Cody took it off speaker. "He said he's fucking fine, okay? Now look…" His voice trailed off as he listened again. Then he said, "Goddamnit," and put the phone back on speaker. "He ain't takin my word for it so tell him yer good."

Blackfoot leaned in. "I'm good."

"Why's he sound so weird?" Kenny said.

Cody took it off speaker again. "I don't know, maybe he's a half retard. Hell, you should know, yer the one sent him. Now look, here's the deal… Would you shut the fuck up and listen! Incubation's twenty-four hours. I'll call back in thirty-six. This fucking piss-ant's my collateral now."

Manuel led Cody out and the shed was dark again, a single streak beneath the door. Blackfoot heard the lock snap shut. Heard a diesel engine turn over, then dissipate. His pants were soaked, the once warm blood beginning to cool.

He'd kill for an Oxy. Shit, even a Klonopin at this point.

He looked at the ropes, the tools mounted on the wall, daydreaming about what he would do if he could reach that machete above the workbench.

14

MORGAN saw the bottle disintegrate in the corner of her eye.

Buck was drunk again. Shooting at beer bottles on a stump, hitting every other one—maybe—saying things like, "Fuck yeah, see that woman?" Morgan would say, "Enough already, 'fore ya shoot the neighbor's dog," but didn't really care one way or another, scrolling on her phone, sitting side-saddle on the porch railing against the vinyl siding of the double-wide—the only spot she could get enough signal to check Instagram.

Morgan liked to follow all the starlets on the red carpet and try to guess the brand of dress they wore. They were all so young now days. She didn't recognize half of them. Sometimes, when Gustavo would come over with a little reefer, she'd get high and picture herself there. Smiling, playing kiss-ass with all the bigwigs.

She touched the bruises on her neck, her face, and wondered if this happened to women in Hollywood. If they ever had to use makeup to cover a strangle mark or a black eye from a backhand.

She couldn't see it. Everyone looked so perfect there. So happy.

Oh, here's a good one: an affair in the Hollywood Hills, something for charity. Demi Moore stepping out of a limo with some young buck—you go girl—rocking a red off-the-shoulder number, pulling it off too for a woman her age. Morgan sure it was an H&M getup, but the footnote listed Zac Posen, whoever that was.

She heard the rack of the 12-gauge, then winced as Buck fired and missed. "I'm serious Buck, someone gonna call the cops you don't let up."

"Shit, let 'em come," Buck said, pumping in a fresh slug. "Them motherfuckers try to take my guns, they'll catch a wad of double-aught buckshot bitch."

He fired. The bottle shattered.

Morgan rolled her eyes. "Yeah, yer a real badass…reg'lar Chris Kyle."

Here was someone she recognized: Bette Midler. Boy, did she look old. Her hair going every which way like she'd fingered a light socket. A caption next to her face said she was bitching about the president again. Something about—

The 12-gauge was pressed against her cheek, the hot steel of the muzzle singeing a circle of skin. Morgan dropped the phone. "Buck, what're you doin?"

"Get up."

She did and could now see the spirals of the milled steel descending into the bore. "Ain't mean nothing by it, I's just making a joke."

"You know, I'm real sick'n tired of you not giving me the respect I deserve."

"I'm sorry, I—"

"Open yer mouth."

Morgan froze. "What?"

"Open. Yer mouth."

She did and Buck slid the barrel into her mouth until she gagged.

"Thaaat's right," he said, getting a sick, vile pleasure from it. "Now, what I cain't member is whether or not they's another shell in here."

Morgan shuddered. Thought about running, but knew she'd be a goner. She tried to plead, but only vowels came out.

Buck told her to shut up.

She saw his trigger finger disappear beneath the receiver; felt a stinging in that little space between her battered legs followed by a rush of warmth as urine flooded her britches.

She heard a click that vibrated up the barrel, into her teeth, and assumed it was the disengagement of the safety.

She tried to picture Gustavo again. His eyes. The life they'd never lead. A black mass bled in from her periphery, consuming her world. She closed her eyes. Accepted death. Earnest to leave it all behind.

Buck pulled the trigger.

Morgan heard the firing pin smack an empty breech, felt it radiate in the back of her throat and dry-heaved as the barrel was pulled out.

Buck laughed. "Guess today's yer lucky day."

The squawk of the siren made her open her eyes. She followed Buck's gaze and saw an old two-door Bronco approaching, a gumball whipping on top of the roof.

Buck looked sober now, the shotgun in a limp hand at his side. He resituated Morgan's sweater, pulled the half-zip up and smiled. "Wanna make it till morning, I suggest stayin on the porch and keepin yer fuckin mouth shut." He flipped the shotgun upside down and cocked it over his shoulder.

Like some big-game hunter.

The cop got out and Morgan thought he had a solid build, a hard face, which might be handsome if he'd shave that rug under his nose. He didn't look like a normal cop with his twill button-down tucked into jeans, a pair of boots similar to the ones she'd seen a few guys wearing over at the Legion—Buck's favorite place because he got drinks for half price claiming to be a war vet. He'd talk in acronyms, saying he did a tour here and a tour there. Saying, "Yeah, it sucked but I cain't complain. End of the day it's still a volunteer job, right?" The bartenders eating it up, calling Buck a true patriot.

Please.

The man never served. Hell, he couldn't even stand authority. Always had to be the big dick. A big fish in a small pond.

The cop drew a flashlight and swept the beam across the yard.

"Howdy, Sheriff," Buck said, stepping off the porch. "Brings you this way?"

Morgan could tell by his tone he was playing the part, acting chummy. The law-abiding, card-carrying, contributing member of society.

The sheriff said, "Received a few calls yer back here getting a little wild with that," nodding at the shotgun. The man wasn't short though he looked it right now.

Buck scoffed. "Just gettin her dialed in for duck season."

"Really, in March?"

"Duck season, self-preservation. You cain't never be too prepared, know what I mean?"

"I don't."

"Well between you and me…" Buck leaned in, kept his voice low. "Last week, a couple spots down that way, a whole buncha spooks moved in. Took all of three double-wides. And I ain't talking no family neither. These guys is military age. Call themselves Mohammed's Chosen Ones or some shit. Wearing the beard, that stupid little hat—"

"You got a beard."

"You know which kind I'm talking about, Sheriff. Them fuckers is passing out prayer rugs round the Vagabond, telling people to get down on they knees and give themselves up to Allah. Know what I say to that? Go fuck yerself. Ain't gettin on my knees for nobody. Shit."

The sheriff waited. Morgan could see he was looking Buck over, sizing him up.

"And I know you heard 'bout that mosque they got in Sheridan now," Buck said. "Only a matter a time till one pops up in these parts."

"What's wrong with that?"

"Shit, how much time you got? Shouldn't have to explain it to a red-blooded ex-solider like yourself."

"Cut the bullshit'n just level with me," the sheriff said with a deadpan expression, flicking his light to the empties on the railing. "You had a few, got bored, thought it'd be fun to throw some lead downrange, smoke a few bottles. Sound about right?"

"Purrty much. Ain't no law against that, is there?"

"There is if you been drinking. How much you had?"

"Only two beers. Ain't even feel nothin yet."

The sheriff looked at the bottles on the railing again. "Then who those belong to?"

"My woman's."

"All four of 'em? What's she weigh, a hunnert pounds soaking wet?"

"You don't believe me, ask her."

The sheriff stared at Buck but didn't answer. He shined his light on the stump. Glass shards glistened like a mound of cane. Then he lifted the beam to light the evergreens huddled beyond. "What's over there, a refuge?"

Buck nodded. "Couple good blinds you ever wanna bag some greenheads."

"There ain't no houses? I go back there I won't find nothing but trees?"

"A whitetail if yer lucky, maybe a fawn this time a year."

The sheriff moved his light around some more. Looking at Buck, at the bottles, the railing. Morgan could tell he was buying time, weighing his options. Then the light disappeared. "Alright, what say y'all call it a night. You make me come out here again, I *will* take you in."

Morgan deflated.

"Absolutely, Sheriff," Buck said. "Thanks for comin out."

Morgan met the sheriff's eyes as he turned to leave, surprised when he stopped and did a double take.

And now, crap, Buck followed his gaze.

Morgan became uncomfortable, aware of her cold, damp britches. The two of them hawking with opposite looks. One inquisitive, the other angry.

The sheriff clicked his light back on. "Ma'am. Come here a sec."

She saw Buck furrow his brow. A look she'd seen a hundred times. The one that told her she was a dead bitch walking if she got out of line.

She wanted to spill the beans. To rat the motherfucker out knowing the shotgun was empty but, crap, now remembering the Colt Cobra always tucked in his waistband.

She couldn't bring herself to do it. Not with the sheriff's welfare at stake. The man didn't deserve to get hurt on account of her opening her fat mouth.

As she approached them she could see Buck smiling, holding his hand out like a doting husband.

The sheriff pointed at her face, asked what happened.

She touched it, saying, "Well, I ah…" and could feel Buck inch closer, a hand moving onto her lower back, gripping the sweater. So Morgan chuckled, said, "Gosh, I'm such a klutz. See, what happened was—"

"She tryin to get a pot down from over the fridge—"

"I ask you?" the sheriff said. He turned back to Morgan. "You were saying?"

"Like he said. I's trying to get a pot down and wasn't payin no attention to what I's doin, so when I pulled it out, the 'nother one behind it came down'n caught me good. Ain't the first time, Sheriff, won't be the last."

Now she was the one acting chummy.

It made her sick to her stomach.

"That's what happened?"

"Yessir," Morgan said.

The sheriff stared for a while. He glanced at Buck, then clicked his light off. "Y'all have a good night."

Morgan watched the Bronco reverse and regretted not saying anything, wondering now if that was her chance to escape. If she would get another.

15

HARRIS was having second thoughts as he pulled the Bronco out of the Vagabond and made a right on Lakota. He didn't like the frail girl's body language, how she was half turned from her husband, almost like she was cowering, anticipating something. Or the way her whole body tensed when the guy touched the small of her back.

Harris was thinking he could've, maybe should've arrested the guy. Handling a firearm while intoxicated. Reckless endangerment. Sort of. It wouldn't stick, not with the refuge downrange. Disturbing the peace, maybe?

Oh, fuck it, Harris thought. Just man up and say it. Assault and battery. Domestic abuse. How about rape or sexual assault? He wouldn't bet against it. No way those bruises came from a damn pot. The girl was lying through her teeth. Protecting him. And for what?

But Harris only had suspicion. He couldn't do jack with that.

He would think about it the rest of the night, tossing, turning in bed. Seeing both of their faces, their eyes. One with the piercing stare of a wild animal. The other with that glazed over look of one in captivity.

Around 2:45 he got dressed and drove back to the Vagabond,

cutting the lights as he pulled up to their trailer. It was quiet. He peeked in a window. The place was a mess, but there weren't any signs of a struggle. He went to another window, saw the girl snuggled in the pocket of the man's shoulder, both of them on top of the sheets in the buff.

Harris went back to the Bronco, berated himself for passing judgement on Buck Taylor. Maybe it was a pot. He looked at the radio clock. Ruth's wouldn't be open for another couple of hours, so he threw in a plug of dip and took the 14 into the Black Hills. Pulled off at one of the outlooks and waited for dawn to break when the radio squawked. A deep voice talking about a woman, late fifties, found dead on the side of the road in a pool of her own blood and vomit. Possible overdose.

Harris snatched the rover, identified himself and asked for their twenty.

He could smell the corpse the second he opened the door. The detective from Rapid City identified himself as Sergeant Bates. He had a flat-top and a thin mustache on a bloated face. Moving under the yellow tape, Bates said, "Lawrence County, uh?" and when Harris nodded, Bates said, "What the hell you doin here?"

Harris thought about it, then made up something about a Missing Person's fitting the description when really he was just bored and had nothing better to do.

"Okay then," Bates said. "Let me show you the body."

Harris followed him along the shoulder. Bates told the forensic tech to pull the tarp, calling him Sport, then said to Harris, "Some biker found her. The poor bastard, out for an evening ride, comes whipping around that turn over there and had to swerve the last second, ended up crashing into the rock wall. Skinned himself up pretty good. Got a big-ass hole the side of his spandex onesie."

Harris was picturing someone on a motorcycle until Bates said spandex.

"Guy thought it was a deer at first. Had to bike his bloody ass back down the hill three miles to get enough service to reach nine-eleven. Then the operator calls us a little suspicious, telling us the guy's out of breath, saying things like, 'No he's fucking not hanging around for the fuzz,' and, 'No he ain't going back.'"

Harris squatted over the body of a female on her stomach, her mouth agape. Unfixed eyes looking back toward the curve. He thought she looked familiar. Something about her eyes, her nose, but he couldn't peg it. Rigor and livor mortis had set in.

Bates said, "We think she's been here about a day, maybe a little less."

Harris nodded at the forensic tech and the guy covered her up. "Got a name to go with her?"

Bates shook his head, pulling a metal case from his shirt pocket. "Nothing on her person. But between the crack pipe, the menthols, and the cash in her pocket, we're ninety-nine percent she's a chicken-head."

"A what?"

"Crack whore," Bates said, pulling a cigarette, putting it to his lips. "You know, way they walk around with their head bobbing, eyes darting." He chuckled, exchanging the case for a book of matches, striking one across the strip and cupping his hands to light the cigarette.

It occurred to Harris that he'd never been in a situation like this, at least since he'd been a civilian. "What happens you can't make a positive ID?"

"We give it thirty days. No one claims her, she'll end up in the incinerator with the rest of the Jane Does."

"You don't bury 'em?"

"Ain't worth the real estate no more and it's a waste of tax dollars. I mean, think about it. Twenty-five percent of yer hard-earned money, you really want it being spent on a proper burial for some dead trick didn't even respect herself? Shit. Easier and cheaper just to throw 'em in the oven."

Harris got the feeling this detective loved to hear himself talk. "Any leads?"

Bates snickered. "Knew that was coming. We made the rounds with the beat cops, circulated a headshot…they all know her, seen her, says she goes by Tracy but we're not getting any hits on that, so obviously it ain't her real name."

"What about a handler?"

"That what you call 'em over in Lawrence?"

"You prefer pimp?"

"We hear 'em all down here. Hustler, whoremonger, flesh-peddler—fuck there's all kinds." Bates took a drag and said, "But what we did? Took a shot in the dark and sent a black and white to locate a known pimp in the area, see if he'd cop to anything."

"When was this?"

"Not but a half hour ago. You mean you didn't hear over the radio?"

Harris shook his head.

"Christ, what a fucking mess. The cops get to the guy's house and knock on the door—"

"This is the pimp?"

"Yeah, and he's there the other side saying he *can't* get up to answer. They wanna come in they better kick the fucking thing down. Course they *do* with an invitation like that. They start clearing rooms and come upon this fat jig on the couch, bag of ice resting on his crotch. One of the uniforms says 'Show me your hands' because—the way the he puts it—the jig's gripping this bag of ice and he can see through it, there's something underneath. It's big, black, he's pretty sure it's a heater. And the jig's pants are on so he knows the guy ain't jerkin off under there. Well when the cop gives him the order, this dumb fucking jig gets wise, starts slipping his hand under the bag and now the cop's positive it's a gun, right? The fuck else would he be doing down there? So the cop shouts at him, 'Put yer fucking hands up,' and what's the guy do but grip whatever it is that's under there and starts lifting the bag with his free hand, saying, 'Fuck you, pig.' So the cop starts shooting, thinking it's life or death. He puts six into the jig, hits the bag with two of 'em, the thing starts leaking all over the goddamn floor. Now, confident the guy's toast, the cop tries to grab the gun so he can clear it only to learn it's not a gun but the guy's junk. His dick *and* his balls, just hanging out of the zipper-hole taking an ice bath—who knows the fuck for. And so the cop's standing there going fuck-fuck-fuck till he hears the jig groan and looks up to see the guy's still clinging. And what does this jig say to the cop, his dying words?"

Harris shook his head.

"If you wanted to grab my dick you fag, all you had to do was ask."

Harris just stared at him.

Bates was cackling. "Can you believe that shit? My God. 'If you wanted to grab my dick all you had to do was ask.' Fucking classic." He drew on his cigarette and blew a stream of smoke into the air. "Tell me something…you said Lawrence County, right?"

Harris, looking at the mass under the tarp, said, "Spearfish, yessir."

"I hear them Injuns is cleaning house over there."

"They've done well for themselves."

"Shit, you must be making out pretty good then."

"Whaddayou mean?"

"Well I don't know about you, but I see a redskin around here? I'll pull 'em over for a missing taillight, not using their blinker, something stupid. Tell 'em I'll let 'em go they give me all the cash in their wallet. And get this…" Bates tapped Harris' chest with the back of his hand. "Ain't been one time I gotten less than two hunnert. Couple stops a month, I can make a few extra grand a year."

The guy was proud of himself. Grinning, arching his eyebrows, chugging the butt all the way to the filter.

"Is that right?" Harris said.

"I'm tellin ya, easy pickings when they're off the rez. Those stupid fuckers ain't learned a thing, don't know shit when it comes to their rights."

Harris waited now for Bates to look at him. "I'm curious about the body being on that side of the road."

"Yeah, what about it?"

"Well I wonder is the perp from Rapid City or if they might be from Deadwood or even Spearfish. Because if you take the 385 going that way," Harris said, pointing past his Bronco, "you'll hit both of 'em."

"Could be from Merritt, too. That's only about a mile, mile and a half."

112

Harris had to grin. "You know Merritt pretty well?"

"Fuck, wish I didn't. Goddamn outlaw bikers are a pain in my ass. Every weekend it seems like there's another stabbing or a fight breaks out. Something." Bates looked at him, getting an idea. "Hang on, you think maybe one of them had something to do with it?"

"No, that's not what I'm thinking. What I'm thinking is…soon as you hit Merritt you cross into *my* county. And if I ever catch you pulling any shit like that with the Indians, I'll throw yer ass in jail."

16

PAPPY had warned Cody about this place. He would say, "Play the hand yer dealt. Do the best you can with what you got, and don't never ask nothing of nobody, 'cause they'll help you today'n take everthing tomorrow when you need it most."

He was right.

But six years ago Cody didn't see they had a choice when a letter arrived, something about a lien on the ranch, failure to pay property taxes. He tried to ask Pappy about it, but all the old man would say is if the goddamn commies working for Uncle Sam wanted it, they'd have to take it from his cold, dead fingers. Acting like he was The Duke or something.

Cody had an affection for whiskey in those days. One night, in a bar called The Maverick, he found himself chatting to a hefty man named Frank Rodale who said he ran the bank. Cody remembered how the guy had shrugged it off, like a property lien was no big deal. Telling Cody to come in, fill out some paperwork, and that lien would be paid off before sundown the next day. The guy, a little twang in his voice, had sounded like a decent person. Someone Cody thought he could trust.

What Cody didn't realize is the interest that would accrue. Or the fact he had to forge Pappy's signature to get it done.

Every year since, after taking the cattle to market, Cody would forgo any salary as foreman and cut a check to the bank, even though it never seemed to make a dent. It bought him time, however, and he was thankful for that. After all, it wasn't just him that depended on the place. The Flying-C housed upwards of five or six hands, more during the busy season. Where would they go? What would they do? As the years passed, Cody believed the operation was more about preserving a way of life than making money.

That's why he was here now, looking at a nice headshot that captured both of Frank Rodale's chins. His thinning, parted hair. A warm, toothless smile. The placard at the top read SPEARFISH BANK & TRUST BOARD OF DIRECTORS.

And wow, what a surprise. The Injun chief idling at the top.

A half hour later, Frank Rodale waddled through a back door wiping his mouth with a handkerchief. He'd smile or nod to just about everyone, saying things like, "Long time no see, pard," or, "What you been up to, man?" as if everyone was a close friend. But when he reached Cody, he said, "And what brings you in today, Mr. Custer?"

Cody looked up at him and came right out with it, telling Rodale it's possible the cows wouldn't make it to market. A few came in underweight—the vet's words, not his—and there's a chance it wouldn't be limited to just a few.

"That don't sound good. What do you mean by *under*weight?" Rodale said.

Cody waited for a patron to pass. He didn't like that Rodale's desk was in the center of the bank. Everyone seeing, hearing what they discussed—as if those half-glass partitions blocked a goddamn thing.

"There's something going around," Cody said. "A virus

maybe, and it might've gotten to my cows."

Rodale swiveled to his computer, fingers hovering the keyboard. "Virus? This the first I heard of it. What kind we talking here?"

"Well hang on, I ain't certain it is a virus."

"But it's got to be *some*thing for the vet to say that. Who was it, Donald Murdoch?"

"Yessir."

"Well, he ain't wrong very often. And when he is, he ain't far out. So tell me, and be honest...he say it might be terminal?"

"Let's say he did. What're my options?"

"How many head you stand to lose?"

Look at him. Using the lingo. A wannabe rancher trying to relate. *How many head you stand to lose?* What a joke. Cody thought the world was backwards. Working as hard as he did and still having to explain yourself, get approval from a man like this.

"I don't know. Could be a few, could be half the herd."

"You culled 'em?"

"Oh come on, Rodale. Bad enough I gotta come here the first place, now you gonna grill me on how I run my outfit?"

"You think I can just punch an application with an approval stamp, throw ya a buncha money and tell the board my reasoning's because you're a good guy and a real hard worker?"

"Sounds good enough for me."

"Well it ain't gonna fly these days."

"Right, 'cause who's on the board?" Cody said, pointing at the headshots on the wall.

"That's got nothing to do with it. It's just protocol now-days. There are certain questions I got to ask—"

"Then let's hear 'em."

"It's no disrespect, Cody."

"Bullshit. I been coming here longer'n that casino's been around. And now, when I need it the most, y'all ain't gonna do shit for me. But some slick with a ponytail and a feather pulls up in a goddamn Nazi sled, y'all meet him at the door asking if there's anything you can get for him. 'Would you like some water, some coffee, how 'bout a pastry?' Shit. I walk inna door nobody even says hello. Be lucky just to get a smile."

"I want to help you, okay? I do. So just do me a favor, answer the questions best you can and we'll see what's what. You good with that?"

Cody wasn't sure. But he nodded and Rodale said, "So tell me again how this occurred?"

"I didn't tell you to begin with 'cause I don't know."

"Then how'd you know to call on Murdoch?"

"I just had a feeling."

Rodale cocked an eyebrow. "What kinda feeling?"

"The kind you get from doing it yer whole life. I thought something looked off with a few of the cows, so I asked Doch to check it out. That good enough for you?"

"And what? This thing, this virus that's not a virus, if it metastasizes and ruins some of the stock, you want to know what's gonna happen if you're not able to keep up with the payments you're making now?"

"That's right."

Rodale leaned in, spoke from the side of his mouth. "Pappy even know about the loan?"

Cody stared at him. "What do you think?"

"That's my point. Because if the Flying-C defaults on that loan, then *technically* we'll have the right to start seizing assets."

"And by technically, you mean…"

"We will."

And if that happens and Pappy finds out, Cody thought, he'd have a heart attack but wouldn't allow himself to die till he could remove me from the will.

God. Damn it.

Cody rubbed his face with both hands, pushing his hat back on his head.

"So you got two options to prevent that from happening," Rodale said. "You could refinance, take out another loan against the business—"

"And get myself into a worse situation than I'm in now? If you'd a told me this was a possibility six years ago, I wouldn't of done it."

"I'm not sure what you want me to say to that."

"Maybe if you'd admit you don't fix people's problems, or even help 'em, you just make 'em worse—"

"I get it, all right? Acts of God are a real bitch, but it's one of the things we have to protect ourselves against."

"But I stand to lose everthing. What're you gonna lose? Nothing. What's the bank gonna lose? A little money? It's bullshit Rodale, and you know it."

"O-kay. So I'm just gonna mark *decline* next to the refinancing option—and I can understand that. But I got something else, and I think you're gonna like it."

Cody waited, looking at Rodale.

"How about investing in a herd of sheep?"

"No."

"Just listen to the numbers."

"I'm a goddamn cattle rancher, Frank."

"You won't be any kind of rancher the livestock don't offset your operating costs. Hear me out."

118

It was an option, Cody reckoned. So he told Rodale to make it quick.

Rodale reached into a drawer, pulled out a one-sheet and handed it to Cody. The grass was green. Too green. The sky was absent of a single cloud and the smiling ranchers were the cleanest damn ranchers Cody had ever seen.

He hated it.

Rodale was pulling out another sheet now, saying, "One cattle unit—a thousand-pound cow with a five hundred-pound calf at her side—is the equivalent of six sheep. Each year, one cow should bring in…" He was holding a hand out, fishing for Cody to answer.

"One calf."

"Bingo-bango. Which equals about five hundred dollars a year income, factoring market prices the last decade. And one ewe'll bring in one point six lambs…"

"Hang on, how'd you get that?"

"Gestation for ewes is a hundred fifty-two days. For cattle, two eighty-three. Some ewes'll yield two lambs a year. So six sheep should bring in ten lambs. One lamb averages a hundred bucks market value, ten lambs, a thousand—still with me?"

To tell the truth, Cody had been lost since he mentioned sheep. He couldn't see himself doing it. Herding the little shits on foot, shearing wool all day.

Shit, he might start drinking again.

He shook his head, said, "Sorry Rodale, it ain't for me," and started to stand.

"Well hang on, here's the kicker. You lose a cow, what's it cost you?"

"Twelve hunnert."

"And the vet bill?"

"Maybe fifteen bucks a year per cow."

The husky banker was grinning now. "You lose a sheep, it's a hundred dollar loss."

Cody looked at Rodale. "And the vet bill?"

"Bout a buck fifty a head."

And that, Cody thought, didn't sound bad at all.

17

THE LAMP rocking on the nightstand—it was a seven-thousand-dollar Demian Quincke—reminded Shea of a metronome. The longer it went on, the less she could tune it out. The clicking, the clacking, the amber glow of the crystal lights bouncing off the headboard. She leaned over and shoved it off, pretending not to hear it break as she continued grinding astride Kenny.

She was surprised he didn't react and thought maybe he didn't hear it. His chin was up, his eyes were squeezed shut, and he wasn't making any noise save a loud breath here and there.

Yeah, Master of the Deal? Top Negotiator? None of that shit was working tonight.

She felt his nails digging into her butt cheeks. At first she liked it, the little bit of pain, but it started itching so she moved his hands onto her boobs and wasn't big on that either because he didn't do anything with them.

Then he started moving his hips, trying too hard to get a rhythm. Shea wanted to say stop, quit fucking up her flow. Instead, she spun around thinking maybe if she didn't have to look at him, she'd get something out of it.

When that didn't work, she stopped and said, "What's

wrong?"

"Huh?"

"What's wrong with you?"

"Nothing. Why?"

"Then stop acting like it's your first time and give it to me."

Kenny flipped her over, got in behind her and forced it.

God, what a joke.

At some point, she started counting pillowcase threads and tried to see the positives: his body wasn't that bad—you know, for a guy who's only exercise was doing laps around the casino. But his arms and shoulders looked like a woman's. Little pipe-cleaners with man-sized hands attached.

She could hear him getting winded now and imagined his face turning red, his pursed lips, really giving it everything. She reached twenty-eight on the thread count before he rolled off, saying, "Goddamnit."

And to think all she wanted was a good lay.

It would have to wait.

She went into the bathroom, catching her reflection in the mirror and thought how gifted she was to have such nice legs and a can that was still considered by modern standards to be tight and perky.

As for those boobs? She'd seen better, though not bad for a bitch pushing forty. She slipped on a robe and pulled a cigarette from the vanity. On her way to the balcony she saw Kenny flaccid on the bed, texting on his phone.

"It was that good you had to tell Hector about it?"

He looked at her from around the phone. "Don't fucking start, all right? I'm working."

Shea went onto the balcony, shut the sliding glass behind her.

She lit up and blew a thin stream of smoke into the air. Leaned over the railing, saw a gradual darkness descending the depth of the high-rise. The reflection of neon across the chrome banister—pink and indigo bleeding together. She drew on her cigarette again, saw the rolling peaks of the Black Hills bumping across a charcoal sky. In a valley off to the left, she could see tiny embers embedded against the void. Lights at the Flying-C. That small one to the left was the front porch. The two off to the right, the barn.

She heard the sliding glass behind her as Kenny stepped out. He started to apologize but she cut him off and said it was fine, forget about it.

"No, it's not. I just can't get it off my mind."

"The situation with your nephew?"

"Yeah. And I swear, if something happens to him—"

"You'll what? All I did was make a suggestion, you're the one who followed through with it. Don't try and pin that on me."

"Are you fucking serious right now?"

"Yeah, and quite frankly I'm beginning to think Blackfoot takes precedence over the ranch."

"He's like a son to me, Shea..."

The chief saying it like she was stupid, that she wasn't getting it. She rolled her eyes. "Yeah, we've been through this 'Only family you have left' bit already."

"I practically raised the kid and he's being held hostage. So forgive me for being a little fucking concerned."

"I didn't say you were concerned. I didn't even say you weren't allowed to be concerned. All I'm saying is, I think you being emotionally attached is causing you to lose focus and it's impacting your decisions."

"Whatever. You're fucking unbelievable, you know that?"

The landline rang.

He looked at it, but didn't move.

"Worst-case scenario. Let's say he didn't get the cows…what's more important? Getting him back, or *that*?" Shea said, pointing at the three embers. "The last piece of the puzzle."

The landline was still ringing.

"That ranch is second fiddle far as I'm concerned."

Shea could see it happening, everything she didn't want. The man losing sight of the objective at the first sign of adversity. But she held the chief's look, wracking her brain, attempting to drum up something that would pull him back to reality. Something that would narrow his focus. "You remember when this town was pitch black? Could look up and see an endless amount of stars?"

Kenny pinched his brow.

"I hated it. Reminds me when I was a girl and my dad would take me on rides in the pasture, just the two of us. Don't think I ever really looked at the sky until that first night. Millions and millions of stars. He'd point out constellations and say that, in the old days, the night sky told a cowboy everything he needed to know. Where he was going, what was coming. It was the only thing he could trust. It wasn't until the third time he took me out that he touched me."

Kenny's head snapped around, shocked.

"And he started slow," Shea said. "Made me feel like it was special. That *I* was special. He kissed me and I knew it was wrong, but for the first time in my life I had his undivided attention. His approval. So I didn't say anything. Of course, my naiveté, I didn't think it would go any further—I didn't even know it could. But every time we went out there, he'd do more and more. If I told him to stop, tried to push him off, it just made him more aggressive. So I let him have his way."

"My God…"

"The stars remind me how powerless, how insignificant I was."

Kenny paced the length of the balcony. His cell rang, the little rectangle illuminating on the mattress. He glanced at it, searching for something to say. "You didn't…"

Spit it out.

"…You didn't tell anyone?"

"I was eight, I thought it was normal. A couple years went by, and finally, I worked up enough courage to tell my mother."

"What'd she say?"

"She lost it. Refused to accept it. Started drinking, popping pills. Stayed in bed all day, not doing shit. Wasn't long after that my dad kicked her out. I tried to tell Pappy, but he wouldn't listen."

"How long did this go on?" Kenny said, genuine concern in his voice.

"Until I was fourteen."

"Why'd he stop?"

"He didn't. Woke up one day and he was gone." She pulled the last of her cigarette and flicked the butt, watching the embers fall until they were swallowed by the void. "So yeah, that's *my* family for ya. That's how I grew up."

Kenny started to speak when his phone rang again. "That's the third fucking time. I'm sorry, I have to get that."

Shea nodded.

As Kenny breached the doorway, he stopped and turned back. "I get it now."

"What?"

"Why you have to have it."

"Yeah."

"Then so be it. If Bodaway didn't get it done, we'll find another way. By the time we're through with that place, you have my word, you won't even recognize it anymore."

She smiled, watching through the window as he answered the phone, listening first, then saying, "I'll be right there."

18

KENNY stood over a surveillance tech watching a feed from the eye in the sky. A slight man wearing a grey suit was in profile. He kept fidgeting with the gold rim of his glasses, and his eyes remained on the felt.

"What's he at?" Kenny said.

"Sixty-seven and some change."

"Thousand?"

"Yessir."

"Why didn't you call me when he got to fifteen?"

The surveillance tech glanced back at Hector Vargas, the Mingan's head of security.

"We tried, sir," Hector said. "The landline, your cell, we couldn't reach you."

And to think he might lose all that dough for some lousy lay and a sob story? Nah. Not tonight. "You figure he's working with someone?"

Hector shook his head. "Too empty, easy to spot."

"Well it ain't luck."

"No, it's skill," the tech said, his eyes on the monitor. "He's counting."

"Bullshit."

"No sir, check it out." The tech pecked a few keys switching the feed to a different angle. This one frontal, closing in.

Kenny turned to Hector. "Got any ID on him?"

"No sir, we don't know if he's local or a tourist."

"The fuck have you been doing?"

"Only thing we could. Watching, waiting for you."

Kenny glared at Hector, holding it long enough until the others in the room noticed.

"See his mouth?" the tech said, pointing at the screen. "He's counting, all right. And watch, the dealer's coming around…there he goes…dishes the card, this guy checks it, then looks up…bam, right there, like he's doing the math in his head."

"What's he holding?" Kenny said.

"Eleven."

"And the dealer?"

The tech punched a few keys. "Fourteen. But he's showing the four, not the fish hook."

"So he should double-down," Hector said.

The dealer checked his bottom card, then signaled the man in glasses. The man waved a palm over his eleven. The dealer hesitated. Now the other player at the table was saying something. But the man in glasses pointed at the guy's stack, then his own stack, looked up and said something to the dealer. It was definitive. The other player paused, then waved a palm over his cards. The dealer revealed his fourteen. Drew a face card and busted.

What a pompous little prick, Kenny thought. He told Hector to intercept, to bring that motherfucker to the office.

* * *

Hector Vargas took the freight elevator down to the main floor.

He didn't take it personal back there, the boss-man's glaring. He knew Mr. Shepard was just trying to assert himself, show some authority in front of the others. He had been with Kenny since the Mingan opened and knew everything there was to know about the man. Shit, he'd served under worse officers in the Marine Corps. Way worse. And the way he saw it? His ass wasn't on the line if he took a little shit from Kenny or didn't like an order. No, this job was kush. What they call smooth sailing. Hector figured he'd just keep cashing checks until he had enough for a place in the mountains and another on the beach.

He radioed security, made everyone aware of the situation and told the exit detail to be on standby, just in case the twerp was a runner.

A voice came through his earpiece saying the man had colored up. He'd left the table, cut past the slots and was heading, it looked like, for the cashier's cage.

Hector radioed the surveillance tech now. "How much is he walking out with?"

"Seventy-two, eight-fifty."

"He tip the dealer?"

"A nickel."

Hector hesitated before putting the mike back to his lips. "Five grand?"

"No, sir. Five bucks. He's a cheap ass."

The doors parted. Hector moved down a drab corridor, hiking his slacks, resituating the .40 Sig on his hip. He swiped his keycard and saw the man through the golden slats of the cage, leaning on the counter watching the cashier work.

Hector forced a smile, buttoned his suit jacket and pointed at the man. "That is quite the stack of chips there. Congratulations, sir."

"Thank you," the man said, though he didn't look up.

Hector extended a hand through the slats. "Hector Vargas. Casino Operations here at the Mingan," already feeling the burn in his cheeks from the fake smile.

The man said, "How do you do," and shook Hector's hand, but still wouldn't look up.

It pissed Hector off. This squat little shit thinking he's the man, counting along with the cashier.

"You from around here, or just passing through?"

"What difference does it make?"

Hector had enough. He put a hand on the cashier's shoulder. "Do me a favor, send all this up with a bottle of some nice champagne to the high-rollers' suite. We'll finish everything up there."

That got his attention.

"You know, that's not really—I'm sort of in a hurry, so..."

Hector waited for him to finish, but apparently that was it. So Hector said, "You don't wanna count this in the open, trust me. Some people lose their nest egg, get desperate, you could find yourself on the receiving end, most likely in the parking garage with no security, no witnesses... I assure you, it's merely a precaution. For your safety, of course." Hector dropped the smile to let the guy know he was serious.

"Fine, whatever." The man looked at the cashier. "Make it a gin martini, would you? I don't drink champagne." He pushed off the counter, straightened and asked Hector which way.

Hector moved out of the cage and guided the man toward the west bank, swiping his keycard to call the elevator. "I'm sorry, I never did get your name."

"Jim," the man said. "Jim Moffat."

When the doors parted, he let Jim Moffat go first. Hector swiped his keycard again and took them up to the penthouse.

On the way, Hector touched his earpiece, pretending to get a transmission. He told Jim Moffat sorry, waited a moment, then lowered his hand. "That was the floor staff. Apparently, they were impressed by how well you took care of the dealers."

"Well, it's important to look after the little people."

Hector rolled his eyes. "What do you do?"

"I'm an attorney. Family planning, real estate law, that kind of thing. It's boring, really, but it pays the bills."

It was quiet now, save the Muzak overhead. Hector didn't speak, curious to see how long this weasel could tolerate the silence.

"So... What was it that drew you into the casino business?"

Hector just looked at him, thinking this dumbshit had no idea of what he was walking into.

When they entered the office, Jim Moffat didn't see anyone because he was too busy looking at all the shit on the walls. A bunch of mounted animal heads. Exotic, big-game types. The kind you see on those wild shows filmed over a decade in places like Africa or Alaska or some undomesticated island you never heard of. Three antelope were stacked staring at a grizzly in contrapposto. There were birds he had never seen. A wolverine. About the only other animal he recognized was a deer—or maybe it was an elk?—an ear cocked like it heard something peculiar before getting its ass blown off.

Moffat stopped at an old photo of some ugly Indian, a head

of greasy hair under a bunch of feathers. The Indian was in profile, pointing at something out of frame. Moffat moved past an ebony desk trimmed in gold, ran his fingers over it and said, "Ohmigod is that real?"

The muscle-dude's response? Shoving him into the next room. He'd been doing it since they got off the elevator. Moffat knew they caught him counting soon as the muscle-dude flashed that fake smile at the cage. He had tried to play it cool, acting like he didn't care. When that didn't work, he made small talk even though the guy didn't have shit to say in the elevator. So he decided he'd wait to meet the honcho, but it wasn't like they could do anything. Counting was frowned upon, not illegal—even if they could prove it. They might ask him to leave for good, maybe blacklist him, but you could bet your ass he wasn't going anywhere without that seventy-two large.

The muscle-dude shoved him again. He saw something flash across his face, inches it seemed, moving left to right. Moffat turned, saw it slam into a mannequin against the wall.

Christ. A damn arrow.

Moffat swiveled left, saw a dude sporting a slick ponytail with his back turned. And behind the dude was a squaw in a calico dress nocking another arrow to a bow almost as tall as the squaw herself. The dude was in a velvet sport coat, the collar popped. When he turned, Moffat saw he wasn't wearing a shirt underneath.

"There's a system in Vegas," the dude said. "And the general rule of thumb is, the more people staring at you, the more trouble you can expect. You win enough, you get the attention, that brings the heat. Soon after, the tap. Nine times out of ten they just ask you to leave, maybe comp you at the restaurant as a parting gift."

"An-an-and," Moffat stopped. The room seemed smaller. He could feel the muscle-dude right behind him, a dozen sets of eyes looking at him. He licked his lips, saying, "An…and the other one?" pretty sure he was looking at Kenny Shepard.

"They call the police. You spend a night in jail, maybe pay a fine. That backroom electric saw shit doesn't happen anymore."

Moffat slumped, sighed relief. "Oh."

The squaw drew the bowstring and fired. The arrow slammed into the mannequin's chest.

Jesus Christ.

On second look, Moffat realized it wasn't a mannequin, but one of those punching bags made to look like a chiseled human—just the head and torso, no arms. It wore a cavalry hat with gold tassels on the brim. A green apple rested atop the hat. And two fucking arrows were now sticking out of its chest, another half dozen in the drywall around it.

Moffat said, "La…la-look," pausing to clear his throat. "It's Mr. Shepard, correct?"

Kenny nodded.

"I re-realize I ma-made a mistake. Please, if you'll just—I don't even care about the money okay, if you'll just let me walk out of here…"

Kenny's laugh filled the room. "The money? Oh, you never had it to begin with. How tall are you?"

Moffat was confused. He said, "Huh," to which Kenny said, "Your height? You know, five-five, five-seven maybe?"

"Right, my height. Yeah, I'm five-nine. Why?"

"Nah, come on."

"I am, sir. I'm five-nine."

"Hmm... Hector, would you mind?"

The muscle-dude grabbed Moffat by the collar and towed him in front of the punching bag mannequin thing. Moffat was saying, "Please, if you'll just let me explain—" but stopped when he saw the hard edges and the little black hole of the automatic. And from where? He didn't even see the muscle-dude reach for it. But there it was, the man's fucking pistol looking right at him.

Hector said, "Move again," like it was a dare.

Moffat didn't.

"Look at that, I can still see the apple," Kenny said, smiling, having a good time. "Kudos to you my friend for not fibbing about your height. Says a lot about you." He pointed at the bow. "That was my great-grandfather's. Apparently it was used in the Great Sioux War of 1876. It's made of the finest ash and juniper on the continent."

"It-it-it's a beautiful piece."

"Personally, I think it's a piece of shit. Even a sharpshooter like Wakhuwa here can't hit anything with it half the time."

Wakhuwa drew the bow back and fired.

Shit!

Moffat squeezed his eyes and screamed until he heard the arrow slam into the wall behind him.

"See what I mean?"

Moffat turned, saw tail-feathers so close he could touch them. Shouldn't there have been a countdown, or a warning? Something?

Kenny said, "But with this..." and reached into the wardrobe, pulling out some kind of modern hunting bow with all sorts of gizmos on it. "She can hit an elk in the heart at seventy-five yards, no problem."

Jim Moffat was certain now it was a fucking elk up there, not a deer. He found it on the wall and swore the elk was smiling at him. The thing looking down from elk heaven, saying, You're next you little turd.

Moffat pleaded, telling Kenny there had to be something he could do.

"What do you think?" Kenny said to Hector.

"Cheater's Justice is my favorite."

"It is. He loves Cheater's Justice. You know what? Fuck it, I'm game for that. Let's do Cheater's Justice."

Moffat looked at Hector. The man was grinning.

"But I want to give her another shot at that apple first," Kenny said, swapping bows with Wakhuwa. "She's so close. I thought she had it with that last one."

"Maybe a degree to the left," Hector said.

"See, I can't remember the last time the sights were zeroed though. So much work, not enough time to go hunting."

The squaw drew another arrow back, the tethers of the bowstring taut. Moffat didn't know what to do but bob and yell please, for God's sake.

"It helps if you close your eyes," Kenny said.

Moffat couldn't. Not with the light glinting off the arrowhead's razor tip. He tightened his sphincter and tried to think. What could he do? This guy was the most powerful man in Spearfish, maybe the Midwest. Between him and that soon-to-be mayor girlfriend, there wasn't anything they didn't have—which meant Moffat didn't have jack he could provide as a peace offering.

Wait a second. That's right. The girlfriend. Whatshername? Custer, right? That was one thing he didn't have. One of the largest ranches in Spearfish and the only one to border the reservation.

"Wait!" Moffat said. "I can give you the Flying-C. The Custer ranch."

19

MANUEL'S VOICE came through the walkie. "A buncha sheep? You gotta be kidding me, *cabron.*"

Cody thumbed the talk button, said, "I know," and eased the flatbed off the dirt trail, heading out to pasture.

Manuel said something else Cody couldn't hear over the growl of the diesel. He clocked a small herd in the distance and angled the truck for them. Some of the cows looked up, curious. Cody looked at their snouts, the way they walked, and saw no sign they were infected.

"Hey, you hear what I say to you?" Manuel said.

Cody said he didn't.

"I say, never trust a fat *gringo* in a suit. Man like that don't work hard enough for the money he makes."

Cody eyed the side-mirror, saw the cows following at a trot. He left the truck in gear, exited, and had to jog to catch up with it before climbing onto the flatbed. He clipped the walkie to his belt, pulled the Kershaw from his pocket and cut the twine around the first bale.

The cows were excited, their bleating audible.

Cody felt better seeing it, thinking no cow would run with blisters on its hoofs, not even for corn gluten.

"You got any idea what it's like raising sheep?"

Cody grabbed the walkie. "Yer still on this?"

"Well do you? I got a few cousins say it's the worst fucking thing there is for a cowboy."

"Rodale gave me the bullet points, it don't sound half bad." He sheered layers from the bale and dumped them as the truck rolled on. A few cows stopped. Others hesitated, then decided there wasn't enough room to munch and caught up with the truck.

"Shit," Manuel said. "You gonna have wool coming out your ears, *cabron*. You gonna be finding wool in places…you gonna wipe your ass, not find no skid marks man, 'cause it's just gonna be a ball of brown wool."

"Less yer the one wiping it, I don't see why yer so concerned."

"Listen to what I'm telling you. And your horse? I know how you love that roan, but he gonna get fat. He gonna be so useless—you won't even be able to sell him he gonna be so fat. I can see it now, all day long, just you and me in a shearing pen, covered in cotton balls."

"Enough."

"Not enough. What in God's name makes you think it's a good idea?"

Cody finished the bale. Hauled the next one to the edge and cut the twine. "I'm sorry, you ever had a hostage? Shit man, I got no idea what to do. I'm hoping for the best, planning for the worst."

"Well you get in bed with the bank again that's where you're going. Nothing good ever comes of it. I told you six years ago and I'm telling you now."

"I don't hear you coming up with anything better."

"That's not my job. I'm the guy tells you when it's a bad idea. Keepin the Injun alive? Bad idea. Taking money from the bank? Bad idea. Buying a buncha fucking sheep? Terrible, awful, no good idea."

Cody shook his head. He looked to the southeast, saw Manuel on the paint among another herd. He thumbed the talk button. "How about you do yer damn job and tell me how them cows look," and made it through another bale before Manuel said they looked fine, but that could all change the drop of a hat.

Then Cody caught something in the corner of his eye. In a thicket, dark in color. Animal for sure. He moved to the cab, used the door frame to swing into the driver's seat and cut the wheel, shifting the truck into second and gunning it—the remaining bales in the flatbed were thrown and the cows stopped running.

"What happens you turn around and all the cows are belly up?" Manuel said. "And you realize, in a matter of seconds, he done more damage than a hundred wolves."

Getting closer Cody could see it was a calf, and for a fleeting second, assumed it was asleep.

No, he thought. It couldn't be. Not this far from the herd.

He was thinking about the wolf now, the one that got away as he hit the brakes and hopped out. He could hear the calf bawling. He ducked under branches, parted the brush and saw the calf foaming at the mouth. Cody pried her jaws, felt warm puss on a fingertip. He said, "No," several times. Grabbed a hoof, saw the blood, the ruptured blisters. He started to lift her, telling her it would be okay when he heard a snort and felt the ground rumble beneath his feet. He pivoted, saw fifteen hundred pounds charging like a freight train and dove out of the way as the Aberdeen slid to a stop over her calf.

Cody rolled to a knee, held his hands out. "Easy. I ain't

hurting her. I'm just trying to help." He thought about it, then said, "The hell'm I telling you for…"

He spat. Looked at the cow again, this time in detail, and saw the phlegm dangling from her nostrils, the raw blisters pocking her deflated utters.

Cody cursed on the way back to his truck. He tore across the ranch and caught a glimpse of the cow settling in next to her calf.

He fishtailed when he hit the dirt trail, thinking about Blackfoot. Wondering just how much Uncle Kenny would fork over in exchange for a safe return.

Blackfoot swore his stomach was trying to eat itself. The contortion. The growling. He was exhausted. Everything was swollen. A fly landed on his nose. He shook his head. The fly hovered and landed again. He wiped at it, catching its flank with a finger and shoving it through the air.

That's when he felt the weight of the rope around his wrist. He lifted the hand, saw the slack dragging in the dirt. Curled his fingers, felt blood circulate over his joints.

Confused, he looked up, saw the frayed tether dangling from the beam. Then he caught the movement. A naked tail of vermin draped over the edge, sweeping the length of the beam.

The rat, Blackfoot thought. It must have chewed through the rope.

It sounded ridiculous, but he didn't care. No time to waste.

He turned to the workbench, saw the machete on the wall and reached for it but fell short. He stretched, contorting his body, feeling the tingle of the taut fibers beneath his skin, a shoulder on the brink of separating from its socket. Blackfoot touched the rusted blade with his fingertips. His legs throbbed. Stretching farther, he curled his fingers around the blade. He grunted, lifted the knife and slid the eyelet off the nail. Pinned the dull side of the blade between his teeth, gripped the handle then chopped down several times, freeing his other arm.

He collapsed and found himself staring at the streak beneath the door again, his cheek in the dirt. An inner voice told him to get out. Now. He got to his knees, cut the ropes around his ankles and crawled to the door and pulled himself up, yanking on the handle several times but the door wouldn't budge. He turned back, looking for a spot he could start to chisel his way out when he heard the sound of the diesel, the tires skidding to a stop.

The engine cut off. Doors popped open. Footsteps could be heard crunching gravel. The hairs on Blackfoot's neck stood tall and the pulsing of his heart swelled. His eyes fell to the dirt, became fixed on the machete.

Manuel had put the paint in the remuda and was riding shotgun as Cody barreled across the ranch, rambling about what he had seen with the cows. Manuel wanted to say he knew the kid was lying. He wanted to say "I told you so." But he looked at Cody and asked what he was planning to do.

"What's the market at, one twenty-six?" Cody said.

"One twenty-five as of yesterday."

"Aright, so get yer damn smartphone out..."

"It's in the tack barn."

"Goddamnit."

"Why? Whaddayou need?"

"A calculator."

"That brick on the dash don't have one?"

"It does, but it don't work 'cause it's been stepped on so many times."

"*Aye-yai-yai, cabron.* Ain't that supposed to withstand a tank or something? Explosions and shit?"

"Not the time, Manuel."

"I mean, what's the point of having it if it can't even take a licking from a few hoofs?"

Cody glared at him.

"Okay, forget about it. What about the Injun's phone? Where's that?"

Cody lifted the center console, said, "Now yer thinkin," and came up with Blackfoot's phone and handed it to Manuel. "You said one twenty-five?"

"*Si*, but with the amount of work it'll take…"

"Already ahead of you. Push it to one-thirty times our best cow last season."

"*Trece, ochenta y siete*," Manuel said, grabbing an oh-shit handle as the truck bounced over the terrain.

"Multiply that by three forty-nine, whattaya get?"

Manuel hesitated, staring at the digital keypad.

"What?"

"I need the passcode."

"Why didn't you say nothing when I's spewing numbers?"

"You were on a roll. I didn't want to interrupt."

Cody shook his head, annoyed. "How many numbers is it?"

"You don't remember the passcode?"

"Just tell me how many numbers."

"*Seis. Seis numeros.*"

"Why'm I thinkin it's four?"

"It's *seis*."

"I know it's *seis*, goddamnit. You were there, you don't member?"

"I wasn't paying no attention," Manuel said. "I didn't know if you were gonna pump that shit into him or not—'cause you didn't tell me it wouldn't do nothing. So when he spit in your face, I thought, I gotta do something drastic, show him I'm no bitch."

"That's why you stabbed him?"

"Don't say it like I did something wrong. What, you can stab him, but I can't?"

As the truck crested a hill, Manuel saw the secluded shed, the ribs of the corrugated metal peaking over a tiny squat box.

"Just think, aright?" Cody said. "It's something simple. Try all zeroes."

Manuel did. Said that wasn't it.

"One, two, three, four, five, six."

Manuel typed that in. Saw the screen shake and return to the keypad, the words INCORRECT, 3 MORE TRIES BEFORE DISABLED written at the top.

"Nope."

Cody gripped the wheel with both hands and roared.

Manuel tried to put himself back in the shed. The kid strung up, bitching about this and that. Cody yelling, acting more like the loudmouth lawman than a cool Eastwood in that revenge western. It was hard to make out what the Indian was saying because the *pinché guey* was missing half his tongue. Manuel ran through combinations until something sounded familiar, the shed swelling in the windshield. He tried two sets of three numbers. Numbers in sequence. No, he thought, that didn't sound right. It was two numbers. Yeah, two numbers three times over. Four. Four three. No. Four seven… No, four, and something that sounded like shits. Manuel pinched his tongue between his teeth and tried to say shits, but it came out sounding like, "Thits."

"What?" Cody said.

"Thit-thit-thits. Four-thits."

"Four tits? The fuck're you saying?"

"Four-thits. Yeah-yeah, that's it. Four-six. Forty-six, three times over." Manuel plugged the numbers, saw a buffet of apps appear. He cycled to the calculator. "Okay, give me those numbers again."

Cody did. And when Manuel showed him the final number, Cody told him to make the call.

When it started ringing, he passed the phone to Cody and drew his Kershaw. Blew some lint clear of the action and flipped it open, believing that, sooner or later, he'd have to use it.

Kenny was on edge. Doing laps around the casino floor, watching everyone, their hands, their bets, the dealers that might be skimming.

He asked Hector how much longer.

"Still another half hour. After that, we can start to worry."

Kenny couldn't understand why he had listened to Shea. He could've used anyone. Any one of the drunks pissing away their royalties at the table. And to think he didn't have to do a damn thing but catch Moffat cheating and he'd be set.

He heard a dealer say, "Full house wins. Sevens over Cowboys," and saw the guy shove a stack of nickels to the player, the chips sliding, catching the felt and spilling.

Kenny beelined for him, collecting the chips, setting them upright. "Who the fuck taught you to deal?"

"Vegas, sir. The Tropicana."

"Well you're in the real-deal now, not that corporate shit they have out West. Do it right, or I'll have you washing dishes."

"Yes, sir."

"And to hell with cowboys. Call them Gorillas or Ace Magnets, anything but cowboys, got it?"

"Yes, sir."

Kenny watched the dealer stiffen. Watched him deal the next hand before moving on, scanning the other tables, gripping a wrist behind his back.

"You all right, sir?" Hector said.

"You don't think Custer has the balls to pull anything, do you?"

"It's the only leverage he's got. He ain't that stupid."

Kenny felt the buzz against his palm. He eyed his phone, saw his nephew's name on the screen. Looked at Hector, said, "Here we go," and answered saying only his name, trying to play it cool like he was busy or expecting a business call.

"Six hunnert thirty thousand," Cody said.

Kenny scoffed. "Little steep considering the market's at what, one-fifteen?"

"One twenty-five."

Kenny guesstimated the amount of cattle and figured the asshole was bluffing. "Then how'd you get six-thirty?"

"'Cause I like the way it looks with all them zeroes after it. So it's either six-thirty, or I tie the sumbitch to my truck and drag him through the streets."

The stupid cowboy had a death wish.

"Fine. You have a deal."

"Three Points above Horsethief Lake at midnight."

Kenny said, "I want to talk to him first," but the line went dead. He cursed at the phone, then told Hector to get cash from the cage.

"Sir, I'd advise against paying him."

Kenny looked at him. "He's not walking away with it."

20

CODY wanted to kill him. Thought about how he'd do it, too. Walk in... No, better yet, kick the fucking door down, shove the Colt in his face and let 'er rip—not say a goddamn word. He could feel Manuel's eyes on him from the passenger seat, so he turned and said, "What?"

"I wanna know what you're thinking?"

"Why?"

"'Cause you got a crazy look in your eye, and I want in."

Cody shook his head. "This far as you go, Manny. I'm goin up there alone."

"*Ni lo sueñes.* Happened on my watch too. I got as much a score to settle."

Cody looked at him. "It's gotta be done my way then. No bullshit, no second guessing."

Manuel grinned. "Hey, you the chief, *cabron*."

He skidded to a stop in front of the shed. Checked the chamber in the 1911, saw a glint of brass, then flicked the safety off and holstered it. At the door, he removed the padlock and heard Manuel say, "*Dia del juicio, pedazo de mierda,*" as he entered first, followed by the Indian kid yelling, "*Hoka Hey,* motherfucker!"

Then Manuel froze.

His arms fell limp, his body lurched. When he dropped to his knees, Cody saw Blackfoot holding a bloody machete. The Indian raked the blade across Manuel's neck and blood sprayed like a geyser.

Cody drew, fired twice as Blackfoot disappeared into the shed. Cody gripped Manuel's collar, dragged him several feet, keeping the gun leveled on the doorway.

Manuel was choking—on his own blood or saliva, Cody wasn't sure. He applied pressure to the well of blood in Manuel's chest. "Stay with me pard, stay with me."

The shed door slammed shut.

Cody stood, fired five rounds through it and could smell the cordite coming off the gun. He dropped the empty mag, shoved a fresh one in and yanked the slide.

Manuel said his name.

Cody knelt, gripped his segundo's hand and said he was sorry.

Manuel said something back in Spanish that Cody couldn't understand, so he leaned closer and heard the segundo whisper, "Kill 'em. Kill 'em all."

Manuel's eyes remained open when he went.

A rage teemed inside Cody. He stood, approached the shed and fired at the door until the gun clicked empty. He found the padlock in the dirt. Removing the key, he snapped it shut on the door and went back to his truck, not entirely convinced of what he was bound to do next.

Blackfoot's adrenaline thumped inside of him. He didn't realize the cowboy was back there till the wetback went to his knees. But man, did that blade move like butter across the dude's neck. When he saw the cowboy come up with the pistol, he dove behind the open door, heard the shots and saw two bullet holes—light spilling through—in a tight grouping opposite the doorway and figured the white man to be a deadeye.

He kicked the door shut, stayed low as five more holes punched through it. Then sat against the door—not wanting any surprises or the cowboy to think he was John Wayne and kick the damn thing down, come in blasting with that old-ass pistol.

Blackfoot watched blood drip off the machete and listened for movement. It wasn't but a few seconds when more rounds came through the door. Blackfoot shrieked, protecting his head when one tore through his shoulder. The force pulled him to the ground. He crawled out of the line of fire, staying low, when he heard the padlock click on the other side of the door.

It was the truck making noise now. Grumbling, belching to life. Tires kicking, speeding off and fading away yet again.

Blackfoot checked his shoulder. Through and through. All meat, no bone. He breathed. Figured the cowboy must have loaded the wetback in the truck and was taking him to get help.

Like it mattered.

The guy was dunzo. Hell yeah, Blackfoot thought. They done fucked with the wrong Injun today.

He sat there in silence as the adrenaline lulled and pain from just about everywhere crept in. His leg, his gut—shit, even the migraine raging in his skull. He couldn't remember the last time he had any water and tried not to think about food. Instead, he would daydream about the kind of drugs they'd put him on in recovery. Probably morphine or fentanyl on a drip. Send him home with some kind of script. Norco. Oxy's if he was lucky.

Focus, he thought. One down. One to go. He couldn't wait to get out of here, see the look on Uncle Kenny's face when he said not only did he get the job done, but took both of 'em out in the process. That's how he'd word it, too. *Took both of 'em out.* Like it was no big deal. Just business.

He heard the diesel again. Faint, but growing, getting closer. Blackfoot got to a knee and peered through a bullet hole.

Hang on. The wetback was still there, a shitload of blood in the dirt. Now the truck filled his frame of view, the engine deafening, and Blackfoot realized it was speeding right the fuck at him, not stopping.

He managed a half turn before the truck bulldozed him, feeling one, then a second tire crushing him.

He was on his back looking at dark, fluffy clouds. The sharp edges of the rubble prodding him from underneath. He couldn't feel his toes, his legs—nothing below the waist. He pulled his chin to his chest, saw the machete sticking out of his rib cage, a trail of broken two-by-fours and tools starting where the shed used to be and ending at his feet. And next to him, emerging from the rubble, was the rat, looking at Blackfoot with its beady eyes, its whiskers twitching. Then it scurried off into the heather.

He knew he was dying. Accepted it. Regretted a wasted life and wondered if all the stories he had heard about "walking on" would be true. The spirit world in the sky, free of pain and suffering.

Sure sounded like a nice place.

The cowboy came limping into view and looked like a giant

150

against the dense storm clouds. No hat. A head of thick, matted hair. The dude didn't say anything, just came down hard with some kind of wrench.

Blackfoot only felt the first blow before everything went black.

Cody Custer grabbed a fist full of the Indian's stringy mane and scalped him with the Kershaw. It was difficult, cutting the fine line of flesh without getting the blade, its serrated edge, caught on the skull—and he did a few times.

He drove back to the shop barn, disconnected from the world around him, devoid of emotion. He passed a few ranch hands. They would wave or nod, but Cody didn't even look at them.

In the shop barn, he grabbed tarps and rope. On his way out, he saw the wolf carcasses in the corner and got what he thought was a clever idea, so he took one and threw it in the truck bed with the rest of the gear. He shut the tailgate, then went back for a shovel.

By the time he got back, it was close to sundown. And a half-hour after that, he drove to the northwest corner of the ranch, then eased the truck up a trail that weaved through the ponderosas.

He parked. Got out, dropped the tailgate and went to a knee. He hoisted Manuel's corpse onto his shoulder. His thighs burned, his calves locked up as he trekked the two hundred or so yards up the hill.

When he reached the eroded crucifix, he set Manuel down, realizing he forgot the goddamn shovel, so he humped it back to his truck.

By the time he reached six feet deep, it was dark. He had broken a sweat, shivered in his damp buckskin and went back to sweating again. The tension in the back of his legs strained his lumbar, forcing him to slouch as he climbed out of the grave.

He rolled Manuel in. Packed and put in a chaw before he started replacing the dirt. He looked at the eroded crucifix, the R.A.C. inscribed—almost illegible now—and thought he should make one for Manuel and did so from broken branches, retrieving a hammer and nail from the toolbox of his truck to fashion them together. He used the tip of his Kershaw to engrave M.F.R., then stuck it in the ground, paid his respects and said goodbye to his only true friend: Manuel Flores Rodriguez.

Thunder pulled his attention to the southwest. A thick layer of clouds encased flashes of lightning. The derecho misting to the earth, sailing through a murky sky toward the Black Hills.

Cody Custer stood there with vengeance on his mind. He turned back to the two crucifixes, said a prayer for Manuel and left, never giving a thought to the man beneath the other one.

Hector Vargas couldn't hear the thunder over the roar of the FN P-90 submachine gun on full-auto. He liked the compact make of the gun, the full-sized stock, the separate foregrips and the short barrel that gave the operator complete control. He could see the U.S. Cavalry hat fluttering on the head of the Century BOB punching bag downrange as the barrage of 5.7s peppered it center-mass.

When the gun clicked empty, he checked the open breech,

confirmed the weapon was clear and safetied it. He went back to the tent reciting the specs of the gun, then looked at Kenny and said, "You want to shred him, this is your girl. Small enough, we can put you in a trench coat and conceal it underneath, no problem."

"That what you would go with?"

Hector shrugged and placed it on the table. "Depends. Close quarters, multiple targets, it's a solid weapon." He moved down the row to the next one, saying, "You want power, though? 12-gauge automatic. This one's got a collapsible stock and several tubes beneath the barrel here giving you sixteen shots a mag."

"That's a bad motherfucker."

Look at him trying to be cool. Acting like he knew about guns. Like he'd actually have to use it.

"What about collateral damage?" Kenny said squinting, his arms crossed.

"Could be an issue depending on what he's planning. Three Points is heavily forested and he'll either lie and wait, or he'll be in the clearing using your nephew as a shield with another guy in a sniper position."

"What if he has Bodaway stashed somewhere and wants to see the cash first?"

"I thought about that, but I'm assuming he's a rookie at all this. He doesn't know what he's doing and wants this to go down as smooth as possible."

Kenny nodded. "But he'll show his face. I'm positive about that."

"Why?"

"Because he's a fucking cowboy. They're nothing if not prideful. Hell, he might even crack a smile as he takes the cash and say something stupid like, 'Nice doin business with ya.'"

Hector forced a laugh and made a mental note to recruit someone else. He moved to the nickel-plated revolver. "So you'll need something reliable. Something you can use up close if it comes to it. This is a .357 Magnum with hollow-points. Enough power to stop a black bear at full sprint." He handed it to Kenny, said to give it a feel.

Kenny took it with an open palm, feeling its weight before wrapping a hand around the polymer grip. He aimed down-range, an eye closed. "You can outfit this with a shoulder holster?"

"Well the thing about shoulder holsters—"

"I didn't ask what the *thing* was, I asked if you could make it happen."

There it was. The hardass coming to the surface again, marking his place in the pecking order. Hector wanted to laugh at the way he was holding the gun like a Hollywood actor. Like he could hit anything in that one-handed, half-cocked stance with the wrong eye closed. It made Hector think about the mail-ordered animal mounts on the wall. Not just the ones in Kenny's office, but the two in the Wagyu steakhouse with the photoshopped pictures of Kenny on a knee, grinning, gripping the antlers. Yeah, the boss-man never killed a thing. When Hector had asked why Kenny wanted the mounts, Kenny told him because people—business associates in particular—would take you more seriously if they thought you killed shit in your spare time. So Hector ordered them and fed the boss-man a few stories that would make sense should anyone with knowledge ask.

"Absolutely, sir," Hector said. "We can outfit it with a shoulder holster, no problem."

"And it shoots true?"

"Only one way to find out." Hector stepped aside, watched the boss-man fire, then saw dirt splash ten meters short and right of the target.

"Where'd it go... I hit it?"

"Right in the chest. Great shot, sir."

21

KENNY had no idea it was supposed to rain. The app on his phone had said cloudy with scattered showers, but only like a thirty percent chance. And when it said "scattered" it never fucking rained, but holy shit was it coming down.

Visibility sucked. He couldn't see the road lines under the glare of his headlights, so he went slow around the turns, snaking up through the thin evergreens—he could never remember their actual name. Part of him felt like a pansy, but how stupid would it look if he had to call Custer and say he'd be late because of a wreck? He came to a stop sign, put the Range Rover in four-wheel drive, just in case, and accelerated.

The .357 Mag stuffed inside the stupid shoulder holster was uncomfortable. The leather was tacky. He had trouble on every practice draw in front of the mirror and couldn't figure out how the tough guys in Hollywood made it look so easy.

He made a right on Hackemore, glanced in the rearview, saw the new guy's box head and told him to pick a side so he could see out the back window. He had an ugly face, acne-scarred worse than Hector's, which was good for intimidating people but no fun to look at.

When the man scooted to the right, Kenny still couldn't see anything, save the wiper blade kicking back and forth. He turned to Hector in the passenger. "What'd you say his name was?"

"Silas Ochoa, sir."

"He looks the part, does he play it?"

"He's the only other Yawakhan to make Force Recon. Multiple combat deployments. Direct action, target acquisition—he's the real deal."

Kenny looked at him in the rearview. "Silas, is it?"

Silas just nodded.

Kenny wondered if the guy was deaf, or maybe a mute. He spoke slower this time. "Did Hector fill you in on everything? You have any questions about tonight?"

Silas shook his head.

"Was that a 'no' to my first question or my second?"

Silas held up two fingers, then used them to rack the slide on the P-90 in his duke, a big-ass silencer on the end of the barrel.

"O-kay... And my first question?"

"Obviously he filled me in," Silas said. "I get the feeling you're a little nervous. And look, it's perfectly normal for someone like you who's never been in a situation like this, so you find the need to fill the silence by asking stupid questions."

Kenny hit the brakes, used Hector's headrest to pull himself around. "Who the fuck do you think you are talking to me like that?"

"Half of the understaffed, underpaid team employed to keep you alive tonight. Look, I know you're the big dick on the rez. I know you're the cheese. But out here, it's guys like me and Vargs who got our shit dragging in the dirt. I promise, execute the plan and we'll walk away with your nephew, the money, and not have to worry about whitey coming back ever again to fuck with us. That all sound good enough for you, *sir*?"

"You think you're underpaid?"

"Considering your net worth and how much you think you're worth… Yes sir, I do."

"What about those tribal checks? Do I get any thanks?"

"I'm only an eighth Yawakhan. Which means, by your standards, I'm good enough to live on the rez but not good enough for profit-share."

"An eighth? What's the other seven?"

"Mexican."

"Jesus Christ," Kenny said. "Then find yourself a full-blood and start climbing the ladder." He turned back to the front, said to Hector, "I liked him better when I thought he was a mute," and drove another mile before they passed a sign reading THREE POINTS: BLACK HILLS, SOUTH DAKOTA.

Kenny kept one eye on the road, the other on the radio clock. When it ticked, he initiated a practice draw, reaching inside his buffalo trench, catching a finger on his shirt pocket before finding the revolver's grip.

Shit, that was bad.

He'd be dead if it were the real thing.

He could feel Hector and Mister One-Eighth back there watching him, so he felt for the shirt pocket again, pulled out an old business card and pretended to be looking for something specific, like the thought had to just occurred to him. He glanced in the rearview again.

Silas was staring, an eyebrow cocked.

"Alright, I can't draw the fucking thing," Kenny said. "Is it supposed to be that difficult?"

Silas looked at the back of Hector's seat.

When Hector hesitated, Kenny said, "You know what, don't

answer that. Just tell me what you'd do if you were in my situation."

They both sat there. Kenny could tell they weren't searching for the words anymore, just refusing to say.

"What, now neither of you speak? Not thirty seconds ago"—looking at Silas now—"you couldn't shut up about how inept I was, and now I'm asking for advice and you got nothing?"

"No one uses a shoulder holster," Hector said. "Except detectives or bounty hunters—guys who don't have to rely on the speed of their draw to save their hide."

"Bullshit detectives don't. You ever see Kenda on Homicide Hunter? Almost every case the guy's drawing on someone. He goes down the wrong alley, or into the wrong bar, and there's the fucking guy that committed the murder. And Kenda, he knows it, right? He's looking at the perp and can tell the dude's thinking it's me or the pig. And what does the perp do? He goes for the gun."

"That's a TV show, ain't it?" Silas said.

"Yeah, but it's based on the man's exploits."

"But generally speaking," Hector said, "detectives come in after the crime has occurred. So ninety-nine percent of the time they're only drawing when they're running caboose on a raid."

"So why the hell would anyone wear a shoulder holster?"

"Because it's more comfortable when you're spending most of the day in a car. Take this next left."

Kenny glanced at him, then made the turn and watched the road narrow to a single lane.

Hector said, "If I were you, sir, I'd just keep it loose in that front pocket."

"What if it goes off? I'm standing there, trying to seal the deal and end up shooting my nuts off. How's that gonna look?"

"That's a double-action Python with an eight-and-a-half-pound trigger pull. Trust me, it won't go off. Keep your finger straight and off the trigger till you clear the pocket and you'll be fine."

"That simple, huh?"

"Long as we do our job, you won't even have to draw it. Stop here."

Kenny hit the brakes. It felt weird taking orders from Hector. He begrudged doing it.

"Flank fifty meters and standby till Mr. Shepard makes contact. Radio when you get eyes on him."

"Roger that." Silas exited the Rover and disappeared into the foliage.

Kenny followed the road into a clearing and parked, leaving the high beams on, asking Hector to walk him through the plan once more.

"We stand by till we hear from Silas. If anyone is out there, he'll sniff 'em out. Odds are, Custer'll come from the south, possibly on horseback since he can access it from his property. After he reveals himself and moves into the clearing, only then do you exit and approach after I receive confirmation from Silas about any possible bogeys. As you make the exchange, secure Blackfoot first, tell him to run—not walk—but *run* back to the vehicle. *Never* turn your back and *never* trust the enemy. Good to go?"

"Well hang on... When do I shoot him? When's the best time to draw?"

"You'll know."

"Okay, but if I don't. If I forget or miss my chance, when,

generally speaking, is a good time to do it."

Hector was staring, his lips parted. "When he looks in the duffel to make sure the money is real, okay?"

"Yeah-yeah, that's good. That's real good."

He felt excitement, then boredom as time dragged. Thirty minutes seemed like half the night. Hector didn't say another word except once into his radio when he asked Silas for something called a sitrep.

Kenny became so bored he started counting the seconds in his head trying to judge the difference between his phone and the radio clock. One time he got thirty-six seconds, another time he got fifty-two.

Midnight came and went.

Kenny's boredom evolved into concern. He asked Hector if he saw anything, if Silas had said anything, though it was clear the answer was no.

"I knew the son of a bitch wouldn't show." Kenny tried calling Blackfoot to no avail and was about to tell Hector to radio Silas when he saw the guy step into the clearing, waving an arm, frantic.

"What's he saying?" Kenny said.

Hector shook his head, listening to Silas's voice siphoning up the pigtail into his ear.

Cody could see the blue tarp flapping against the wind in the truck bed when the brake lights illuminated. The rain was dumping, drumming the truck's metal roof. He preferred listening to that over any of the shit on the radio, the DJ doing more talking than playing, reminding listeners he was coming at them live from his corner booth at Bear Republic Coffee

Roasters, "The new, hot coffee joint in town. Pun intended, bros."

Cody had been avoiding Pappy since everything had started, only tending to him when he called. He didn't know what Pappy knew about the cows, or what he could have seen from the window. But after Cody buried Manuel, he had driven back to replenish the spent ammo and was caught off-guard when he saw the old man on the porch with a jar of whiskey. He seemed better than usual, sitting erect, sucking deep breaths through his nose. The oxygen machine was on a dolly nearby.

"What're you doing out here? You aright?" When Pappy didn't respond, Cody said it again, this time louder over the hum of the oxygen machine.

"I miss this smell," Pappy said. "Tired a sittin in that goddamn room all day, staring out the window at what I used to be."

"Ain't missing much, trust me."

A gust of wind carried the sour mash and oak into Cody's nostrils. He lifted his chin. Became fixed on the russet liquid. He inhaled again, long and slow. Could feel an empty sensation in the pit of his stomach, a tingling in the back of his throat. The inside of his cheeks began to salivate and he took a step toward Pappy.

"Didn't see nobody down the corrals today. Give everone the day off, or what?"

Cody blurted the first thing that came to mind. "Had 'em mending fence lines yonder."

"It affect the count?"

"No, sir. Count's solid since we took care the wolf problem."

Pappy half nodded. "What I like to hear."

162

The thought of an imminent relapse consumed Cody as he found himself stealing glances of the whiskey, pining for that buzz. A voice in his head said grab the jar and down it, or walk away, but stop standing there and being a bitch about it. So Cody shoved his hands in his pockets and started for the steps, but felt the lawyer's crumpled business card and remembered what that weasel had said about the ranch being a sole prop. "Can I ask you something?"

"Depends on the question."

"How come I ain't got a stake in this ranch?"

Pappy drank, clenched his teeth as he swallowed and said, "What're you talking about?" like it was news to him.

"Don't play stupid. I talked to that lawyer was over here."

"Yer foreman. What more you want?"

"I want a guarantee. I want to know I ain't busting my ass everday for nothing."

"Only guarantee in this life are death and taxes."

"Goddamnit, that ain't good enough. For once in yer life will you give me an honest fucking answer?"

"It's yers alright!" Pappy said, slamming the mason jar on the side table. "Jesus Christ. When yer dying the only thing anyone gives a shit about is what yer leaving behind."

"I didn't mean it like that."

"The fuck you didn't. Don't get remorse for saying what you really felt."

"Pappy, when yer gone, it's all I got."

"And I been trying to tell you it's over. Yer still out there working cows on horseback, and for what? To prove a point? The biggest and best outfits this country're using helicopters, quads, trucks, you name it. Got twice—shit, four times the cattle'n work 'em in half the time. You can't keep up."

Cody cocked his head. "I don't believe you just said that. Yer the one used to tell me a cowboy's about being connected to the land, to the horse between his knees. That it's the reason we're put here on this Earth."

"That sounds romantic, but it don't pay the bills. He who fails to evolve gets left behind, and that casino ain't nothing but a fatal reminder of that. Yer a hell of a cowboy, I'll give you that. But don't let it be yer demise."

Cody spat. "I'd rather die young doing what I love instead of waiting to die with nothing but regret."

The squawk of the siren brought Cody back to the present.

He eased the truck onto the shoulder and came to a stop. He couldn't see a damn thing but a red light twirling and wondered if the cop would look under the tarp, whether or not he could by law.

The cruiser door opened, an amber light filled the interior and Cody caught a glimpse of the man's thick mustache before he slid out and shut the door. The next thing Cody saw was a cool white beam flick on, lingering on the tarp before moving to the cab.

When the cop knocked on the window with the butt of his flashlight, Cody cranked it down and heard the rain smacking the cop's canvas jacket. A nametape over a chest pocket read HARRIS in block letters.

Harris spoke first.

"Know why I pulled you over?"

"Sure don't."

"Got a busted headlight. Happened to yer truck?"

"I, ah, hit a wolf coming up 75."

"A wolf?"

Cody could tell he wasn't buying it, the man's nostrils flaring like he was smelling bullshit. "Oh yeah. Big grey one. Jumped out right in front of me. Tried to swerve, but with the rain you know, there's only so much I could do."

"When?"

"Just now."

His nostrils were flaring again. He asked if Cody had been drinking. Cody said, No, he didn't touch the stuff no more.

Harris stared for a moment, then pulled the door open and told Cody to step out.

"Come on, you gotta be shitting me."

"Get. Out. Of the truck," Harris said, blinding Cody with the Maglite.

Cody took his time, glaring at the sheriff.

"Where's yer gun?" Harris said.

"Makes you think I got one?"

Harris lowered the light to reveal a deadpan expression. "Really? Ya wanna go that route?"

"Left hip." Cody unbuttoned his coat and let Harris pull it from the holster. Before he could ask, Cody told him, Of course it was loaded, and, Yes, the safety was engaged.

Harris didn't skip a beat. He dropped the mag, cleared the chamber, and laid it on the roof. Now he turned to the truck bed. "What's under the tarp?"

"Like I said, I hit a wolf."

"Show me."

Cody watched Harris take a step back, a hand hovering his sidearm. When Cody pulled the tarp, its lips were curled revealing two-inch fangs and gnarled teeth. Cody turned back, saw Harris deflate, and wondered if Kenny or his goon had found the Injun kid yet.

* * *

All kinds of shit smacked him in the face. Leaves, branches, hell, a spider web went into his mouth, you name it. Silas was leading them through the forest, talking a mile a minute, but all Kenny could make out was, "Up here, just a little further."

He asked if there was any sign of Custer, but didn't hear the guy's response because he was too busy trying to stay on his feet, climbing over uprooted trees or skating across patches of slick moss blanketing jagged rocks. The traction on his suede Kiton's sucked. He had fallen on his ass about twenty yards back, splashing down in a mud puddle, soaking his buffalo trench through the polyester lining. And now the damn thing weighed a ton which meant he could no longer feel the Python in the front pocket and thought maybe it had fallen out, but Kenny didn't give a flying fuck because he wasn't about to stop and make this bullshit rendezvous last any longer than it had to. He said, "You know what would come in handy right now? A fucking machete," but no one responded as they moved into a clearing and he saw Bodaway lynched, dangling from a tree. He could see the stark alabaster of the kid's skull, rinsed clean from the rain. Bodaway's face was black and blue, swollen the size of a basketball. Kenny wouldn't have recognized him if it weren't for the Yawakhan tat on his shirtless shoulder.

Kenny fell to his knees. He tried to speak, tried to yell, but nothing came out. He put his face in the dirt and sobbed, clawing at the earth, craving vengeance but overwhelmed by sorrow at the same time.

22

MORGAN sat on the bed watching him bounce from one side of the room to the other, grabbing everything he thought was hers and shoving it into a duffel. He was spewing Spanish, amped up, calling her husband a *pinche*-something. Talking about what he'd do the next time he saw Buck Taylor—something with his hands, maybe that he'd cut them fuckers off, because that's what they did to people who pulled this shit back in El Salvador.

Morgan didn't actually know. She was making it up as he rambled on.

This mocha-soaked dreamboat with the combed hair that always stayed put—even after sex—standing up for his woman. Yeah, she could see herself with him for the rest of her life. A litter of half-breeds playing in the sand, the smell of salt water in the air, some exotic beach town, streets lined with palm trees.

What had they been waiting for?

Gustavo was in the underwear drawer now, extracting wadded panties. Neutral tones, raggedy pieces with frays and holes. A decade of periods and skid marks the trailer park's well water couldn't erase. Morgan wondered if Gustavo would like the way she looked in a thong, something bold, neon orange or fire-engine red. The kind with a thick waistband and some guy's name written across.

Morgan's eyes drifted to the dresser, landing on a picture framed of her and Buck. They were on a quad, mudding in one of those parks you had to pay to enter just so you could tear your own shit up, get it all dirty. Buck was smiling, sure, but Morgan could see the menace lingering in the back of his eyes. It made her paranoid. She felt a mass caving her shoulders, rounding her back. She became short of breath. Could hear Buck's voice in her head saying he would find her wherever she went. Saying he'd kill her then torture Gustavo before killing him too.

She said Gustavo's name several times.

He was still jabbering in Spanish. Morgan couldn't imagine what he was saying anymore. It didn't matter, all of this was a pipe dream anyway.

She stood, intercepting him as he turned back for the duffel and shouted at him to stop.

"No, I won't. I'm taking jou tonight."

"Where we gonna go, huh? We don't got no money. It ain't like we can skip town, catch a flight out the country some place he cain't track us."

Gustavo shook his head, baffled. "What other option jou have? Jou wanna stay, what happens next time the gun is loaded?"

She hesitated, didn't have a good answer.

He said, "That's what I thought," and brushed past her.

"I cain't just up and leave everthing, aright? It's more complicated'n that. Believe it or not, he's been there for me."

Gustavo muttered something in Spanish as he mashed and pulled the zipper on the duffel.

"He took me in when I's a little girl, when I had no place to go."

Gustavo smacked the duffel. *"Maldita sea, cariña!"* He turned back, pointed at the full-length mirror. "Look at jourself. Look what this man has done to jou."

She saw the bruised cheekbones. The bags under her eyes. The heavy lines across her neck. She was sore, had constipated herself for several days because she didn't think she could bear to go number two.

She caught Gussy's eyes in the mirror, his head perched over her shoulder, and felt a sense of security when his arms closed around her.

"I swear," Gustavo said, "so long I have breath, I be there for jou. I take care of jou. Provide for jou. Love jou. And this," he caressed her jawline, "will never, ever happen again."

Morgan wasn't sure. It sounded good, but she couldn't shake the feeling that Buck was always around.

Had they been facing each other, one of them would have caught the headlights coming through the window, careening the wall.

"Eres mi persona favorita, amor. Please, leave with me. *Por* jourself and no one else."

She turned, saw the yearning in her man's eyes. "Okay."

"Sí?"

"Let's do it."

"Listo."

He moved past her, grabbed the duffel. She managed to take just one step forward in this new life, this new outlook, when Buck Taylor entered the house. He didn't notice at first, looking down at his boots, calling her by name.

Morgan felt a chill climb her spine.

When Buck looked up, he stopped mid-step and his eyes shifted from her to Gustavo and back again. He said, "Motherfucker," then advanced.

She heard Gustavo yell for her to run, saw the duffel come flying past and Buck spike it to the ground.

She couldn't move, frozen with fear as Gustavo darted past her and leapt for Buck.

Buck caught him, spun and chucked Gustavo through the gypsum wallboard into the living room, leaving a gaping hole. Now Morgan could see Dr. Phil on the flat screen, an arm draped over a man dressed like a woman, but not fooling anyone. Dr. Phil pumping some encouragement into the guy's ear.

Buck went after Gustavo, ripping the bedroom door off its hinges.

Morgan let out a primal scream, an octave she didn't know could be reached, and jumped onto Buck's back, digging her nails into his eye sockets. He twisted, roared, and bucked out of the bedroom. Morgan saw a quick flash of Gustavo reeling on the floor, moving right to left. She saw the card table, the gypsum-floured sofa. Dr. Phil. Gustavo again. She beared down, felt blood seeping onto her fingers and dug deeper.

They bounced from one wall to the next. Her hip rammed the card table. She could feel the snub-nosed Cobra in his waistband, digging into her groin. She was getting dizzy, nauseous. She saw cabinets. The hot plate. The sink. Buck lunged back against the counter, gripped an arm and slung her to the ground.

She looked up, saw his boots stomping away. Saw Gussy come in with a chair across her husband's face. Buck's neck snapped then returned to the front like it was spring-loaded.

Morgan rolled, curled her fingers around the edge of the counter and got to her knees. She heard something break behind her, glass or porcelain. She ran her arm across the counter, her palm molding to the handle of the cast-iron skillet. Before she could lift it, her eyes were pulled to the wooden block, the black handles jutting from the slits.

She plucked the biggest one, turned, saw Gustavo swing the chair again, but Buck parried the blow and shoved him to the ground, moving to the TV now, reaching behind it and coming out with...

Oh, shit.

The shotgun belched and blood painted the flower-patterned gypsum.

Morgan moved up on Buck, saw a grin stretching across his mouth, the satisfaction in his eyes as he turned back.

The knife didn't go in as far as she hoped. Halfway, maybe.

Buck dropped the shotgun, looked at her surprised, his hands hovering the knife. He went to his knees first, then fell onto his stomach.

Morgan rushed to Gustavo. Hysterical, she buried her face in his chest. "Oh Gustavo, God no." She held his limp body, sobbing until she heard him groan.

At least she thought it was him.

She looked up, felt a cool breeze against the warm blood on her face and heard the groaning again.

Behind her.

She turned, saw the burly man getting to a knee, calling her a fucking whore, blood seeping from a corner of his mouth. He started to stand when he saw the 12-gauge nearby.

She ran for the back door, pulling it open, crow-hopping when the slug punched the gypsum wallboard adjacent. In the backyard, shards from the shattered bottles bit her bare feet as she sprinted into the refuge. She heard the shotgun's report again and tripped over a shrub, scraping her legs on the stiff, naked bushes. She could hear the crunch of leaves and sticks beneath Buck's boots and knew she didn't stand a chance out here, even with the knife in his chest. Then, through the trees, she saw a pair of headlights hugging a turn. She diverted, and prayed she would see another passing car.

23

HARRIS pulled the Bronco to a stop at the three-way, thinking the road ahead looked familiar. No doubt he'd seen it before. Hell, he'd been down it several times. But he recalled seeing it somewhere other than here. It had been daytime, the colors were brighter, the trees were thicker, and that row of solar panels along the fence line hadn't been there. Still, he couldn't quite peg it.

It would come to him.

He pulled coffee through the oval in the plastic lid, lukewarm now, and thought it was weak. Thinking now, whatever happened to that strong, bitter coffee? The kind that put hair on your chest. No one made good coffee anymore. The label on the Thermos at the Pump N' Stuff said it was from Ethiopia. That it was full-bodied—whatever that meant—with notes of berry, deep earth, and a hint of butterscotch.

Harris tasted nothing but shitty coffee. More and more he was thinking he might have to stop in some day, try that new hipster joint, see what all the fuss was about.

He snatched the rover clipped to the visor and radioed Thelma.

She didn't answer right away. He could see her hunched over the keyboard, grinding out a game of Solitaire. So he said her name multiple times every few seconds until the frequency squawked and her voice came through. "What? Whadaya need?"

Harris thumbed the talk button. "Would you quit playin on that damn computer. What if there's an emergency?"

"You get that herd a goats offa 42?"

"I did."

"And y'all finished with that traffic stop?"

"I am."

"Then I 'spect that's the end the 'mergencies in Spearfish tonight. Hell, a busted headlight—I got a busted headlight."

"Thank you, that's enough."

"What're you callin me for?"

"See if you wanna go to Denny's, get a cuppa coffee."

"No I don't wanna get a cuppa coffee. I wanna sit here'n finish my damn game, maybe catch a few Z's on the clock, waste some taxpayer dollars."

"Okay," Harris said. "A simple no woulda been fine."

"Why're you even out there? Can you tell me that?"

"I don't patrol this town, who's gonna?"

"Well when that busted-ass Bronco breaks down 'cause you put so many goddamn miles on it, don't call me to come pick you up."

"Watch it, Thelma. You know how I feel about this truck."

"The thing's a piece of shit. And if you want people to take you serious, use what's left of the budget to buy ya a new squad car—Lord knows ya ain't gonna do no upgrades here at the station."

"Thelma—

"I mean, it's only got two doors for Christ's sake. What happens you actually gotta arrest somebody? You gonna let 'em ride shotgun, take 'em through the drive-thru on the way back, ask if they want a cheeseburger?"

"I ain't never getting rid of it, okay? So drop it."

Still at the stop sign, he looked up the road and realized where he had seen it before. A Yawakhan commercial. The production value was crap—even Harris could tell. It was a first-person point of view inside a moving car, like the viewer was the one driving, a pair of feminine hands on the wheel. It made Spearfish look nice, Harris reckoned, even the backroads like this one that ran past the trailer park. The car in the commercial glided over several dotted yellows before the whole screen peeled back like a pair of playing cards, an Ace of Spades and a Jack of Clubs. A voiceover could be heard of a female shushing someone, whispering, "It can be our little secret." Then the screen went black and Harris remembered seeing the Yawakhan logo appear.

It kind of pissed him off, thinking people traveled all this way to spend the duration in a windowless, timeless room, jiving to the incessant jingle of a broke man's tune.

"Weston, you still there?"

"Yeah. Go ahead."

"Yer Bronco sucks."

Harris shook his head, saying, "You know what—" when a strawberry blonde covered in blood came out of the heather and slammed her hands on the hood, yelling for help.

Harris jumped out of the Bronco.

She was out of breath, in baggy sweats, a stretched tank, and kept looking back the way she came. Harris knew it was the girl with the bruises.

"Ma'am what's wrong? What happened?"

"Helpme, please. Heonnafuckinkillme."

Harris told her to slow down, breathe.

Before she could respond, he heard a deep, raspy voice bellow from the heather. Then he saw Buck Taylor stagger onto the tarmac. The Bronco's headlights reflected off the blade coming out of his chest. Off the gunmetal on the barrel of the shotgun. Harris corralled the girl behind him. Drew his H&K .45, shoved the Truglos out front and shouted for Buck to drop the weapon.

Buck didn't stop coming. "Get out the way, Sheriff."

"I said drop it."

"That cheating bitch is my property, I'll deal with her how I see fit."

Harris felt the girl cower behind him. He slid his finger inside the trigger guard. "Take another step it will be your last, I guarantee that."

Buck stopped.

And Harris couldn't tell what the big guy was thinking, so he kept his eyes on Buck's hands, waiting for movement.

Buck dropped the shotgun.

Harris heard the girl exhale. Heard her say, "Oh thank God," as he lowered the .45 and started for Buck, ordering him to turn around, to put his hands behind his back.

Buck swayed. It looked like he might collapse, but he straightened and Harris caught his hand coming around with it, gripping what looked like a compact revolver.

Harris lifted the Truglos to center-mass, firing, tasting a hint of metal under his tongue when saw the muzzle on Buck's gun flash and kick.

The big man took four to the chest before he dropped, disappearing into the heather. Harris felt his body: chest, arms, legs, neck—he wasn't hit. When he turned back he didn't see the girl at first because she was flat on the ground.

He rushed to her. A hole in her neck leaked like a sieve and blood filled the cracks between his fingers as he applied pressure.

Dialing 9-1-1, Harris told her it would be okay, but didn't believe it. Her eyes began to drift and Harris smacked her face, told her to focus.

She blinked. Caressed his face and mouthed what looked like, *Thank you.*

He started CPR soon as she went limp, doing it until he was dizzy and realized she was never coming back.

24

SHEA could hear him bitching in the other room, unloading on the phone to Hector about her brother. He was saying, "I want him dead, and now wouldn't be soon enough you understand? I want to watch him bleed. I want to hear the way he cries when I take that scalp from his head. And I want to see him beg before I kill him with my bare fucking hands. Bring him to me. Whatever it takes."

God, was he emotional. The desperation in his voice. No confidence. Pulling the words from his throat like he was staving off a good cry instead of reaching deep into his diaphragm, speaking with some conviction.

Shea wanted to tell him how bad he was at this. That maybe he should stick to business deals. And he was confusing everyone. Saying he wanted Cody dead *now*, but then the grocery list of everything he wanted to do—none of which the Kenny Shepard she knew had the stomach for.

She leaned towards the mirror, pulled the skin taut at the corners of her eyes and thought about Los Angeles, the Botox clinics on every block. When all this malarkey was over she'd take a trip, get some injections, then hit up Boa on the Sunset Strip, get a filet and a seafood tower, a table-side Caesar maybe, and tell the waiter—probably a wannabe actor—to keep the scotches coming.

She heard Kenny slam the phone on the receiver, then huff and puff as he paced around the penthouse. She heard ice rattle crystal. A cork went *phunk* as it was yanked from the moist throat of a bottle and the ice crackled and popped when the liquid rushed over. Shea wondered if it was for her, getting an answer when she heard Kenny gulping, the audible exhale as the glass thudded atop the leather coaster.

She released the skin and the wrinkles returned. "God, all this stress is giving me crow's feet." She thought about taking a sleeping pill to put the night behind her, but said, "Kenneth, come hither," and waited for him to appear in the doorway. "You some kind of Yawakhan Mafioso now?"

He held a hand up. "Look, I'm sure this is difficult, considering it is your brother—"

"There's nothing difficult about it because it's not going to happen."

Kenny furrowed his brow.

"Don't look at me like that," Shea said. "Your deal with Moffat is what?"

"I think there are bigger issues at hand."

"Regardless, the end goal is the same and I want to make sure we're on the same page. Your emotions are a little haywire and my concern is that you're losing focus."

"You don't think I'm fucking entitled to that?"

"Take it down a notch. We don't need the entire casino, all your employees, to hear about the woes of unclehood. Just tell me—"

"Get the fuck out."

Shea scoffed. She turned back to the vanity, tucked a strand of hair behind her ear. "And go where?"

"Not my problem, long as it's off the rez. Go to the ranch for all I care, just get the fuck out. I'm done with you." He disappeared from the doorway.

Shea grabbed her empty glass, followed him through the bedroom and out to the living room.

He was at the bar pouring another drink, his back to her. She felt the weight of the crystal in her hand, a rush in her head when she thought about smashing it over his skull.

She breathed, curbing the inclination. Walked up next to him and poured a drink from the tall, emerald bottle. "It's not that I don't want revenge. But we get one shot at this. And all I'm saying is that you're fueled on emotion right now. I mean, Hector and that new guy, whatshisname?"

"I can't remember," Kenny said, looking down at his drink.

"It doesn't matter. Those two guys, they'll do what*ever* you say, *when*ever you say it. And what happens if they go out, do the job on some poorly executed plan and get caught, botch the entire thing? The media would come in, the tourists would evaporate, and you could kiss *everything* goodbye."

Kenny took a drink. He seemed calmer now. "He murdered him, Shea. You can't expect me to sit here and do nothing."

"It's what you have to do. Like it or not, it was the risk you were willing to take when you agreed to send him in—"

"But it pisses me off because it seems like you couldn't care less."

"That's not true."

"The hell it's not. All you're talking about—all you've *ever* talked about is that goddamn ranch."

Shea put a hand on his shoulder, trying to show she cared. "Because it's the only thing that matters now. It *is* the means to the end. We can't bring Blackfoot back. Killing Cody isn't

180

going to bring him back. And it'll blow the lid off everything we're trying to do." She paused to drink. "All I'm asking for is a little more patience. After that, you have my word, you're free to do whatever."

Kenny looked at her for a while, then dropped his head. "Fine."

She smiled. "Now tell me about Moffat."

"It's simple. He'll restructure the will so when your grandfather dies, the ranch becomes yours."

Music to her ears. She headed back to the bedroom thinking about her outfit. Something on the casual side. Jeans and a blazer. "Better call David. We break ground Friday."

"Why Friday?"

Shea grinned, but didn't look back. "Let me worry about that."

Thelma was getting tired of hearing those bristles scrape the stainless receiver.

Gosh dang. The man had been at it over an hour.

She hung the twill button down in the locker, dragged on her cigarette and blew two columns of smoke through her nostrils. She was hungry. She patted her stomach, pinched a love handle and wished there was something decent open twenty-four hours in this town other than a damn Denny's—their food gave her the shits—or the Pump N' Stuff.

Heck. Go in the Pump N' Stuff this hour you're liable to come out with a hot dog been cooking since eight yesterday morning. And Thelma knew she couldn't resist once she was inside, smelling that pork. She'd cover the dog in liquid cheese and chili with no beans even though she knew the Pump N'

Stuff's fare would have the opposite effect of a Denny's meal.

Not tonight, she thought.

When she lifted the DSLR—a neat little camera with a big-ol' lens—a still from the first crime scene appeared in the display panel. It was a wide shot of the county road. She could see the gal's body against the asphalt. Bare feet looking at a set of boots, big ones, that disappeared at the knees into the heather. There was a shotgun between them. Harris was standing in the middle, pointing at the Bronco. She recalled him saying how he pulled up and the girl came out of nowhere. It was so random, unexpected. His military training had kicked in and part of him thought it was a setup.

Thelma zoomed in on the girl, unable to see where the bullet had entered from all the blood.

Damn lucky shot, she thought.

At the scene, Thelma had figured an azimuth with the girl's height and the man's height according to their IDs, then held her pincer fingers an inch apart. "Bullet missed ya by that much."

Harris hadn't said anything. He just looked down at his boots and shook his head, a hand perched on the handle of his sidearm.

Thelma cycled through a series of photos until she was inside the double-wide, stopping on a close up of the Latin boy. He had died with his eyes open, a hand extending out of frame like he was reaching for someone.

The next photo: blood spatter on the wall in a circular pattern. Rivulets running, pooling into the hunter-green carpet. She remembered snapping the photo as Harris was telling her the boy was Salvadorian, reading it from a green card in his wallet, an issuance date of less than a year ago.

Twenty years old, Harris had said—which surprised Thelma because he looked like he was still in high school.

Thelma felt sorry for him. Winning the visa lottery to meet this kind of fate. But Jesus, that's what happens when you play with fire.

She heard the slide on Harris's .45 clicking, the walls of the magazine brushing steel as it slid in and out of the grip. She powered off the camera, placed it in her locker and shut the door. Slipped on her backpack, went through the swinging doors and saw Harris hunched over his desk, the lamp on.

She went for the front door, said, "I'm a call it a night," but stopped when she saw her bottom drawer open. She turned back, saw the bottle on his desk, a third of it missing. The magazine of the .45 was set aside and Harris was holding the hollow grip up to the lamp, working the bristles back and forth.

"How many times you gonna clean that? It ain't that it don't work right."

He didn't look up, just sat there scraping. His shirt was unbuttoned and Thelma could see the girl's blood had gone through, staining his undershirt—a dark maroon color now.

"Fine. You wanna sit there'n sulk all night, be my guest." She turned for the exit, kicked the drawer shut on the way past when Harris mumbled something under his breath.

"What was that?" Thelma said.

"I coulda saved her."

"Yeah, maybe for tonight."

"If only I'd a trusted my gut."

"Yer gut? The hell're you talking about?"

"I knew she lied about them bruises," Harris said, looking up. "And I didn't do a damn thing about it. She sat there on the porch our whole conversation trying to be invisible. And when I called her down I saw that sumbitch stand a little taller, and I'm thinking he don't want me talking to her. He don't want her coming down here. Then I see the bruises and I knew, I just knew."

"Yeah, and what would you of done? Been focused on taking the 12-gauge when he pulls the snub-nose from the back a his britches. He had the drop on you and you damn-well know it."

"That ain't the point."

Harris grabbed the bottle, leaned against the back of his chair and drank. Doing too much thinking, over-analyzing.

Thelma took a few steps at him. "Fine, say you locked him up on battery… You think he gonna turn over a new leaf, come out a better man? No, he'll sit there stewin, blaming her for what happened to him and come down ten times as hard. Demented prick like that, ain't no telling what he'd do."

"Woulda least given her time to get out."

"Oh don't give me that shit," Thelma said, flopping a hand through the air. "They never leave the abuser. It's like a drug that beats ya down till there ain't nothing left, telling yer brain you need them for survival."

"How do you know?"

"They done studies on this kinda shit. It's all over the innernet. Yeah, I do more'n just play Solitaire on there. Something like ninety percent of 'em never leave, never tell no one about it. Just put up with it the rest of their sorry-ass lives. So if it's that, or the alternative, I'd say she's better off wherever she's at now."

Harris shook his head then took another swig. He looked off, the soft glow from the lamp was lighting half his face.

184

Thelma could tell he saw it different.

She thought about cracking a mustache joke, try to lighten him up, but said, "Go ahead, get bent and analyze the details all you want. But the only time you ever had *any* control is that split second 'fore ya told him to drop it."

She looked at her watch. Half past four. "Come on, Ruth's'll be open in half an hour. Let me buy ya some breakfast."

Harris just looked away, gripping the slender neck of the bottle.

25

THE RAIN let up around three. Cody had expected some kind of Indian war party to come charging under the overhang, but the only action was a dually driving along the 75, headed for town.

During the night, he had canvassed the property looking for trespassers just about anywhere the pickup would take him. All he found were a couple whitetails, a coon digging through the trash behind the bunkhouse, and a small herd of cows that had evaded the virus—fourteen in total, a handful of unbranded calves among them. It gave Cody little hope as he watched them dawdle.

He wrestled demons, reasoned with himself why he did what he did.

He threw in a dip and couldn't recall any details about the scalping, nor the lynching save the fact he did it. He remembered driving toward the shed, Manuel's voice coming from the passenger, that hint of an accent, but he could no longer picture his segundo's face, nor any features.

On occasion, he'd come to a stop, absorb his surroundings, the serenity, and forget what he was doing. He would nod off until he saw the Indian bloody and screaming and it would jolt him awake. He cranked the window down on the way back to the house, cowboy-striping the truck as he spat tobacco juice against the breeze. He heard the blue tarp popping against the wind, could see it in the rearview and remembered trekking back down the mountain after he buried Manuel to catch the paint in the remuda and saddle it in the middle of a goddamn thunderstorm. He recalled passing Horsethief Lake. The rain going sideways. The kid's body folded over the saddle. Reaching Three Points and thinking he still had a chance to turn himself in, explain to the Sheriff what happened.

It felt like there were two sides to him. One, the Cody Custer he always knew with sound morals. And this other guy, someone new, blinded with hate, fueled by rage. Warding off the latter proved a constant struggle in the dark of night.

He remembered getting back to his pickup, driving toward the casino with every intention of leaving the wolf carcass in the lobby, thinking, at the time, a dead wolf in the Mingan would really send a message.

It sounded juvenile now.

Morning came without much sleep. And now, in a chair on the front porch, the repeater on his lap, Cody could see the hands staggering out of the bunkhouse, selecting their mounts for the day. Cody thought about telling them to leave, find work elsewhere, but then he remembered the small herd of cows and knew Pappy would be watching through the window. So to keep the old man from prodding, Cody told the hands to catch the cows, run them into the branding corral.

The barrel-chested one named Randy stood there, watching the paint pluck grass. "Happened to Rodriguez?"

"He's gone," Cody said. "Found somethin somewhere else."

"Are you shittin me?"

Cody didn't respond. Didn't even look at him.

"Who you fixin to make yer number two then?"

"I ain't. Least not today."

"You know, something occurred to me last night… What's gonna happen with our bonuses now that all them cows are belly up?"

"That ain't none yer bidness."

"It is when it's *my* money."

"Ain't yers till I cut the check. You don't like the way that taste all a sudden, pack yer shit, let me know where I can mail it."

Randy spat. "That paint fair game now that he gone?"

Cody nodded, said, "Be my guest," to keep the status quo and moved on.

It didn't take long to round up the strays. They had sorted a few heifers, loaded them in the chute lane and by midmorning, Cody was elbow deep in one of them when a black town car pulled up along the fence line. Cody could feel the uterus, the ovaries. They were sitting high. He pulled his arm out, the latex sleeve covered in fecal matter. "Nope. Not pregnant. Next."

He turned to look at the black car, saw what seemed to be two figures inside but couldn't tell for sure with the dark windows. He turned back, said, "Come on, let's go," to a long and lean pale-faced kid with peach fuzz on his chin. The kid trying his damnedest to shove the next heifer into the chute. "Zap that sumbitch."

The pale-faced kid jabbed a hot-shot into the cow's flank and did just that, jolting her into the chute.

"Wake up, Jackson. Ain't got all day to do this shit." Cody latched the gate. Lifted the heifer's tail, shoved an arm up her rectum. Feeling around, he looked to the fence line, saw the passenger window of the town car was down, an ugly Indian with a box head looking this way through binoculars.

This heifer was also barren.

Cody removed his arm, released her into the pen when he heard someone yell, "Hold him! Hold him!"

He turned, saw an ornery bull calf on the ground in the arena with lariats around its hoofs. A few hands struggled to hold it down, making injections, tagging an ear, castrating it. The bull was kicking, bucking, and it looked like the cowboys atop were riding a wave.

Randy had been the one yelling as he approached with a hot-iron, the Flying-C brand glowing orange. Cody noticed the guy was being lazy, approaching the calf at its belly. Soon as Randy touched hide, the calf bucked loose, kicked Randy in the hip, knocking him to the ground.

Cody sprinted for the corral, told Jackson—a half step behind—to grab another iron.

He scaled the pipe-fence. A cowboy on foot shouted for someone to get a rope on the calf which was now cantering, looking for an exit. Cody moved past a buckskin, told its rider to throw him a pigging string as another mounted cowboy slung a lariat around the calf's neck. Cody used his thighs for leverage and flanked the calf, letting it splash in the dirt. He jammed a knee into its neck. Grabbed the pigging string clenched between his teeth and hog tied the hoofs.

Jackson came in with a hot iron and stuck it against hide. White smoke floated. Cody sucked it through his nostrils, waiting for Jackson to clear out before releasing the calf. Then he stood, chest heaving, and faced the other hands. "Goddamnit! I gotta do everthing around here now or what? Quit fucking around."

"Lighten up, would ya," Randy said. "Damn near cauterized my nut sack."

Cody turned, saw the loudmouth in the dirt brushing off his Wranglers, the skin of his thigh peeking through singed denim. "What'd you say?"

"I said lighten up,"—Randy was getting to his feet now, strutting this way—"we're short-handed as it is, don't need you barking orders at us all goddamn day."

Cody let him take another step before belting him across the chin. The guy's knees buckled and he dropped to the dirt, out cold before impact.

"Anyone else care to lay their two cents on me?"

Silence.

"Then get back to work."

Cody walked back to the heifers. The town car was still there. The one with the box-head was standing outside now, no qualms about being in the open.

"Hey, Cody…" Jackson said, jogging to catch up. "Them cows back there? They ain't even BCS-3 and most the pastures I seen, 'specially the one we pulled 'em from, is moisture deficient…"

Not that it mattered, but Cody was impressed. "Yeah? You think a few blocks of SmartLic'll do the job?"

"Maybe even some flaxseed. We gotta put some good weight on, else they won't be worth a shit we take 'em to market. You want, I can head in town, get everthing."

Cody looked at the town car again.

He told Jackson not to worry, he would take care of it. Jackson walked off and Cody said, "Hey…" waiting for him to stop and look back. "Nice work out there."

Jackson tipped his hat, moved back to the heifers with a

little pep in his step.

Cody took the flatbed because the weight would make it easier to run the town car off the road if it came to it.

Coming up the drive, he could see the one with the box-head tracking, standing erect like he was caught off-guard. Then the man scrambled, rushing to get in the car.

Cody grinned as he went under the overhang, cutting the wheel when he hit the main road. Another hundred feet, he'd be passing them. He drew the 1911 and switched it to his right hand, holding it across his body, below the window.

He was passing them now. His chest throbbed, his hand shook. The two Indians looked like they could be twins in their black suits and matching shades. The one in the driver's seat waved, a smile on his face like a damn tourist taking in the sights.

Cody relaxed his gun hand, watching the side mirror, expecting them to flip a U and follow.

But they just sat there.

"The fuck?" Cody said.

When he could no longer see the town car, Cody phoned one of the hands and asked what they were doing.

"What car?" the hand said.

"The black one. Side of the road on 75."

"Uh…"

"Right there. Just up from the entrance."

The hand paused. "I don't see nothin."

"Maybe it's moving now, or something… Anything going away from the ranch, headed for town?"

"Cody, ain't a goddamn thing on the road, period."

He was confused. It couldn't have gone the way it was facing. Nothing but ranches and wilderness that way, the road dead-ending. "But you *did* see a black car there all morning, right?"

"Shit, I don't know man. I ain't pay no attention."

Cody smacked the phone shut and wondered if he was losing it. He waited for the next driveway before he turned around. By the time he could see the overhang, he was pushing sixty in the flatbed but the black car was gone.

He drove past the ranch, past Bobby Cooper's ranch all the way to the dead-end and still, no sign of it.

He vacillated between mirrors on the way to Bomgaars, slowing every time he saw a black car. And when he found a space next to the stacks of lumber, he wasn't sure he ever saw the town car to begin with.

26

HE grabbed a cart and paced the aisles, keeping a feel on the 1911 at his waist. He watched the patrons, their hands, their body language. A few would look up and smile, women for the most part. They'd say, Hi, ask how he was doing, holding eye contact until he said something back. An employee in a green coat with yellow embroidery asked if he needed help. Cody said, No, he was just looking.

He spent twenty minutes poring through the store, looking out the windows, watching the automated doors open and close.

No sign of the Indians.

He returned the cart. Walked back to the truck but stopped as he gripped the door handle. Something wasn't right. A nerve at the base of his spine tightened. He turned, saw an irritated mother dragging her rebellious daughter over a crosswalk. Behind them, loitering on the corner, was a Yawakhan in dark sunglasses, a phone to his ear. The Bronco was pulling out of Ruth's on Third, the one named Harris in the passenger seat, some older woman with frizzy hair driving.

The Yawakhan was moving over the crosswalk now, looking this way.

Every fiber told him to run. But he was scared to turn his

back, scared to brandish the 1911 with the kid around.

He felt someone coming up quick and turned as a dark-skinned man spear-tackled him to the ground and started choking him.

It was Manuel. Dried crimson on his shirt, a crusted gash across his neck.

Cody couldn't breathe.

Blood, cold and thick like mud, poured from Manuel's neck onto Cody's face. "Why didn't you fucking listen?"

Cody shouted at him to stop.

But Manuel gripped tighter. "Look what you did to me. Look at what you did!"

The blood splotched Cody's vision, a black mass consuming everything in sight, until he heard a voice.

It was the Yawakhan man, yelling, "Hey," clapping his hands, trying to break it up and get Cody's attention.

When Cody snapped out of it, the black mass was sucked from view. He looked around. Manuel was gone.

And now, Cody realized, he had his own hands around his own neck. He released his grip, wiped at his face catching sweat, but nothing else.

The Yawakhan offered a hand, asked if Cody was all right.

Cody said he was, but couldn't stop his hands from shaking. A group of twenty-somethings coming out of the Bomgaar's were staring and it made Cody feel vulnerable, awkward. Then he saw a neon light winking at the end of the road.

No, Cody thought. It's a dumb idea.

But it kept enticing him, sucking him in. Cody relented, telling himself he'd have just one, something to soften the edge. He walked toward The Maverick and convinced himself he never saw a town car to begin with.

He went through the swinging doors, saw a few felts and a straw—no feathers in the hat bands—which made him feel good.

Still some places left, Cody thought. He bellied up to the bar, could smell the mixture of urine and stale beer as his palms stuck to the dried, crusted puddles staining the wooden top.

A heavyset gal in a spaghetti tank sat at the end of the bar, an unlit 100 pinched between her lips, a pint of AmberBock in her duke. Cody had to say excuse me three or four times before she looked up.

"Where's the barkeep?"

The heavyset gal rolled her eyes. She said, "Gimme a sec," then chugged her beer without removing the cigarette. She limped behind the bar and lighted up. "What're you havin?"

Cody hesitated. "Double rye straight with a beer back."

She didn't move right away. Just stood there, an arm braced on the bar exposing drooping cleavage. She grabbed a glass with her free hand, smacked it on the bartop and fetched a bottle with a label that looked like Jack Daniel's but had a different name on it—some distillery in Kentucky.

"I said rye."

"And this here's got rye in it. Now what flavor beer you want, and don't tell me none a that pussy light shit 'cause it's outta my reach."

"Okay... What *can* you reach?"

She drew on her cigarette, squinted through a haze of smoke. "Coors. 'Riginal."

He waited for more, but apparently that was it, so he said, "Sounds good to me," and stared at the glass of whiskey with some rye in it. He put it to his lips but his hands tremored so bad he had to set it down. He took a breath, composed himself. Decided it was what he wanted, then downed it in one swift motion, spilling a little on his chin.

It burned his throat. Felt worse in his stomach.

Other than that, he didn't feel much of anything. The edge was still there. His hands were still shaking. He wiped his chin, pushed the glass back at her. "I'll take another."

"Nother double?"

"If ya please."

She kept her eyes level and poured another.

Cody didn't hesitate this time. Not bad, he thought. A little smoother. The edge was beginning to soften. His head and shoulders felt lighter. He liked where this was going.

He pushed the glass back at her. "Again."

She was still holding the bottle but didn't pour. "There's a limit of what I'm supposed to serve—"

"I'll nurse it, aright?"

She didn't budge.

"Please. It's been a real shitty twenty-four hours."

She poured.

Cody kept his eyes on her as he lifted the glass, his hand steady, and holy shit did he miss the way this felt. He had stopped thinking about Manuel. About the ranch. The cows. The only thing he cared about was chasing this feeling. Intensifying it.

He downed it.

The bartender started swaying. At least that's the way Cody saw it. She took the glass, told him to get out.

"Come on, one more," Cody said.

"Ya got two options. Hit the road, or I'll call Mule, have him throw yer ass out."

"Look, I don't want no trouble. Lemme just pay you'n I'll go sit in the corner, won't bother nobody."

She leaned in, both hands crutched on the bar—the sacks forming her cleavage swaying like a curtain. "Last chance, and I promise you don't wanna play this game with me."

"I'm sure I don't. Here… Just run my card. I don't finish the beer by the time you do, I'll leave."

"Mule…" the bartender said. She was looking toward the door.

Cody saw the guy stand and thought Mule was a crap name. It should've been Ox, or fucking Tank, anything but Mule.

"…This douchebag done had too much. Just tried to grab my tits."

Cody swiveled back, saying, "The fuck I did," but his word was shit because Mule was already coming. Cody tried to stand but fell back onto his barstool.

Best case scenario, Mule would kill him with one punch.

And Mule was getting closer, getting bigger, making a fist and reeling it back.

"Hold it Mules, take it easy," a man said from the corner.

And Mule did. Stopped dead in his tracks.

It was dark and hazy, but Cody could see the oversized brim leading to a ten-gallon crown. He was in a bowler's shirt, something tropical with little designs on it.

"He's good people," the man said, approaching the bar. "And I been watching… Trust me. He ain't make no pass at her."

Mule deflated, went back to his stool.

"And buddy, you gotta stop believing that shit. Ain't nobody under seventy without dementia would ever attempt a pass at that."

As the man drew closer, the neon coming off the back bar lighted a grinning, jovial face that Cody recognized. "Thanks Bobby. Owe ya one."

"Don't sweat it, pard," Bobby Cooper said, flopping a hand through the air. "Buy ya another drink?"

"I'm good, thanks."

Cody swigged beer, staring at Bobby's shirt. "The hell is that?"

"What?"

"That shit yer wearin." Cody leaned in, felt himself going cross-eyed. "Are those sailboats and hula dancers?"

"Oh, Marnie got this for me. Apparently, this what they wear in the tropics. Got breathability."

"Shit, must be nice. How long you goin?"

"Rest of my life, far as I'm concerned."

"What're you talkin about?"

"You didn't hear? I sold. I'm out, man. Got a place on the beach in Florida and it's goodbye South Dakota winters."

The room began to spin. Cody could taste stomach acid rising in the back of his throat. "Who'd you sell to? And don't tell me—"

"Kenny Shepard. Gave me a helluva good offer too, I couldn't say no."

Cody had trouble breathing. He stood, slammed a fist on the bartop which got everyone's attention. "Goddamnit! He owns both my fucking fence-lines now. Don't you see what he's doing?"

"Take it easy."

"No, fuck that. He's taken everthing in this town and he's doing it right in front of yer face. People died for this shit, wars were started over this fucking land and people like you are giving it up, pissing away two hunnert years of a way a life for some fucking money?" Cody jammed a finger into Bobby's chest. "Yer nothing but a coward, taking the easy way out. Before you know it, that sumbitch gonna own everone and everthing in this town."

"Fuck you, Cody. I got mine. Ain't nothing wrong with that."

"You got yers... You'll wake up on the beach one day a fat, worthless piece a shit who only tells stories about the way things used to be. That hat on yer head used to mean something, used to stand for something. Now yer nothin but a fucking joke."

Bobby Cooper's grin had since faded. He finished his cocktail and placed it on the bar. "Mule, throw his ass out."

Cody managed to keep the beer bottle from breaking when Mule tossed him into the alley. He made it to his feet in time to upchuck the whiskey back onto them. If it burned going down, it wasn't anything compared to how it felt coming up. He heaved five times before he felt stable enough to wash the taste out of his mouth with the last of his beer. He threw the bottle—it didn't break—and exited the alley, crossing Main Street when he saw the town car again.

He stopped, saw two sets of shades floating behind the windshield. So he turned and moved toward the green glow coming off the BOMGAARS façade. A hundred yards, maybe. He could hear the slow churn of the tires creeping behind him, gripping tarmac.

His first thought was to draw. Get the drop on the Injun bastards. Aim for the shades and light that fucking car up. But a couple was nearby sharing a cigarette. Someone else was closing up shop a few doors down.

Too many bystanders.

So Cody ran, drawing a bead on the flatbed before cutting into a nearby alley.

The town car followed, gaining speed.

A skinny man wearing an apron exited a door, lighting a thin cigar. Cody knocked him off the stoop and darted into the building. Two line cooks, black coats over herringbone pants, looked up at him. Cody turned back, saw the town car stopping, the box-headed one emerging. Shit. Some kind of compact machine gun in his duke.

Cody slammed the door, twisted the deadbolt when a server entered the opposite side of the kitchen, saying, "I need another order of sweet tots on the fly." Another one came in just behind her yelling about four rodeo burgers all day, hold the onion rings on two.

Cody ran through the swinging doors, past the jam-packed high-tops with pitchers of beer and three-hundred sixty degrees of spring training. Someone against the Dodgers. Cody wondered what these people did for a living that allowed them to be drinking beer, watching baseball before sundown the middle of the week.

Then again, Cody thought, who was he to judge?

He filtered into the street, sprinting for his truck when he saw taillights rushing at him, the town car reversing from the alley.

He dove onto the sidewalk.

When he stood, he was looking down the barrel of that high-tech machine gun for what seemed a long time.

The Indian pulled the trigger.

Cody lurched when he heard the gun click.

The box-headed one chuckled and Cody stood there, feeling weak in the legs, thinking his only option was to feint and draw, put one on target before the Indian could chamber a round.

Which was a good idea until he saw the Sig in the driver's hand. The man said, "Go ahead, cowboy, make my day."

Both of them chuckled now, having some fun, butchering the Eastwood line. The driver removed his shades and spoke in Yawakhan. Then he pointed a finger gun and fired it, clucking his tongue at the same time.

The window lifted as the town car drove off.

What the hell? Why didn't they shoot? What were they waiting for?

Cody couldn't figure it out as he cranked the ignition in the flatbed. They were so casual with the guns. Pros, no doubt about it. Men that had seen a thing or two. Cody could tell by the blank, mechanical stare in the driver's eyes. Joking, but not joking.

The only reason they didn't fire, Cody figured, was because they were under orders.

He pulled Blackfoot's phone from the glovebox and phoned Kenny Shepard, ready to make a deal. It went to voicemail twice. On the third, Cody got the fuck-you button before the first ring finished.

It was dusk when he made it back to the ranch. And Cody knew he was in for another long night when he saw the black town car parked along the fence line.

27

SHEA turned into the drive and saw her brother on the porch holding that stupid, antiquated cowboy gun. The boy was pissing in the wind if he thought it was a match for the firepower Hector and the other guy had in the town car.

When she reached the porch, Cody was looking past her. He had dark rings beneath his eyes. His hat was back on his head and strands of mussed hair curled over his brow.

"What's the matter, something got you on edge?"

"What're you doing here?"

"Last time I checked he's still my grandfather, I don't need a reason to see him." She tried to move past, but Cody blocked her route.

"What, no doughnuts this time?"

"You know what? I don't need this shit. I didn't come here to argue, I came to say goodbye."

Cody stared for a moment. "You know about the plan to kill my cows?"

"Not until Kenny found his nephew lynched in a fucking tree. You're a savage, a bottom feeder. And if I were you I'd stand guard with a lot more than that repeater." She tried to slide past him again but was pinned against the house, the cold steel of a gun prodding her chin.

"You mean something like this?"

His breath was rotten. At first, Shea thought it was alcohol, but there was something more foul in play. Stomach acid, vomit perhaps.

"I's gonna return that kid, gotten a payout and that woulda been the end of it. But not now. No, I'm coming after everone—"

"That why you're sitting here like a little bitch, waiting for them to make the first move? Don't try and act like a hardass Cody, it's not your nature."

"You think I won't do it?"

"Then get it started. Right here, right now."

He didn't move. Didn't blink. Just stood there. So Shea grabbed the gun, shoved it deeper into her chin, saying, "Here, let me help you..."

Cody smacked her hand away and pinned her by the neck, moving the muzzle to her cheekbone. "Get the fuck off. I'll do it, I swear to God."

"Please. You don't have the balls. It ain't like killing some Native you hate." She leaned in, staring at his crazed, blood-shot eyes. "Killing *blood* is different."

"The fuck would you know about it?"

Shea wanted to tell him. Wanted to cut him down right here and see the look on his face, but there would be a time and place for that. "Go ahead, prove me wrong. You gonna scalp me too when it's done?"

His eyes shifted back and forth, focusing on one of hers, then the other. She could see the tip of Cody's finger turning white against the trigger, but knew he didn't have it in him. It was in the way he loosened his grip around her neck. The delicate way he placed the gun under her chin or against her cheekbone. The way he shoved her against the house but seemed to catch her before she slammed into it.

Cody lowered the gun, released his grip.

"Jesus," Shea said. "You really are pathetic, you know that?"

"You got five minutes. After that, I don't ever wanna see you again."

Shea pulled the storm door open, looked in the direction of the pasture and imagined a pipeline running through it as money rained from the sky. She looked at her brother—he was refusing to make eye contact. "You proved her right, you know."

"Who?"

"Mama. That you're all hat and no cattle."

Shea entered the house and stopped short of Pappy's room, waiting to see if Cody would follow. She could hear the muffled drum of the oxygen machine and wondered if Pappy was asleep, whether he would be in the chair or in bed—not that it made any difference. Getting a rush now, the same feeling when that bitch hit the pipe laced with fentanyl.

Hector had wanted a piece of the guy ever since he saw Blackfoot in the tree, hanging there like an animal, like this was the 1800s. He appreciated the diplomacy, the brains and the wherewithal Mr. Shepard had used in advancing the Nation, but that shit only got you so far. And Hector was excited when the boss-man showed a little aggression, asking for the cowboy's head. Then, not five minutes later, he calls back with a change of heart. Told them to follow, but not engage, saying he had other plans.

Other plans? Like what?

So when Hector saw the cowboy draw on the boss-man's honey, he had opened his door, figuring the situation to be just-cause to split the cowboy's grape and pock a few holes in that stupid fucking hat. He was able to swing a leg out before Silas grabbed him by the shoulder, asking what the hell he was doing.

"What's it look like?"

"We don't intercept."

"And when her brains're all over the fucking siding, what're we gonna tell him?"

"Consider the situation," Silas said. "He takes her out, we're the only witnesses. Which means both of them'll be gone for good."

"We need her."

"Please man. I don't know why the boss wants this place so bad, but he don't need her to get it. The casino's hopping, the money's coming in—he's got nothin but time. You know what these dumbshit cowboys got? Jack. Shit. And they can go down with the ship, or not, but you better believe that motherfucker's sinking."

Hector had to agree.

"And think about it. Mr. Shepard tells us he wants the guy dead, then goes back on it? Why? Because of her. Which means we're now taking orders from a white bitch with the last name Custer. I don't know about you, but that don't sit well with me."

That had never occurred to Hector. It ticked him off a little. But he still wanted a piece of that motherfucker. So when Shea entered the house, he got out of the car.

"Goddamnit," Silas said. "Hector—"

"Stand down. It's my detail." Hector rounded the car,

shouted the cowboy's name which got the guy to turn and approach the steps. "Why don't you try that shit with someone your own size?" He removed his coat, his tie. Drew the Sig and placed it on the hood.

And the cowboy, he was getting the picture. He moved down the steps and drew what looked like an old Army-issued Colt from inside his coat. He cleared the weapon, threw the pieces in the bed of his truck and laid his hat—crown-side down—on the hood, moving from a brisk walk into a trot.

Hector loved this feeling. The blood surging, the adrenaline teeming. He ran under the overhang, was at full-sprint by the time he reached the cowboy. He feigned a kick, snapping his leg back to throw a cross, but felt a blow to his sternum before the ground thumped against his back.

Cody had spear-tackled him.

Hector parried the first two punches but caught a third beneath the eye. The man's fists seemed to be the size of softballs and hard as granite, but Hector could tell by his movements the cowboy was all piss and vinegar, no training. So he left himself open, and when the cowboy came down with a hard left, Hector caught his wrist, using the momentum to roll and flip the cowboy onto his back.

Hector pinned and popped him in the nose with two quick rights—blood smeared across his face on the second. Hector launched another right hand, but the cowboy slipped the punch, wrapped Hector in a bear hug, saying, "Come on bitch, that all you got?"

Hector tried to get leverage with a foot, but the damn guy was strong and he couldn't make enough space. So he worked an elbow between them, ground it into the cowboy's rib cage until the man loosened his grip enough so Hector could push back and spike down with a hammer-fist.

Hector rolled off, sprung to his feet.

The cowboy was slow getting up. Not because he was hurt, more like this was all a nuisance. He spat blood, wiped his mouth. "Round two?"

"Long as you promise not to run this time."

The cowboy flashed blood-coated teeth, getting to his feet now, raising his fists.

Hector moved in, open palms in a Muy-Thai stance. He smacked away the first two punches before catching a Mexican uppercut to the ribs—something cracking—the blow so powerful it lifted his feet off the ground. It hurt to breathe. Hector pushed away and circled the cowboy, stepping in again to trade punches. Hector favored his rib, trying to show the cowboy he was in pain, giving the guy a target.

Cody telegraphed his next punch. Hector parried, threw a knee into the cowboy's side and ripped an elbow across his jaw. It should have been enough to put him down.

But the cowboy didn't fall, didn't shy away. He took the blow and kept coming. He grabbed Hector by the collar and came down with a barrage of lefts.

Hector ducked, tried to tuck himself close to the cowboy, inside the effective range of his punches, but the man shoved him back to arm's length and belted him again.

Hector's knees buckled. The cowboy yanked him to his feet, swung again—wild this time—and Hector ducked, slipped behind the cowboy and suplexed him to the ground. Hector rolled, straddled the cowboy and ended the fight with three straights to the nose.

Or so he thought.

Hector was walking away, licking blood from his lip, clutching his fractured rib when the cowboy said, "Where you goin?" The guy pinched a nostril, blew a snot-rocket into the gravel and was now coming this way, like a motherfucking machine.

Hector knew he'd have to kill the guy. So he pulled his pocket knife and was aiming for the cowboy's lungs when Shea screaming from inside the house stopped the guy in his tracks.

The cowboy looked back, then at Hector again.

"Don't worry," Hector said. "We'll finish another time."

The cowboy backpedaled a few steps before turning and running into the house.

28

CODY rounded the corner, saw the old man in bed with a hand draped over his chest, the other beneath the covers.

Shea was sobbing, her face buried in the pocket of Pappy's shoulder.

"What happened?" Cody said.

Looking up, she balked—Cody assumed because of his newly battered face. Her makeup was running. "I... I don't know. I thought he fell asleep, but he's not breathing. You have to do something Cody, please."

He approached the bed. Pressed two fingers against the old man's carotid and felt nothing. "He's dead."

Her sobs grew as she stood and fell into Cody. He hesitated at first, but wrapped her in a hug, laying a gentle hand on the back of her head. He could sense the little girl inside, the yearning and the sorrow, letting her remain there until she pushed back, never mentioning nor thinking of bygones.

She walked over, knelt before the oxygen machine and clicked it off. "I'm sorry. It's just too much right now."

"It's fine."

When the ambulance arrived, Cody helped the paramedics load the gurney into its belly and told one of them he wanted an autopsy.

"But you said he was stage four…"

Cody arched his brow, glaring, until the guy said, "Hey it's your call. Morgue it is."

On his way back to the house, Shea asked what Cody had said. He looked at the fleeing taillights through a cloud of dust. "Nothin. Just told him take good care a Pappy."

Cody would sit in the recliner until sunrise, watching but never realizing what was on the tube: sound bites of news spliced with infomercials about estate planning or mutual funds or the rising prices of silver.

Halfway through the night, he had turned the oxygen machine back on. The silence was uncomfortable. He would close his eyes only to find himself watching the tube light flicker against his eyelids. He wanted a drink to soften the edge, to force himself into a slumber, but fought the urge and abstained.

When the landline rang that morning, Cody couldn't breathe through his nose. The blood had dried and crusted on his face and lips. He lifted the phone, said, "Hello?" and listened as a woman told him she was sorry for his loss before rifling off a block of appointment times.

The voice was familiar, but he couldn't peg it. When he asked who she was, the woman said, "Oh sorry, I assumed you knew. That's my bad. This is Janice from the Law Office of Jim Moffat? We heard about your grandfather and, first and foremost let me just say, we are so very sorry for your loss and we apologize for reaching out to you in such a grieving and troubling time. And we understand that the legality of everything is probably the last thing on your mind, but it is important to set up a time so we can move forward with Mr. Custer's last stand…Oops, pardon me, don't know where that came from. I meant his last *will*. Last will and testament."

"Okay…" Cody was baffled they already knew.

"So what times work best for you today?"

"The man ain't even cold yet."

"Mm-hmm, it's just…well, I have no doubt you've a lot going on—"

"How about you just read it to me over the phone?"

"Well that's the tricky part, because there are some things we would need you to sign."

"So read it to me, put the goddamn thing in the mail. When I get it, I'll sign it'n send the shit back. How's that?"

There was a pause. "I'm sorry, could I please place you on a brief hold?"

"And if I say no?"

"Uhh…Uhh…"

"That's what I figured," Cody said. "I'll hold, but when you come back, you best have the answer I want."

"Yes, you got it. Thank you sir."

The line clicked over to Frank Sinatra singing about doing things his way. On the tube, several women were on a couch talking about the president. He was in one of the Koreas again, shaking hands with that squat little gook with the bad haircut. There was one gal, heftier than the others, that seemed to disagree with everything the other four said. She wouldn't shut up either, so the other four started to gang up on her, and now Cody couldn't understand what anyone was saying, nor could he gather if they were still talking about the president, the Korean, or what.

When Sinatra cut out there was another familiar voice, and Cody got the feeling the people at the Law Office of Jim Moffat weren't going to read anything over the phone.

* * *

Janice had to put the jackass on hold and wondered why everyone was so damn difficult. It was always the blue-collars too, because they didn't understand any of it.

Mail it to me, he says. Ever heard of email? Docusign? Anything from the twenty-first century?

She knocked on Moffat's door, waited for him to say, "You may enter," before pushing it open. He was doing yoga, the warrior pose, or one of those deals that looked like he got stuck doing the splits. She eyed the contours of his butt, the firm, tight way it looked in those biker shorts and thought she'd like a piece of that. Give it a pinch or a swat one day, see what he'd do.

She averted her eyes, pretended to be surprised. "Oh, sorry sir, I didn't realize…"

"It's all right, Janice. You know what I would just kill for right now?"

"What's that?"

"A velvet, black-tie cold brew. The big one too."

"You mean the old big one or the new big one?"

"The one with thirty ounces."

"That'd be the new big one," Janice said. "With six pumps of sugar-free vanilla?"

"Yes, but make sure they froth the cream in a separate tin, then layer it on top of the coffee. They've been getting lazy, and by the time it gets to me it's already mixed. I want it to look the way it does in the picture, you understand?"

Janice nodded as her mind drifted to the way it played out last time.

The barista was moving slower than dirt. Capping the thing,

sliding it across bar at the pick-up window, saying, "Janice, your black-tie with six pumps is now on the bar." She had checked the clock on her cell, saw she only had two minutes to make it back before Mr. Moffat called her bitching up a storm, asking what in the holy heck took so long to make one drink. Then she went sprinting down Main toward the office, the perfectly layered cold brew swishing and swashing, getting all kinds of fucked up en route.

Shoot. The boy in Spandex getting his cake, wanting to eat it too.

Janice said, "I will make it happen, sir."

He popped up with his feet together on the mat. Bent at the hips, pressed his palms together and whispered something that sounded like, "Mama stay." He did it every time, and still, Janice could never figure out what he said. She had a fear of feeling stupid and unhip, so she never asked.

"Now, what is it that has you knocking on my door during quiet time?" Moffat opened a door leading to a small three-quarter bath, removed his aqua tank and threw it at Janice's feet. His body was polished with sweat. Janice could see those two tiny, rock-hard nipples and it made her a little excited. She never could understand what attracted women to the beefcake type. They were always so dense, never playful or willing to explore. And Jim Moffat? Well Janice believed he was quite the opposite—never mind that he seemed to always have a stick up his ass. Or that he was wiry and short, and all the hair on his head had migrated to his chest. No, Janice could overlook all that. Because what she longed for most was some company on those long winter nights. Someone she could have deep conversations with. That's what turned her on, that big brain of his.

"Hellooo?"

Janice snapped out of it. "Sorry. What'd you say?"

"Why are you bothering me?"

She hesitated. "Uh, because I—I g-got a…"

"No, you have a…"

"Right. I…I have a—"

Moffat sighed. "This is why I wrote the script for you, Janice. So you don't sound like a hillbilly over the phone. Learn it. Memorize it. Use it in everyday life. It will make you a better person."

"Yes, Mister Moffat. My…my apologies." She squatted to lift the damp tank. The intellectual had disappeared into the bathroom. She saw his reflection in the shower door as he stepped out of those shorts—ooh-la-la—no briefs in sight. She watched him for a minute, could tell he was checking out his physique by the way he was posing, turning and looking back. "See, I have a gentleman on the phone,"—she paused to look at the legal pad—"a Cody Custer."

"Don't tell me. He's refusing to come in."

"That's correct."

"I figured he would give us flak. What's he on?"

"Um, well if I had to guess, I would say that usually the ones of his demographic prefer methamphetamine."

"I meant what line is he on?"

"Oh, right. Line one, sir."

Moffat came out of the bathroom, a towel around his waist—dang it—a handsome trail of fur running from his navel, disappearing behind the towel. He handed the shorts to Janice and snatched the phone from his desk. "Mr. Custer? Jim Moffat here… Yes, sir, it's a terrible, tragic situation… We can discuss all of that when you come in… No, actually it

214

doesn't work like that… Because the residence is on the land owned by the business so it complicates things a tad… Well, for instance, section thirteen-point-five-B of the South Dakota Estate Code says you cannot operate the business, you cannot legally live in the house until ownership is established… Well no, that's not what *I'm* saying, that's unfortunately the law. But the good news is…"

Moffat stopped.

He lowered the phone, said, "O-kay," then returned it to the receiver.

"What happened?" Janice said, the sweat from his garments bleeding through the sleeve of her blouse.

"I believe he's on his way."

"Really, just like that?"

"Well, no. First he told me to fuck off. Then he told me the law was stupid."

"What law is that by the way? Because I never heard a…"

"I *have* never heard *of*… Jesus, I mean the laziness with which you speak."

"Right, sorry sir. Do not take this the wrong way, but I have never heard of any section thirteen-point-five-B."

"That's because it does not exist. But for reasons above your pay grade, I need his signature on these documents as soon as possible."

"I see." She stood there, correcting her eyes every time they drifted to his happy trail.

"Now if you'll excuse me. I need to 'drop-trou,' as they say, and rinse off before he gets here."

Janice giggled. "Oh, yes sir. I will be sure to have these washed and folded before day's end."

When Cody entered the Law Office of Jim Moffat, he didn't barge through this time. He waited for the plump secretary to say, "Ah, Mr. Custer I presume. Please, have a seat and Mr. Moffat will be with you shortly."

Cody sat, scanned the magazines fanned on the coffee table and didn't care for any of them. He had drunk a pot of coffee and felt the urge to wiz, so he asked Janice where the bathroom was.

"Sorry. It's for employees only."

"What about customers?"

"You mean clients?"

"Whatever."

"Sorry," Janice said, shaking her head. "Employees only."

What was the world coming to?

Cody sat for what seemed like five minutes before lifting a magazine with a bunch of photos, long shots of actors and celebrities who looked hungover, like they had just rolled out of bed. The captions talked about how normal they were. Picking produce at a "farmers" market in the middle of some urban street—no dirt in sight. Or this one, some broad in sweatpants grabbing a latté, sipping it from a biodegradable cup. The caption talking about how woke and aware she was, saving the Earth one cup of joe at a time.

Never mind the fossil fuels it takes to produce what's in the cup and import it to the States. But hey, it's a helluva start...a helluva start to battle the harm done from all them mangy cow farts.

Cody tossed the mag back on the coffee table. It ticked him off, the warped reality these people lived in.

The secretary's phone rang. She answered. Paused. Said, "Yes, sir," then hung up and craned her neck. "Mr. Moffat will see you now."

Cody stood. He lifted his hat, finger-combed his hair back then funneled the brim low. He entered the office, saw the lawyer behind the desk, occupied with the computer.

"Have a seat, Mr. Custer."

"I'm good. Let's just get on with it."

"Very well." Moffat pushed off his desk to a bank of file cabinets and grabbed a Manila folder.

"There's something bothering me," Cody said.

"And what is that?"

"How, or why, you knew about Pappy dying so quick."

The lawyer made eye contact. "Well, your sister of course. She called me, absolutely devastated, and asked if I had any referrals for a funeral home, since, you know, I deal with this sort of thing quite often."

"Ain't no funeral home needed. He'll be buried at the ranch."

"Well whatever you decide, that's between the two of you. I just sent over what I had."

Cody suspected her not being here was a good thing, though he harbored guilt for thinking it. "Shall we get on with it?"

"Absolutely. I have a lunch meeting in twenty and we have some of paperwork to get through."

Cody couldn't stand the way this guy talked. How he put emphasis on, or annunciated certain words to drive home how smart he was.

Moffat pulled a stack of papers from the folder and spun them so Cody could read along as he spoke.

And he did. A mile a minute.

Cody had trouble keeping up. He leaned over the desk, read the first few sentences and had no idea what any of it meant. A bunch of words he had never seen before.

Jim Moffat paused, took a breath. "Now we're getting to the meat and potatoes here. And as I was trying to inform you over the phone, it's what we deem a special situation because it has been divided into two sections, business and personal, because obviously he lived where he worked, but legally the two could not be combined, so…"

"Yeah, I got all that. Dakota code thirteen-point-five-B."

"…Right…" Moffat said, blinking. He fingered the frames higher on his nose. "So… On the personal side, he wrote: to my grandson Cody, you are to receive the ranch house and everything in it." The lawyer flipped the page and looked up. "And that's all there is for that. So initial here, here, sign and date here."

Cody reckoned that all sounded fine, so he did.

"Now, to the business side. To my grandson Cody, I leave you all the horses, the cattle, and any livestock that may generate revenue this season." Moffat flipped to the next page. "Now if I could just get you to sign here and initial—"

"The hell's the rest of it?"

"That's the extent of which pertains to you."

"Fuck you. Show me where it says that," Cody said, reaching across the desk.

Moffat retracted the folder. "It's confidential. You are entitled to only *your* portion—"

Cody ripped it from his hands and Moffat lunged across the desk, saying, "Sir, you can't—"

In a single motion, Cody shoved him back into his chair and drew the 1911, asking if he wanted to die over a piece of paper.

The lawyer offered no more protests as Cody read the following sentence:

218

To my granddaughter Shea,
On the business side, I hereby name you the sole proprietor
of the Flying-C, and heiress to all its land totaling fifteen
thousand seven hundred eighty-nine acres.

Cody shot the man, unloading on him until the gun clicked empty. Blood spattered onto the desktop, the wall of framed accolades behind him.

There were three quick knocks at the door. "Five-minute warning, Mr. Moffat." Janice sounded calm, run of the mill.

The hell? She had to've heard, right?

Cody half turned, listening, waiting to see if she would enter. He'd have to grab her, throw her in Moffat's direction and reload or stick her with the Kershaw, though he wasn't sure he could muster it.

"Thank you, Janice."

Cody snapped back. The lawyer was in his seat, alive and well. The room devoid of blood.

Jesus. Another hallucination.

Moffat looked annoyed, unfazed, flicking his finger. "The document, if you please."

Cody became aware of his audible breath, the sweat on the small of his back. He handed it to the lawyer and exited the office, wondering if that's how the place would look after a barrage from the 1911.

29

FRANK RODALE said, "Can you prove it?"

"Not yet, but there's gotta be something you can do." Cody made a left on Main, the flip-phone warm against his ear. He didn't know who else to call, or even what Rodale could do. Hell, he didn't even know what he was trying to prove, just that he kept hearing Pappy's words in his brain, saying the ranch would be his one day.

So he couldn't take the lawyer at face value. Something was going on.

"Like what?" Rodale said.

"Stall it."

"Stall it?"

"Shit, I don't know Frank. Something, anything to keep that bitch from taking over, 'cause I'm telling ya it ain't true. It can't be."

"Cody, there ain't nothing *I* can do. Far as will and testaments go, they're pretty ironclad."

The damn guy was chewing as he talked, enjoying his lunch.

"What about all the bidness we done over the years?"

"What about it?"

"Don't it mean somethin? Don't I get a say in the matter?"

"It was a sole-prop," Rodale said. "Technically, I believe it still is."

Cody shook his head, turning right on Caprock, moving past the petting zoo. A new sign over the awning read: FUNDED AND DONATED BY THE SPEARFISH BAND OF YAWAKHAN INDIANS. Adults were at the bar playing video poker while an Indian guide supervised a group of kids, a few billies munching seed from their palms.

"How 'bout that initial loan?" Cody said.

"That was extended in good faith to the Flying-C as an enterprise, not to you personally. That kind of thing we could get away with five years ago. But not today, not with the way things are run, the board we got in place."

"Frank, I'm the one signed for everthing."

"Because I assumed it'd be yers one day. Had no idea Pappy'd pull some shit like this."

Cody put the microphone against his lips. "He didn't goddamnit, he told me to my face it'd be mine!"

There was a pause. Cody assumed the man had hung up until he heard slurping, what sounded like the last of a soda being sucked through a straw. "Pardon me, Frank, don't let me interrupt yer fucking lunch."

The slurping stopped.

A muffled belch reverberated through the earpiece. "Ooh, excuse me. Goddamn pinto beans. Look"—his voice was low—"I know yer going through a lot, but my hands are tied. Hell, I could lose my job the board found out I let you forge Pappy's signature."

Cody shook his head as he came to a four-way stop. And there was Shea on the corner, three-stories tall. Her hair pulled up in a neat bun. A denim button-down cut a little too low and pulled tight across her chest. Trying to keep it casual. Her way of telling the ranchers she was a friend. She had closed fists resting on her hips and a serious look on her face. As if to say she wasn't running to be popular, she was doing it to get shit done. And that's what it said at the bottom:

SHEA CUSTER FOR MAYOR.
"GETTIN'. SHIT. DONE."

"So I got fourteen fuckin cows and not a pot to piss in. Whaddayou suggest I do?"

"Nothing you can do except try to liquidate 'em. Take 'em to auction."

"Fuck that."

"Look at the bright side, could fetch ya enough dough to get a one bedroom over at Mallard Pointe."

"A one bedroom?" Cody said.

"For six months, pending market value for them cows of course. And listen, you pay up front I can probly get a deal, your first month free or something."

Cody went straight at the intersection another half block. He put a tire up on the curb and looked through the windows at all the staffers running around, answering phones, holding meetings. Headless chickens. He saw Shea in a glass-encased conference room, talking to some guy in a suit.

The bitch was smiling, on cloud nine.

Cody put the truck in park. Said, "Hey Frank?" and waited for him to say, "Yeah," before asking if that was a chicken or steak burrito he was chewing on.

"How'd you know it was a burrito?"

"Just a hunch…lotta bang for yer buck over there."

Frank told Cody he was right. They're the best. The best. Had what they call a half 'n half. Chicken and steak, boy, bingo-bango.

"You get it with *guacamolé*?"

"Got to man, only way to go," Rodale said.

"Well, be careful. I read the paper some guy not as big as you, I'm betting a lot slower eater too, choked to death on the flour tortilla. Just blocked his windpipe like a damn exhaust flap that didn't flap, know what I mean?"

Rodale swallowed. "Well good thing I got me a corn tortilla."

"Oh, well shit, that's even worse."

"What? Why?"

"All 'em got recalled. Yeah, apparently some terrible E. coli outbreak in all the maize coming out the Midwest. People're dropping like flies."

Cody heard him cough. Heard the phone drop before the chair hissed and squeaked as it decompressed. He could see it now, the man chugging his fat ass across the bank, trying to reach the head before puking his guts out.

Cody had to grin.

He left the keys in the ignition and exited the truck. Blew through the entry door and past the gal wearing glasses at the front desk. She said, "Sir" several times, asking if she could be of assistance.

Cody didn't respond. He snaked his way between the desks. Shea didn't even look or seem to notice. When he passed the last desk, Cody asked the gal to stand up, even said please. He took her chair, wheeled himself around like he was throwing shotput and chucked it through the glass.

Shea was looking now.

On her feet, her arms out like a woman on the cross. "Jesus Christ, what the hell is wrong with you?"

"You fucking bitch," Cody said, moving up on her. "What'd you say to him?"

"What're you talking about?"

Cody looked in her eyes, trying to see if she was playing dumb. "Pappy. What'd you tell him to make him give you the land?"

"He gave me the land?"

"Don't play this goddamn game."

"Cody, I have no idea what you're talking about."

"His will. He gave you the land and all he left me was that stupid house and I know it's 'cause you manipulated him you backstabbing cunt."

"Excuse me, I don't appreciate you coming in here, making a scene in front of my staff. Unlike you…" She paused, placed a fist over her mouth and started producing tears. A real show, like she was fighting it. Half turning, biting it back. She opened the fist, patted her heart and said, "I'm really struggling with all of this because he meant so much to me."

"Are you fucking serious?"

"You think I care about any of it? I'd trade it all to have *one* day with him."

"Then hand it over. If it's worth one fucking day, hand it over."

Someone behind him said the police were on their way.

"Please leave," Shea said. It was abrasive, dramatic. And Cody knew it was all a show. Everything for the audience.

"This ain't done. Not by a long shot. You better bring a fuckin army you wanna get rid of me."

He hadn't made it to the end of the street when the phone rang. He grabbed it—his hand numb from wringing the steering wheel—and saw his sister's name in teal on the square-inch black screen.

Cody answered. "Ready to talk now?"

"Well something just occurred to me."

"Yeah, what's that?"

"Your new house is on my land."

Cody knew where she was going before it came through.

"So I think thirty-five hundred a month is a fair price," Shea said. "But all the stock, all the horses, I want them gone."

Cody tried to muster some kind of rebuttal, but she beat him to it. "You said bring an army? What makes you think we haven't already?"

He slammed the phone on the dash until the top half snapped off. He saw everything for what it was now. Shea had planned this. She was methodical, manipulative. No shot in hell did it *just occur to her*. He thought about Pappy, believing now the old man didn't die the way God intended. Shea had done something.

And the autopsy would prove it.

Cody berated himself. Everything happening right in front of his face and he was too stupid to see it. Goddamn was he sick of the bullshit, this game she played.

He wasn't going down like this. Not a fucking chance.

Then he saw it, not thirty seconds after he hit the 75. The six-foot, galvanized chain links. The signs every fifty feet. PROPERTY OF EXCEL CORPORATION. TRESPASSERS SUBJECT TO CRIMINAL PROSECUTION. Behind the fencing, he saw light towers over generators over hard hats against the setting sun.

The ranch hands were at the end of the drive. A few of them loitered with duffels, others were moving down the road, their thumbs cocked toward passing cars.

Cody found Jackson among them. He cranked the window down and called the pale-faced kid over. "The hell's going on?"

"Wish I knew. They kicked us out, said the place was under new ownership or somethin. Won't even let us stay the night."

"Where you gonna go?"

"We're all splittin rooms over the Crow Peak. Figure we'd come back in the mornin."

"Don't."

The kid squinted, looking in the truck now.

"I were you, I'd split town."

Jackson scoffed. "And do what?"

"Still some decent outfits west of here. Wyoming. Montana. Yer a good enough cowboy—"

"Wyoming? The hell you talkin about? Ain't got no money for that. Shit, I barely gotta'nuff for the motel tonight."

Cody watched the kid watching the commotion. The uncertainty in his eyes. The confusion.

He told Jackson to get in the truck. He had the others pile into the bed and shuttled them to the Crow Peak, a quaint two-story with a vaulted roof. When the hands hopped out, Cody wished them luck and apologized for the situation. Someone asked if they should stick around, wait it out.

Cody said he wouldn't bet on it.

When Jackson opened the passenger door, Cody grabbed his shoulder. "Hang on. Got another stop to make."

Rodale was nowhere in sight as Cody filled out the withdrawal slip. At the counter, he asked the teller for his balance.

He dropped Jackson at the Crow Peak with seven hundred fifteen dollars, keeping the remaining two dollars and eighty-six cents in his pocket out of embarrassment. He wished the

226

kid luck, then said, "You ever find yerself in Kaycee, look for an outfit by the name a Double-H. Tell 'em I sent ya."

"And what do I say happened to you?"

Cody looked off, didn't say anything for a while. "This town's changing, and I'm afraid there ain't no stopping it. But I'm gonna see just how bad they want it, whether or not they're willing to die for it."

"Are you?"

Cody didn't answer. He wasn't sure yet. He gave Jackson a nod, tipped his hat, and drove off.

30

THE TRUCK leaned as Cody swung into the drive. Over white knuckles, he could see a blue hard hat in a chair at the entry gate. He put the pedal to the floor, saw the man stiffen, flagging a pair of hands in rapid fashion before diving out of the way as Cody demolished the chair, plowing through the gate and smashing his remaining headlight.

Cody sped to the end of the drive, hitting the brakes when he saw two men hunched over the hood of a corporate truck, examining what looked like a map or a blueprint. He hopped out, said, "Who's in charge...you?" pointing at the slick in the suit.

"That's right."

"Get all yer shit'n get off my property. Now."

The suit scoffed. "You're the one trespassing, Brokeback. Take a hike."

They turned back to the map. The other one—he looked more like a superintendent—called the slick David and started talking about the elevation, all the timber they'll need to clear.

Cody grabbed David by the shoulder, spun him and dropped him with a left cross. Cody's other hand shot to the super's neck, pinning him against the hood, the man's red face turning purple.

That's when Cody heard the engines. A convoy of identical white pickups barreling up the drive. He turned to the super. "Call 'em off."

"It's not your land no more."

Cody drew the 1911, put two rounds through the lead truck's windshield. It ripped a chaotic U-turn and rolled onto its side. The rest of the convoy halted.

Cody swiveled, laid the muzzle between the super's eyes. "You were sayin?"

The super grabbed the walkie off the truck. "All units turn around now. Go back to base camp."

Cody watched the clusterfuck of trucks reverse onto the 75. He holstered the 1911. "Next time won't be no warning shot."

The super, helping David into the truck, told Cody this was bullshit, that he was coming back with the sheriff.

"Yeah, well tell that sumbitch he better bring backup." Cody went into the house, made the turn into the kitchen and grabbed the cordless from the wall, dialing the number for the morgue.

A lady answered. "Lawrence County Morgue."

"Yeah, y'all're doin an autopsy on my grandpappy and I was callin to see if ya got the results yet."

"Name?"

"Gerald Armstrong Custer."

"One moment."

Cody could hear computer keys clicking, the lady humming to herself. After a moment, she said, "Um, sir...you said Gerald Armstrong Custer?"

"That's right."

"At 52-16 County Road 75?"

"Yeah," Cody said, anxious.

"And who are you?"

"His grandson."

"Well, there's, um… See the thing is, we were unable to commence the autopsy."

"Why?"

"Maybe this is something you should consult his granddaughter on."

"I ain't doin that, so tell me what the hell's going on."

"Mr. Custer's will stated that he be cremated, and the point of contact was actually the granddaughter. I see here you mentioned you wanted an autopsy, but unfortunately, because of the will, you don't have the power to actually make that decision."

"Bullshit, I'm coming down there. Do not touch him, you understand me?"

Cody was lowering the phone, moving his thumb over the END button when he heard the lady through the earpiece. "Sir, it's too late."

He put the phone to his ear. "Whaddyou mean it's too late?"

"He's…he's already in the chamber."

Cody paced the hallway after breaking that phone too.

Voices teemed between his ears. One hammering him about how stupid he was. The other convincing him what he should do next. He cursed, punched holes in the drywall. Flipped the credenza. At the painting of Custer's Last Stand, he saw the rage, the resolve burning in the colonel's eyes. The man steadfast amidst an all but certain death.

"There are not enough Indians in the world to the defeat the Seventh Cavalry." Cody had said it as he read it from the placard below. He caught his reflection in the window. Imagined himself with a mustache and saw, for the first time, some resemblance to the colonel.

He had an answer to Jackson's question now. He wasn't prepared to die for this place, but man-oh-man was he ready to kill for it.

Cody moved to the window, saw no traffic on the 75. He drove out to the shop barn and collected every jerrycan he could find. Plastic red ones, rusted metal ones. He loaded the truck bed, then reversed to the overhead tanks—drums of red diesel on stilts, three hundred gallons apiece.

When the nozzle clicked off on the last canister, Cody returned it to the receptacle. Put the canister in the truck bed, shoved it flush against the others and shut the tailgate.

He drove out to the corrals, checking the radio clock several times a minute along the way. He haltered and led the roan down the lane when another horse nickered from the shadows. Turning now as the paint appeared in the remuda, moving into the soft glow coming off the barn's naked bulbs. It whinnied and clouded breath drifted from its nostrils.

It put a lump in Cody's throat.

He haltered the paint. Hitched both horses to the rail and saddled the roan. Then buckled the reins over the roan's halter and let the horses trot alongside the pickup, holding their lead ropes out the window as he drove back to the house.

He gathered supplies. A bedroll. Sleeping bag. Instant coffee. Non-perishables. A pot for boiling water. He went to the gun case, pulled out the over-under and the M1A Scout. He loaded most of the gear on the paint. Slipped the over-under in the roan's scabbard and slung the Scout across his back.

He used two jerrycans in Pappy's room, starting with the recliner, moving to the bed, the rug and the floor. He dumped gas on the walls in the hallway, the credenza, even poured some in the new holes in the drywall. He doused his room. The kitchen. Made a trail from the hallway to the front door. Chucked the canister, stepped onto the porch and looked over the railing—three remained in the truck bed. Then, his gaze lifted and he saw two sets of headlights moving south on the 75.

Cody struck a match and looked down the hallway, trying to recall better times past.

He couldn't.

He dropped the match, watched the flames grow and race along the glistening path. He mounted the roan and, towing the paint alongside, set out for the Black Hills and was enveloped by ponderosas when the headlights swung into the drive, moving past the rolled corporate truck, coming to a stop next to his pickup.

It was Harris in that beat-up Bronco, the two corporate jabronies tailing him.

Cody watched through binoculars as Harris emerged, talking into a handheld.

The suit named David exited the corporate truck, shouting at Harris. Harris turned back, pointed and yelled like he was telling David to back off.

David stopped moving but didn't stop talking.

Cody dismounted, swung the reins and the lead rope around a tree branch. He laid prone, swapped the binoculars for the Scout and peered through the scope, finding some amusement as he watched them bicker without hearing what they were saying.

He disengaged the safety.

The superintendent was getting involved now, pulling David back to the truck—the heels of his loafers raking lines in the dirt.

Cody turned the yardage dial and David swelled, filling the frame of the reticule. Cotton balls plugged his nose. His hair was mussed. Dirt was matted up the side and the front of his jacket.

Cody swiveled to see Harris, his back to the jabronies now, shielding his face from the heat coming off the flames of the engulfed house.

Cody estimated twenty yards between them, another fifteen or twenty between the jabronies and his truck. He had no beef with Harris. After all, the man was just doing his job—even if it was something stupid like a busted headlight.

So Cody waited for the jabronies to go back to their truck before putting the crosshairs on a jerrycan. He said, "Suck on this ya corporate fucks," but stopped short of squeezing the trigger when Harris darted into frame, reaching in through the driver's side door of the Bronco, coming out with something—a phone or a radio, he couldn't tell. Harris turned back to yell at David who was still yelling at him. They exchanged a few more words before Harris trotted back toward the house, wait no, moving around it now, heading to the shop barn—the hell was he doing?

Cody swiveled back. The jabronies were somber now, halfway to their truck. He put the crosshairs on a jerrycan again, waited for them to get closer and fired.

His truck combusted in a massive fireball causing a chain reaction and all three vehicles exploded.

"Shit," Cody said. "Did not see that comin."

The force of the explosion had knocked the jabronies to the ground. Harris was crouched, looking back at them, halfway to the shop barn.

Cody zoomed in on David. He had a mouth full of dirt and was pushing his tongue out, doing his best to spit out grit and gravel.

When Cody found Harris in the reticule again, the man was looking this way, it seemed, right into the lens of the scope. It startled Cody, made him lift up and look with his naked eye. The flames became miniature, the men just three small specks.

No way could he draw a bead, Cody thought, lowering his eye to the scope again. But there he was, unblinking, saying something to someone on the other end of that handheld.

31

THELMA had a new personal best going—three aces in under eight minutes—when Harris had radioed the first time saying it was a code eleven, a house afire. He had been in a pissy mood since he left the station because the douche in the suit and his sidekick had come in raising hell, telling Harris he needed to get up off his ass, do his damn job since they were just assaulted—with a cheap shot, mind you—because that Custer asshole was allegedly out there shooting at people like he was a gunslinger and this was the Old West. So Thelma dispatched the fire and EMT units without skipping a beat, but when Harris radioed a second time, she couldn't hear a thing he was saying. She told him to call back using his cellular which gave her enough time to make another move, attaching the two of spades under a three of hearts, before the cordless on her desk started ringing.

She answered, tried to ask what he was doing but he cut her off, saying, "Hold on a minute." She could hear his heavy breaths. Could hear him rummaging through things. Tools, maybe. Something made of iron or metal. Then, what sounded like a car door opened and slammed shut.

Harris said, "Came from the north, shit, musta been seven, eight hunnert yards."

"Wait, you talking to me?"

"Not really, just thinking out loud."

"The hell're you doing?" Thelma said.

"There's a flatbed in here. I'm trying to find the keys."

"Flatbed? What good's that gonna do?"

"Hang on a sec."

"Goddamnit Weston, just tell me what yer doing. And I swear to Jesus, you tell me hold on again—"

"My Bronco got blown up Thelma, so forgive me if I'm a little off-kilter."

"I am this close to dragging my fat-ass down there. You think you got problems now, it'll be a helluva lot worse you make me schlep it out there in the cold."

There was a pause. The background chatter had ceased, like he stopped moving altogether, and a heavy sigh made its way through the earpiece. "Guy said an access point's at the northwest corner, all right? And if I were him—"

"Yer not goin up there."

"Well he'll come down Thelma, and correct me if I'm wrong, but I don't believe it'll be civil when he does."

Thelma bit her lip. She zipped across the station in her desk chair, the wheels squeaking, wobbling over the polyurethaned vinyl. She stood as she reached the topographic map and her chair continued rolling, crashing into Weston's desk. She found the Flying-C—a large parcel outlined in black. Grabbed a marker and plucked the top with her teeth. "Ya said from the north?"

"'Bout eight hunnert yards."

Thelma guesstimated, put a black dot in the vicinity. She ran a finger along the closest contour until she saw the number, then wrote "6k+" next to the dot. She searched for the access point but couldn't remember if he had said northeast or west.

Harris was saying, "And if I were him, I'd wanna do two things—"

"Where's the access point again?"

"You listening to me?"

Her first thought was to hammer-fist the map in frustration, but that would hurt and Weston probably wouldn't even hear it. So she smacked the map instead, gave it a good one. "Where's the goddamn access point, Weston?"

"Northwest corner," his voice drab.

Thelma marked it. Ran a finger along the contour then marked a "4" next to that dot.

"And listen, if I were him, I'd wanna do two things. Keep eyes on the ranch, and be near a water source."

Thelma circled the closest body of water. "Iron Creek Lake."

"Not with that open stretch a beach they got. Ain't enough concealment or escape routes."

Thelma put an "X" through it. The next one would be Horsethief Lake. She circled it, marked the elevation and told Harris.

"That's the one," Harris said. "So I'm betting somewhere in that vicinity he'll set up camp."

Thelma connected the dots which formed a triangle. She capped the marker. "Kay. Y'all done?"

"That's all I got."

"Then lemme break it down for ya. The elevation from where the shot occurred to the lake is anywhere from forty-five hunnert to over six thousand plus."

"And the access point?"

"In the four hunnert range."

"So what's yer point?"

"Yer just gonna hike yer old ass up there at night in the goddamn freezing cold, track him down, most likely engage in a gunfight since we ardy established ya ain't great at talking these types off the ledge. Then—and this if you don't kill him first—bring his ass all the way back down, still in the goddamn freezing cold."

There was another pause. This one longer than the last. "Well I ain't thank about all that."

"Course not," Thelma said, dragging the chair back to her desk. "So 'less you can shit out a Humvee—'cause a goddamn flatbed won't do nothing but cause ya more problems—then I suggest you do one of two things: find an alternate means of transportation, such as a horse. Or, and what I mean by *that* is it's really yer only option 'cause I know you cain't ride for shit—"

"I can too."

"Well ya ain't no reining champion. And I don't think anyone in this town'd be willing to go so far as to call you a *good*, let alone a *great* horseman like I 'magine ol' Custer probly is."

"Fair point, I reckon."

"Great. Then ya ready to hear what I thank you oughta do?"

"Lay it on me."

"Get yer ass back to the station so we can formulate a plan of action, track this bastard down come morning."

"Cain't do it," Harris said.

"See this is where we got a misunderstanding, 'cause that wasn't no goddamn suggestion."

"It ain't that I don't think it's logical. But imagine what would happen word gets out I came to the station for a cup of joe and some shuteye when the town's got a maniac running around blowing his own shit up! I cain't do it. I won't do it—"

238

"Weston—"

"I'm goin up there, into the mountains, the middle of the night the goddamn freezing cold and bringing his ass to justice. 'Cause nobody blows up my Bronco and gets away with it."

"You cain't take it personal—"

"I loved that truck."

"And we'll find ya another one. You know how many mid-life crises's are tooling around the Midwest?"

A horse neighed or snorted or whatever damn noise it was that horses made. It was distinct, clear. Thelma said, "The hell was that?"

Harris didn't respond.

"Weston, don't be a goddamn fool. I'm begging ya."

"Wow, it's like you care about me."

"For Pete's sake, you know I do. But this ain't the right move." She could feel her heart fluttering, her cheeks getting warm.

"Keep a radio on you. I'll let you know when I get 'im."

"The hell with the damn radio, that shit don't work. Take yer cellular. Weston? Weston, you hear me?"

When he didn't respond she yelled, tried to tell him to stop, to think about it for Christ's sake, but all she heard was his distant voice talking to the horse like it was a toddler. "Easy boy, easy. It's okay, yer okay." And the last thing she heard before the line went dead was him saying, "This is so goddamn stupid."

32

SHEA CUSTER thought the place wasn't befitting of a mayor. It was dark, depressing. Everything was black, trimmed with gold. The gator-print bed frame. The silk sheets. The coffee table with the smoked glass. The side tables. The desk. The dresser. The couch. Shoot, even that entry tree with the coat rack and the storage lockers. The place could've been a film set from that one starring Al Pacino playing the big dog with the bad accent, pushing drugs in Miami's heyday; the title evading her as she watched the flat screen, waiting for the guy with the dreadful haircut and the fake teeth to start talking about her.

Kenny was on the pot in the next room going number two.

Shea could tell because he always turned the faucet on like a little girl, trying to drown out all the noise he made.

The anchor swiveled to meet the new camera angle, this one moving in on his face. "And now, as we have a look at some recent polling, if the election was today, Shea Custer with a near double digit victory over the Republican incumbent..."

Christ, what a terrible photo, Shea thought. It was straight on, had no depth, idling next to the anchor's head.

"I mean those numbers are staggering, are they not?"

The feed cut to a middle-aged woman with lipstick on her

teeth. "They really are. Not but a few days ago she has a two-point lead, and now this? It's staggering, it's stunning, I'm excited, and quite frankly it confirms the one thing we already knew..." She arched her eyebrows and waited for the others to lean in.

"Which is?"

"This town is ready for new blood in the mayor's office."

"No doubt about that."

Wow. Could they get any cornier?

The amber flickering in Shea's periphery pulled her attention from the screen as they motored on about how great she was, how excited they were. At first, Shea thought Kenny had fixed and moved that stupid lamp, the Demian-whatchamacallit. But when she turned, she saw it was in the distance, beyond the sliding-glass. It took her a minute to get the door unlocked because she couldn't take her eyes off what looked like a fire raging, a plume of smoke rising, blending with the charcoal sky. Stepping onto the balcony, she knew it was the ranch house because the barn lights were still visible to the right.

The toilet flushed. The faucet turned off.

Kenny came out of the bathroom chuckling. "I'm talking dividends son..."

"Kenneth."

"...Twenty-five miles—"

"Kenny."

"—of the transportation system for fifty-four percent of America's crude..."

Shea turned back, saw the phone to his ear and yelled his name.

He started to shout back until he saw the flames. He said, "I have to call you back," and hung up, wading onto the balcony. "Is that…"

"Yep."

Kenny's phone started beeping. Texts coming so quick the phone couldn't finish its jingle. "Fucking David. He's trying to stop production."

"Why? What's going on?"

Kenny shook his head. "He didn't say. Just, 'This is bullshit. I'm shutting it down until further notice.' And he sent the crew back to base, told them to standby. Fire department's on the way."

And they were indeed.

Shea could see the flashing reds and yellows carving their way down the 75. Two of the big ones, an ambulance, and a volunteer pickup in caboose.

"That's not his decision to make."

"I'm aware."

"Call him, and if you don't set him straight, I will."

"That's what I'm doing, Shea. For fuck's sake." Kenny put the phone to his ear, his eyes racing back and forth.

Shea wanted to move. Wanted a drink. Wanted to do something, but felt cornered, sitting up here in this ivory fucking tower. The anchor on TV was talking about some earthquake in central California that hit seven on the Richter. The one with lipstick on her teeth said, "Ohmigod, how awful," and the anchor said, "Yes, a terrible, terrible tragedy. We're sending thoughts and prayers from the studio."

Half of Shea wanted to vomit, like thoughts and prayers did a goddamn thing. The other half thinking it would make for a nice talking point, mention something at the next speech since it sounded like the quake had hit farm country.

Interesting.

Kenny lowered the phone. "He's not answering. This is unbelievable." He dialed another number. Put the phone back to his ear. "A hundred and fifty union dicks on the clock hanging out in a parking lot... Goddamnit! Answer the fucking phone!"

"Screw this." Shea moved past him, grabbed her mink off the entry tree.

"You're not going over there."

"Watch me."

"Would you please—and this is me trying to be polite here—but would you please stand the fuck down and let me deal with it?"

"Because you want to feel like the big dick or because you're actually concerned for my welfare?"

"Ohmigod, I can't talk to you when you're like this."

"Stop pacing, okay, you look ridiculous."

Kenny stopped, arched his brow. "The man just lost everything. Literally everything. And you're just going to waltz right over there?"

"Well, I can tell you what he won't do, Kenneth: shoot us down in cold blood with half the fire department on site as spectators. So we can sit here, do this bullshit all night if you want, but the fact of the matter is simple: it's my ranch. It's my land. I'm an equal fucking partner which means I don't take orders from you. And if you'd like me to do your job while I'm over there, then just say the word and I'm happy to oblige."

Kenny could see the fire almost the entire way as the town car sped toward the ranch; Hector and the box-headed dude up front, Shea in the seat next to him, refusing to make eye contact.

They passed a parking lot crowded with hard hats and reflector vests. A bunch of white men and a few coloreds huddled around space heaters and barrel fires, shooting the shit. One guy looked up, drawing on his cigarette, and watched the town car as it passed.

Hector said, "Sir, I strongly advise you to reconsider."

"I will not be confined to the rez because this asshole's off his rocker."

"Just till the situation's resolved. We're going into his territory, we don't know what he's capable of."

Shea scoffed. "Please…"

"All due respect ma'am, the circumstances are different. He's desperate."

Jesus. Everyone talking, giving their two cents. Soon the box-headed one who used to talk a lot but now wasn't saying shit would chime in. Kenny felt he was losing control of the situation. Losing it to her. Shit. Even Hector was offering unsolicited opinions. So Kenny eyed him in the rearview. "I'm sorry, what do I pay you for?"

"To keep you secure, and that's what I'm trying to do."

"No, you're trying to hinder my business, there's a difference. I don't tell you how to set a perimeter so the aesthetics are better at my meetings, I just let you operate. So do your job correctly, and it won't be a problem, understood?"

Hector nodded. "Yes, sir." Then, he touched his earpiece. "Hang on, I'm getting something here. Fire department was dispatched about thirty minutes ago. House is toast." He eyed Shea in the rearview. "Sorry, ma'am. They're hosing it down as we speak."

"What about Custer?" Kenny said. "Any sign of him?"

Hector shook his head. "Nothing from the local P.D. But I am..."—he stopped to chuckle—"there is something coming through on the medic's end, they're talking to David."

"What's he whining about?"

"Hang on..." Hector looked at the box-headed one now. "You hearing this?"

Silas nodded, but that was it. He had been on high alert since they left the rez, scanning a hundred eighty degrees, lingering on the shadows when the town car would come to a stop. It made Kenny nervous.

"One of them is saying his eyebrows and eyelashes were burnt off. Half the hair on his head has been singed. When they found him, he was dazed. They asked him regular questions, you know, what's your name, what day is it? But when they asked what state he was in, they're saying he said, 'One of the goddamn piece of shit flyover states.' That he's going to sue everyone who's ever had contact with the little asshole."

Kenny laughed, feeling better now. Picturing David all fucked up, having one hell of a first day. If the city slicker was talking like that, it meant the area was secure. Yeah, nothing to worry about. That Custer prick was long gone.

When they pulled into the ranch, Kenny waited for Hector and Silas to run a quick sweep. He tried looking at Shea, but she wouldn't meet him halfway. He was about to apologize when she cut him off, told him she wasn't staying in the car so don't try and pull any shit.

What the fuck ever.

Hector opened the door, told Kenny it was clear. He beelined for David the Douche who was on a gurney in the back of an ambulance. Bandages were on half his face—only one eye visible—and a medic was wrapping an arm in gauze. His shirt had either been ripped or burnt, Kenny couldn't tell.

"What the hell happened to you?"

"I don't wanna get into it," David said. "He is certifiable."

"Where is he?"

"Playing G.I. Joe Mountain Man up in the fucking hills apparently."

Kenny leaned back, clearing the door to glance at the hills. A fluctuating canopy of evergreens lit by the pale hue of a full moon. "How do you know that?"

"Overheard some hag on this guy's radio talking," David said, cocking a thumb at the medic. Then he looked at Kenny with his good eye. "You gotta stop production. Now. At least till they catch him."

"I already told you that's not happening."

"I didn't sign up for this shit."

"David—"

"Look at my face! This is not okay, bro!"

"Shut up." Kenny stepped into the ambulance. "You will press on because everything I do is what?"

"There has to be extenuating circumstances."

"Everything I do is what, David!?"

"…On time…and on budget."

"And that's my legacy, and I won't let that piece of shit ruin it for me. You got it?"

"I got it."

Kenny patted the medic on the back. "Now tell this man to give you a Percocet and get back to work."

"He can't go back to work, he needs help."

"Zip it, Poncho. This doesn't concern you." Kenny turned

to exit the ambulance.

Shea was there, arms crossed, looking at David. "Who's they?"

David perked up. "Shea...hi..."

"Who's *they*, David?"

"Whaddaya mean?"

"You said until *they* catch him," Kenny said.

David seemed confused, his eye doing laps around the ambulance. "Are you all talking about the same thing?"

"You said *they* went up into the hills to try and catch him. Who is they?"

David was still searching, still confused. The medic looked at Kenny. "Give him space. He's had a couple good blows to the head, and he's probly experiencing some short-term memory loss."

"Okay, well it's imperative we know who *they* is," Kenny said. "So smack him on the head, do whatever you have to do—"

"Smack him on the head?"

"I don't know, these Wall Street types, maybe he's like an old TV, a good smack'll get him working again."

"He needs time, and proper medical attention."

"You're not taking him to the hospital, he has work to do."

"Legally, I can't leave him here, okay? He may have a concussion, he may have brain damage, I don't know... But he's got to get somewhere where they can take a better look at him—"

"Okay-okay, I get it, you fucking boy scout. Just let me tell him one more thing..." Kenny paused, leaned closer. "David. David, over here. Yeah, right here. Listen. Take care of yourself in the hospital all right? And when you get better, don't bother coming back because you're fucking fired."

On the way back to the town car, Kenny found the superintendent and told him to bring the cavalry, start drilling.

Kenny was thinking about the way David had looked at her with his one eye and didn't like it at all. Looking at her like they had history. His whole demeanor had changed too. Like it was a pleasant surprise or some shit.

By the time Hector made a left on 75, Kenny was surprised there wasn't a convoy of trucks going the other way. In fact, he didn't see any vehicles, nor could he see the few speckled lights in town.

Odd as it was, he shrugged it off and looked out the window at the Black Hills.

"Who do you think *they* are?" Shea said.

"There is no they. It's just that sheriff. The good ol' boy, whatshisname?"

"Harris."

"There you go. It's just him, which is why I didn't even ask in the first place. Then you come along with your stupid question asking who they are."

"If it was stupid, why'd you follow it up, hammer him about it?"

Kenny turned. "Because it's my show. I can't have some broad demanding this and that from my staff, talking over me. Makes me look weak."

"Some broad?"

"Oh please, don't act like you're offended. What? You can insinuate I'm some kind bitch, but I can't refer to you as a *broad*?"

"What are you talking about?"

248

"You give me shit all the time. It's exactly what you did before we left, saying you'll do my job for me. Acting like I'm scared, like I'm too big a bitch to handle my own shit with your brother out there, doing whatever the fuck he's doing."

"Well you're not helping your case right now, that's for sure."

"You know what? I've had it. I'm fucking done with you, this double standard bullshit. I can't do it anymore—"

"Heard that before."

"This time I'm for real. We need each other only so far as the money and the operation goes, but that's it. Personally, you can pack your shit, get the fuck out."

She didn't even flinch. Just came right back. "Pssh, no skin off my back. In fact, I prefer it that way. Hector, would you mind dropping me at the office?"

"Um, I'm not certain that's a good id—"

"Don't answer that," Kenny said. "You don't work for her."

"Oh, I see. You want me out, but on your terms, right? Or were you expecting me to beg and grovel? 'Kenny, please, I have no place to go, what ever will I do?'"

He couldn't take it anymore.

He lunged at her, clamped his hands around her neck and felt her skin compress at the gaps in her spinal cord. One of the guys up front was yelling for him stop. But he didn't want to. He wanted to feel her neck pop, to feel her body go limp.

Silas leaped into the back and broke them apart. Shea gasped for air, calling Kenny a motherfucker before yelling at Hector to stop the car.

"I can't do that ma'am."

"Pull the fucking car over now!" her voice was hoarse.

"Everyone calm down," Silas said. "We're not stopping till we get back to the rez, period."

Hector slammed on the brakes, throwing Silas over the center console, crashing into the dash.

"What the fuck, man!?"

Kenny looked ahead, saw cows swarming in the road. Big black ones and ones with spots. It seemed like a lot, but what did he know? He couldn't tell where one ended and the other began.

Hector said, "Get down and stay low," then ordered Silas to clear the cows.

Kenny sunk into his seat as the box-headed one pulled the P-90 from the floorboard—this time without the silencer—and exited the car. He moved into the headlights, shouting, mock-charing the cows, but they wouldn't budge.

Kenny felt a shadow creeping outside his window and yelped.

"Jesus, get it together," Shea said.

He followed her gaze, saw it was only a curious horse craned over a string of barbed wire.

Hector keyed his radio. "Cook a few."

Kenny saw him point the gun skyward. Saw him hesitate. Then saw his head snap and a gush of pink mist before he dropped like a rag doll.

33

THE HILLS had seemed haunting ever since he shot the canisters. Like there was something out there. Something following him. The fog had started high but was beginning to settle, framing the ponderosas in a slate grey backdrop. It was frigid. He heard no wildlife and figured all of them were hunkered down for the night. Smart little buggers.

He could see most of the Mingan from his original vantage point, but had to trek higher to see the penthouse. Through binoculars, he saw the two of them bickering. The chief pointing at the flames, the television flashing in the background. He watched Shea grab a coat—some kind of fur—then say something before both of them exited.

They were headed for the ranch. He was sure of it. Where else would they be going? So Cody heeled the roan and started moving down the mountain, the paint mare alongside. When the roan slipped, he checked the reins. Said, "Woah," and fed slack on the paint's lead rope, allowing her to lag behind. The horses weren't fond at the lack of visibility. They would jump or yip at every little sound. It was a constant effort to keep them in check, to maintain discipline. If they tried to look anywhere but straight, he'd neck-rein the roan or yank on the paint's lead-rope.

When they reached a flat with a small break in the fog, Cody clucked his tongue, sending the horses into a canter. The more they ran, the calmer they became. They snaked their way through the trees, came to a clearing and saw a lone wolf with its nose to the ground, looking up at them.

Cody halted, feeling the over-under against his knee in the scabbard. The paint nickered, reared up and started turning. Cody tugged the reins, had the roan back up so he didn't lose the mare. He tried saying, "*Yay-wa-buena*," and "*Dalé*," words he'd heard Manuel use in the past. But when that didn't work, he resorted to a few lashes with the lead rope until the paint settled and started listening again.

When he looked up the wolf was still there, revealing teeth under a pair of flaxen eyes. Cody grouped the lead rope with the reins, then pulled the over-under across his lap.

The wolf lifted a lead leg, twitched its nose.

Something was familiar. Cody wondered if this was the one that got away when the errant shot hit Blackfoot. He thought of Manuel, his dying words. "Kill 'em. Kill 'em all."

So Cody shouldered the over-under, put the front sight just below its snout. He stared into wolf's burning, unwavering eyes. And somewhere in the depths of them, Cody Custer saw himself.

He returned the shotgun to the scabbard and waited until the wolf disappeared. It was too far anyway, Cody told himself. The scatter of the 12-gauge would've been ineffective.

From the base of the mountain he saw the fire trucks. Streams from mounted water canons rushed at the flames. The town car was in the driveway. The chief and his sister were huddled around an ambulance.

He could train the Scout, find that ponytail in the reticule and get the party started. See what the two goons standing next to the town car would do. But he needed Shea alive, and contemplated how he'd do it when he clocked the small herd of cows in the adjacent pasture.

He moved out of the tree line. Dipped into an arroyo, following it until he reached the barbed wire. He dismounted. Used the Kershaw to cut three rows and peeled back a good-sized gap.

Back in the pasture, using the roan and the paint together, he circled the cows and pushed them towards the 75.

It was a pain in the ass. Some of the cows wouldn't move at first. Cody would rifle the lariat at their backs, cutting his horses left and right until he worked them into a soft trot and herded them to the fence line. A few slipped when their hooves hit tarmac. It caused confusion, pandemonium among the herd.

Cody rode into a gulch running parallel to the road. Hitched the horses to a telephone pole and waited for the town car.

Harris couldn't figure the damn thing out. It just wanted to trot. The pads of his palms were swollen. His biceps burned from squeezing and pulling the lead rope. He would put a heel into the thing and its whole body would jolt, but it wouldn't go any faster or straighter or smoother.

And it would only turn right. He tried pulling the halter to the left, but that only made the horse look left and trot straight, which Harris thought was ridiculous.

Shitting out a Humvee sounded like a viable solution at this point.

He found the access point and made it a hundred yards up

the grade before his balls hurt so bad he had to dismount and walk until he could climb no more—sweating inside his canvas jacket.

The horse would stop when he stopped. And every time, it would turn back and try to head home. Still, it wouldn't turn left. So Harris would have to make a full circle to keep pushing forward.

The fog was thick, concealing trees not twenty feet in front of him. When the pain in his knees and lower back surpassed the pain in his balls and lower stomach, he found a boulder and used it as a mounting block. But when he put a hand on the horse's back this time, it bolted, skipping the canter, going straight to full gallop. He gripped a handful of mane and cursed. Swung a leg over, pulled the lead rope as hard as he could, but the horse ran harder, faster.

Tree branches whipped past his head. He yelled fuck and shit and stop, but the thing surged like a goddamn locomotive. He pleaded, begged for it to stop to no avail.

It wasn't until he almost fell, saying, "Woah," that the horse halted, throwing Harris over top, hugging the horse's neck. When he pushed himself back, he noticed the horse's ears were no longer pinned against its skull. No, now those fuckers were perked and listening.

Harris bounced a heel off its flank.

It walked forward.

He said, "Woah," and it stopped which made him chuckle, shivering now from the moisture on his clothes. He said, "Left," and tried to turn but that didn't work, so he decided he'd be content with the "woah" bit and continued up the mountain.

He saw two wooden crucifixes nestled within a grouping of trees. One crucifix was more weathered than the other.

Something was engraved on each of them, though he couldn't steer the horse close enough to see and wouldn't push his luck to find out.

Harris climbed another few hundred feet thinking about how he'd do it—approach Cody when they came face to face. He'd have to be first to draw. It'd be the only way. Harris told himself he wouldn't hesitate this time. No sir. If the guy was dumb enough to reach for the 1911, Harris would have no qualms about dropping him.

That's when Harris heard the gunshot.

He said, "Woah," and the horse stopped. It sounded like a high-powered rifle. A .308 or a .30-06. He turned the horse, listening as the echo washed up the mountain.

It had come from down below, near the Flying-C. And now, shit, more of them. A lot more. One after another, snapping and cracking, blending together like rolling thunder.

Harris came up with the radio, pushed the talk button. "Thelma, come in."

The radio squawked, hissed an ear-piercing frequency and the horse spooked, kicking, bucking, then rearing back and throwing Harris.

He tumbled down the mountain, the rocky terrain assaulting him from every angle. He ricocheted off trees, went through shrubs, none of which seemed to slow him down. When he felt the ground beneath him no more, he flailed his hands and managed to grasp a tuft of stiff branches, squeezing a fist around them. He looked down, saw his feet dangling over a rock shelf two hundred feet below. He looked up, along his arm to the bare shrub in his duke and saw the taut roots stretching from the dirt.

* * *

Hector said, "Get down," as he threw the car in reverse and floored it. Bullets shattered the back window. One made the rearview disappear.

Kenny tried but couldn't get any lower than he was, watching Hector turn back, navigating, flinching, as more rounds peppered the car. A tire blew and Kenny felt his side drop a few inches. Another bullet went through Hector's seat and into his shoulder causing him to lose grip of the wheel, the car crashing into an embankment.

Hector worked the lever on the steering column. The car jerked forward and backwards but didn't yield any progress.

Kenny asked if Shea was okay.

"Like you give a shit." Her head was buried in her arms.

Kenny turned to Hector. "Get us outta here."

Hector glanced in the side-mirror. It exploded from the impact of a bullet.

"Shit." Hector peeled himself around the edge of the seat. "I'll lay down cover-fire—"

"No-no-no."

"It's our only option. There's a gun under your seat."

Kenny cocked his head to one side. Reached down there and came up with a pistol that looked identical to Hector's.

"It's loaded," Hector said. "All you gotta do is flick the safety off."

Kenny did, saw the little red dot appear.

"Okay. On three I want you to exit that way and run"—he was pointing at Shea's door to the right—"I'll cover you."

Kenny looked at him. "That's your fucking plan?"

"See those headlights the other side of the cows? That's the convoy. Get to them, then hightail it back to rez."

Kenny nodded, but looked at Hector again. "What about you?"

"End of the line, boss." Hector drew his pistol. Turned to the front and unlatched the door.

A lump swelled in Kenny's throat. He eyed Shea, asked if she was ready.

She nodded, curling her bony fingers around the door handle.

Hector peeled himself around again. "One...two..."

Kenny saw Hector's tongue pinched between his teeth as he started to say *three*, but the word never came. A bullet slammed through his upper-lip, blood and brain matter painted the windshield.

Shea had thrown her door open, was half out of the car when two more rounds battered the door, sending her back for cover.

"Fuck." Kenny saw Hector slumped over the center console, a gaping exit wound in the back of his head. "What do we do?"

"Be a man and fight back."

Kenny wanted to pistol-whip her. Or better yet, give her the gun, see how fucking tough she was with John Wick back there.

But he didn't, because Kenny Shepard saw an opportunity. A way to be the hero. To become famous. Famous for saving the town from a crazed killer. A racist, xenophobic, white killer. He could see the headlines: BLOODSHED AND BORDER WARS ON THE RESERVATION. Or better yet: YAWAKHAN CHIEF, DESCENDENT OF CRAZY HORSE, A TRUE AMERICAN HERO.

A *real* American Hero?

True.

No, real.

It could go either way. He'd let it marinate for now.

Kenny peeked over the seat and saw a figure advancing, straddling the dotted yellows on the asphalt. The guy's muzzle belched fire and Kenny ducked as bullets snapped overhead.

He felt Shea watching, judging him, but he wasn't deterred. He rose above the seat again, aimed and pulled the trigger as fast as he could.

He caught movement in his periphery, the figure filling the door frame—instincts telling him it wasn't a curious horse this time. He tasted metal on his teeth. Saw Shea reeled from the car by her hair, then caught a glimpse of the muzzle from an old pistol before everything went black.

Cody had a chunk of blonde hair in his duke when he put one between the eyes of the Injun bastard. Shea's hair hadn't ripped out on the initial yank, thank God, but rather as she flew past him, clear of the door, her roots acting as the fulcrum, ripping as she pivoted around him and hit the pavement.

She was on the ground, writhing, yelling the chief's name. Calling Cody a savage and a motherfucker.

Real original, Cody thought.

He got her upright, moved her to the paint and told her to mount up.

"Fuck you."

He pistol-whipped her. Her knees buckled and she slumped to the deck. When she didn't move, he knelt, thinking he didn't hit her that hard. He prodded her, said her name, but she remained flaccid, unconscious.

He holstered the Colt, folded her over the roan's saddle, then mounted up and headed for the hills.

He was shrouded in darkness again, secluded from civilization. Even still, he couldn't shake the feeling that someone was out there. That same feeling had left with the wolf, but now it was back and it made him nervous. He sat his horse and watched for movement.

When Shea woke, Cody let her fall from the horse, feet first. She gasped for air.

Cody dismounted. Fixed the loop of his rope around her midriff, dallied it around the saddle horn, then told her to get up, start walking.

When she didn't, Cody swung up on the roan, clucked his tongue and let the horse drag her a few steps.

She clawed at the rocky ground, yelling, pleading for him to stop.

"Woah." Cody shifted in the saddle. "Only one way this gonna work, Shea."

She got to her knees, wiped at her face. "Let's just talk about it, okay? You know how much money's at stake? We can split it down the middle, fifty-fifty, you'll never have to work—"

Cody popped a heel into the roan. It lurched forward, pulling Shea flush against the ground, dragging her further.

"Motherfucker! Cody, Cody—stop!"

He tugged the reins. Allowed Shea to get her bearings, watching her deep breaths flush and cloud against the ambient moonlight.

"Fucking kill me if you want. I'm not doing this bullshit. I'm not walking my ass to death up a fucking mountain in a pair of eight-hundred dollar Louboutins."

Cody dismounted, assuming she was talking about the heels

on her feet, the ones that made her almost as tall as him. "Kill you?"

"Oh that's right…" Shea spat over her shoulder, a lot of force behind it. "We already established you're too big a pussy."

Cody drew his Kershaw, cut the lariat and told her to walk. "Where?"

He nodded past her. "Straight. Want you to turn, I'll fucking tell ya."

Shea removed her heels, discarded them down the mountain. And Cody followed her through the forest, awaiting the look on her face when she reached the crucifixes.

34

HARRIS thought he was screwed, hanging there with one hand around a half-frozen shrub. Pain radiated throughout his body, and the rocks below seemed to be getting further and further away.

He pulled up, felt the shrub start to give and knew it wouldn't support him much longer. He reached for the cliff's edge, but fell inches short. Ran both feet along the rock wall and felt a branch or a root swelling in the cracks. So he dug his toes into it, tested for stability before shifting his weight, getting enough leverage to lunge for the shelf.

But his foot slipped.

The sudden deadweight uprooted the shrub and he was falling fast. He kept his hands against the wall, clawing the jagged rock, closing his fingers around the first thing he could—a thin ledge the width of the top half of his fingers. Wailing through gritted teeth, he looked up and saw the rock shelf was several feet higher now.

His fingers were slipping.

A small jut along the cliff badgered the side of his knee. So he put the inside of his boot flush against the wall and hiked his leg until his sole was gripping the protruded rock. He scaled a few feet and used the momentum to leap, getting both hands to the shelf. Pebbles and grit stung the flayed skin on his fingertips.

And there, waist high, was an impression in the wall. He sucked in through his nose and pulled himself higher. Dug his foot into the dimple and was able to get one elbow over the shelf, then the other, bracing himself before his foot slipped again.

Dangling now, folded at the waist around the ledge, he worked one elbow in front of the other until he felt the rock shelf beneath his entire body. When his breathing slowed, he began to doze until he heard the gal's voice from above.

Harris sat erect, unable to see more than a dozen feet through the fog. Then he heard a man's voice and knew it belonged to Cody Custer.

He steeled himself. Drew the .45 and stalked the man that destroyed his Bronco.

Shea could feel her little brother back there, five paces, half a step to the left. She walked for what felt a while, weaving through the stout, barren trunks, wondering what in God's name they were doing up here. She went back and forth in her mind about whether or not Cody had it in him.

Earlier, she was sure he didn't. Now, it seemed like a tossup.

She remembered the look in his eye. The way he blinked twice when she told him killing blood was different. He showed weakness then, was showing it now ever since he put that knife away. And the pistol he always carried? She knew it'd be on his left hip.

"Stop."

Shea turned to see him looking every which way. She said,

"Don't tell me you're lost," and he came back with a nice, "Shut the fuck up'n turn around."

Shea rolled her eyes. When Cody told her to angle left forty-five degrees, Shea let a hand drop and smack her thigh. "This is ridiculous. I've got other shit to do tonight. Why don't you just lead the way so we can get this over with?"

He looked up, eyes squinted, and started on about what a cold-hearted bitch she was and blah bla-blah, bla-blah, bla-blah… She couldn't tell if he was being serious or sarcastic, so she tuned him out. The man-child getting more worked up the more he talked.

"Look, I can't see anything, okay? Can't see five feet in front of me, and I don't know what forty-five degrees is. So come up here, point me in the direction, and I'll go."

She hadn't expected him to come up so quick, but now was her chance. When she felt his hands on her shoulders, she spun and reached for the gun, feeling the textured wood inserts of the grip before he squeezed her wrist. His other hand—this one a closed fist—crashed hard into her nose.

She saw a flash of red and tasted the warm blood as it leaked from her nose and over her lip. By the time she realized she was on her back, she was hoisted to her feet again. His grip like a vise around her jaw, their eyes inches apart.

"Pull that shit again, I'll just fucking kill you. Got it?"

She believed him.

They walked down a grade, forty-five degrees to the left. Neither spoke for a while. Shea grabbed anything she could for balance. Tree limbs. Boulders. Her calloused feet held up well from years of high heels.

"You ever wonder about Pop? Where he might be?"

Shea blotted her nose with the sleeve of her mink. "Like I

care."

"Pappy was convinced he went to California—"

"I wouldn't be surprised if he had another family, living like none of this ever existed."

"What if I told ya he's here. Ain't never left."

"I'd say you need to get your head checked, but you've made that abundantly clear tonight."

The crunch beneath his boots stopped. Shea turned back, saw him perked like a prairie dog.

He told her to get down and fired several shots into the forest.

"The hell's wrong with you!?" Shea said.

"Shut up. You hear that?" He had an ear turned and his eyes were bouncing all over the place.

Of course she heard it—footsteps pattering below. But couldn't hear shit now because her ears where ringing from all the gunshots. So she said, "Hear what?" unaware of how loud she was yelling.

"Shut. Up."

"You can't ask a question, then tell me to shut up."

He raised the gun at her. "Try me."

"Cody, there's nothing out there. You're fucking delusional. Contrary to what you think, no one in town really gives a shit the ranch is up in flames. No one is looking for you. No one *cares* about you. So stop."

After a moment, he lowered the gun halfway. "Walk."

She did.

"November eleventh, ninety-seven...that ring a bell?"

She pretended to think about it. "No."

"You went to bed early, said if Pop thought you were asleep, he wouldn't take you out to pasture..."

34

She could see the bastard in the recliner. A fire going. Empty beer cans on the foldout.

"…When I asked what that meant, you broke down, finally told me what he'd been doing all them years."

She was back in the cold again. Could hear footsteps, down and to the left, getting closer. Have to stall, she thought. Get loud, draw attention. "Oh for the love of God, that's what this is about?"

"Yeah—"

"Then you'll fucking love this. I mean, what are we, two decades later and you're still on that shit? You remember the date?"

"What're you talkin about?"

"I made it up."

"You what?"

"That's right," Shea said. "I made it all up and you know why? Because it proved how easy it was to manipulate those blinded by sympathy."

"Bullshit."

"Come on, don't be so naive. You remember Gretchen that little cunt Watkins? She claimed that shit in the third grade—that her uncle gave it to her good—and she got to do *any*thing she wanted, my God, she got away with *whatever* she did. This whole fucking town catered to her."

"Shut up."

She heard the footsteps again. Cody didn't seem to notice. The boy was in his own head, pacing, pulling the brim of his hat.

"So you know what?" Shea said. "I started with Mom, just to try it out, see if it worked. And she went off the fucking deep end, boy. I caught her turning tricks down in Rapid City,

265

sucking off all the roughnecks for a quarter."

Harris heard Cody yell shut up again.

They were above him, off to the right. Every time Shea Custer would start rambling, he'd move a few quick steps, clawing at the dirt with his free hand, staying low after the gunshots—which didn't come close, but Harris sure as hell didn't want the sumbitch getting lucky.

He heard a branch—or maybe it was a limb—crack. He gasped, thinking Cody had hit her, but seconds later Shea was off to the races again. "And you? God, once I saw the power I had over you"—go, go, go, move, move, move—"with such a simple statement and a few crocodile tears, I knew I'd be able to afford anything and everything I wanted in this life."

"Goddamnit, I said shut the fuck up!"

Harris heard the limb again, this time an insulated thud, followed by a second and a third and a forth.

No doubt Cody was beating her.

The gal was yelling, cursing, trying to utter phrases between blows.

Harris rushed, pursuing the sounds until the forest fell quiet again. He stopped and listened, trying to curb his heavy breaths.

He heard Cody swear, a subdued yell, then what sounded like something being dragged across the ground. Harris dug his boots in and moved onto a flat. He saw the crucifixes first, and beyond, a faint silhouette. A man for sure—tall, broad shouldered, walking backwards in a wide, wonky stance. Harris trained the .45, but couldn't muster a clear shot with all the foliage.

He crouched, moved in closer, flanking the silhouette, and saw her ankles in Cody's grip, the man dragging her toward the crucifixes. Harris assumed she was dead or unconscious.

He leveled the .45, hovered the Truglos over Cody's frame.

Cody didn't mean to beat her so bad. It just happened.

He couldn't get her to shut up and didn't know what else to do. He dragged her to the weathered crucifix, making no mention of Manuel because what difference did it make? It was all over.

No one would leave this mountain.

Vengeance was his on the Yawakhans, and he was about to get it with Shea. And one thing he was sure of? No shot in hell was he spending the rest of his life in a tiny cell.

He mounted her. Grabbed a fist-full of mane and lifted her head so she could see the initials inscribed. "Open yer eyes. I want this to be the last thing you see 'fore I fucking kill you."

She was shaking, muttering the name that fit the letters. Saying now, "Why are dad's initials—"

"'Cause I fucking killed him that night."

"What?"

Cody drew the 1911, seeing flashes of his father in the pasture after he had lured the piece of shit on that cold, winter night. Cody had fed him some crap that he saw Shea sneaking out to the barn with that new guy, Manuel. He could see his hand out front, the 1911 in it. He saw himself pulling the trigger until the gun was empty, his dad cursing up to the moment he perished.

And now, with the muzzle on the back of Shea's head, Cody knew he had been a murderer his entire life. He would never forgive himself, never be able to live with it.

He shoved her face in the dirt, said, "I loved you. I protected you. And you fucking shit on me." He cocked the hammer, curled a finger around the trigger when everything went black.

EPILOGUE

TAMMY had seen the commercial quite a bit. It came on at least three times before noon during *The Price is Right* and *Let's Make a Deal*, then twice more during *Barry*, that talk show where they did more fighting than talking.

What a paradise, she thought. And great production value. The casino, the rooms, everything looked immaculate.

And you know what? This place didn't seem stuffy like the corporate shitholes they had in Vegas now-days. No, you could take vineyard tours (blackout dates applied). You could do a trail ride on horseback, hit the bars on Main Street—and boy was there as a shit-ton of 'em. You could learn something at the cultural museum during the day, check out *Gary Flatts and the Taphandles* in the amphitheater at night—the stud doing a residency there. Or hell, look at that: new double-decker bus tours that'll let you do it *all* over the course of two days. Get off the bus whenever, hop on another one and continue the tour which ended at a brand new historic monument with a gift shop and a full-scale reenactment and... Are you shittin me? Having its Grand Opening the end of summer.

They even got the guy with the sexy, deep voice to do the narration. The one who did the previews for the Hollywood pictures.

The opening quote hooked her. The movie-preview-guy saying, "Life. It's not measured by the breaths we take, but by the moments that take our breath away."

Heck yeah.

The screen was now showing a group of hip dudes shooting craps, just the right amount of scruff on their faces.

What a great idea, Tammy thought. Convince the hubby, a craps man himself. Say, Baby, you been working hard. Let's do a vacation.

He could roll the dice all day and she could sip on tequila sunrises, check out the hot pieces of ass like the ones squinting and grinning on screen now. Maybe sneak one of 'em up to the room, or take him in the bathroom, show him what he'd been missing. What a farm girl from Topeka was all about.

The possibilities seemed endless.

It showed the pool now. A great big one. Girls in bikinis with tiny waists and huge boobs—bodies she had never seen in real life—walking along the edge. One of them had sunglasses covering half her face, sipping what looked like Tammy's gosh-darn tequila sunrise.

Whatever. Not like that balding, muffin-top hubby could score a broad like that anyway. But what if he got lucky, won a million bucks? All them gold diggers—and that's what they were—would be fawning and frolicking.

Screw it, Tammy thought, convincing herself the hubby didn't stand a chance.

And she just had to be there for the grand opening of this reenactment thing.

The voiceover guy must have read her mind because now he was talking about the unlimited possibilities. The memories.

And this place, Tammy still didn't know the name or where it was, had a waterfall three stories high, dumping into a koi pond the middle of the gosh-dang lobby.

Get out. A waterfall? Three stories high?

That's when she phoned Eugene at work, but got the floor-manager instead. He said Eugene was busy, would have to call her back.

So Tammy told him it was urgent, for Christ's sake. Eugene's mother was dying of the colon cancer. Put his ass on the phone now.

When Eugene came on, all she had to do was mention the Vegas-style games and the unlimited cocktails, and then tried to be clever, telling him if he played his cards right, he'd get lucky every night.

He didn't even ask how far it was, just the name of the place.

"I cain't member," Tammy said. "Something starts with an 'M' or maybe a 'Y.' But listen to this: it's got a fucking waterfall right in the lobby, three-stories high, the thing just spilling right over the edge of the balcony, splashing into a pond with a bunch of Indian statues guarding it."

A month later they were coming out of the Mingan, heading for the valet, Eugene bitching like always. "I just don't understand why I can't hit the tables while you go do this sightseeing thing?

Because they didn't offer free fucking drinks, that's why. And had a twenty-dollar minimum. But what Tammy said was, "Oh shut up, not like ya ever come out ahead anyway." She saw the shuttles pull up. A whole gosh-dang fleet of 'em. "Thank that's us, lemme just double-check with this nice Indian fella."

She approached the Mexican in the valet jacket, said they were trying to get to Little Bighorn.

"Yes, ma'am," the valet said. "That shuttle right over there." He was pointing at a different shuttle. This one, a red double-decker, had a stream of people snaking in the door.

Tammy thanked the valet. Grabbed Eugene by the belt loop. "Let's go. Such nice people you know it? Even after all the shit they been through."

She found a spot near the center, giving Eugene an ear-full in front of the entire bus for jacking the window seat until the sumbitch got his fat ass up and let Tammy slide in.

As the bus drove through town, Tammy could see the bars on Main were jam packed. She saw a coffee shop, and a law office—some guy named Moffat. A slogan at the bottom of the signage claimed he was *South Dakota's Hammer*.

Tammy had her smartphone out, was snapping photos left and right. Taking candids of Eugene just to piss him off, only to spin it later on, show him what a sourpuss he was being.

They came to a roundabout, what the guide dubbed City Center. Traffic was swirling around a massive statue of some Indian riding horseback, pointing the way they were going, a bunch of feathers coming down off his head. The guide said it was Crazy Horse.

Which confused Tammy, so she raised a hand and asked the guy what the Indian's name was.

The town wasn't anything like she had ever seen in the Midwest. There was only one route in, a big green sign that said you are now entering something-something-something reservation. It had all new construction. Subdivisions, strip malls, restaurants, beautiful estates without fences or security gates. And everyone seemed to be hanging in their front yards, or out on the town having fun. The middle of the day all these people relaxing, no one working. A bunch of gosh-darn Indians living the good life.

They turned on a two-lane the guide said was Kenneth Way. He said that if you happen to look at an older map, you'll see it says they're on County Road 75, but that all changed two years ago when the southern section of the city was officially annexed back to the Yawakhan tribe.

The guide said, "Looking out to your right, you'll see the Black Hills. Once a spiritual and sacred place to the indigenous, it became a sight of major conflict after the imperialists settled and gold was discovered."

They looked no different than any other mountain, Tammy thought. And shoot, certainly more green than they were black. But what she wondered about was that gigantic pipeline going through the hills, painted hunter green like they tried to conceal it.

They passed several sets of bleachers out in the middle of a pasture. A podium on a stage faced the bleachers. Behind it was an open field with cannons on one side. The bus turned into a long driveway and passed under an overhang that read WELCOME TO on the top and LITTLE BIGHORN on the bottom.

The bus dropped them at the gift shop which was a small house with the same paint job as the other buildings on the spread. The gift shop though? It had fresh paint and newer siding.

Inside, the shelves were lined with what they called U.S. Cavalry and Yawakhan memorabilia. Tammy saw a burnt American flag in a shadowbox on the wall, a little of the blue and one star remaining in the corner.

Someone asked the guide about it and he said something about a guy named Custard, or something or another. Tammy didn't pay much attention. She moved on to a kiosk, with a picture of that guy Crazy Horse. She pushed an illuminated button and heard the movie-preview-guy's voice. "Hoka Hey, today is a good day to die, said Crazy Horse before leading two thousand men in a bloody victory over Lieutenant Colonel George Armstrong Custer…"

Tammy hadn't planned on buying anything until she saw the cute Crazy Horse bobblehead and thought it would look good standing guard on the dash of her Beetle. A lot more pleasant to look at than the one of the president Eugene had gotten her.

Sitting in the bleachers she took a few selfies, telling Eugene if he couldn't muster a smile, then get the hell out of frame, stop being such a Debbie Downer.

Then a brunette woman in a sharp pant suit stepped behind the podium. Tammy recognized her right away as that provocative senator that was in the news all the time. The fresh blood on Capitol Hill everyone fussed about. How she wouldn't follow any code, adhere to any party B-S. There was footage every day of her on those steps, the white dome in the background, the gal talking about fighting the good fight for the common man. All the news anchors could talk about was how she would win if she ever decided to run for president.

Tammy would vote for her.

Mainly because she looked like a badass chick that could run circles around all the men. Put her fine ass in office see what Saddam-bin-whatever in some shithole country had to say about that.

Shea. Shea McNally. That was her name. She had married

the vice president and then bam, just like that, was a junior senator making waves in the swamp.

There were a handful of Indians in slick suits sitting in chairs next to the podium. Tammy overheard someone in the audience talking about how they were the tribal leadership of the town.

After the handsome Indian in the sheriff's outfit introduced her, Shea McNally talked about how this place was a landmark, how important it was to transfer the land back to its rightful owners, the Yawakhan Nation, so they could flourish. She talked about her roots growing up here, and apologized for the sins of her ancestors, how much shame and guilt she harbored for being related to them. She talked about the impact the Yawakhan had on her as a young girl. And it's because of them why she continues to fight for the freedom of all the other tribes.

So well spoken, Tammy thought. What a rockstar.

Shea said, "And that's why it gives me great pleasure to unveil this historic landmark and museum in the new Shepard, South Dakota, on the very same day Bighorn was won. So without further ado, let the battle begin!"

Tammy clapped, totally invested, as the cannons went boom and an actor dressed like Crazy Horse moved over the ridge at full gallop on a grey gelding, an army of mounted Indians behind him.

And now the cavalry, the boys in blue were charging from the other direction. They fired blanks and yelled, "Kill them redskins! Kill 'em all!"

But Crazy Horse pressed on, fearless. He charged right through them, yelling "Hoka Hey" just like the kiosk.

And Tammy, she wasn't sure who she was rooting for,

though she could see herself leaning towards the Indians.

Shoot, maybe next year she'd just sack up, make it a girl's trip.

Harris pulled into the drive-thru, surprised the fly rods were still on the hood of his '72 Bronco FastTrac. The Weather Channel predicted the mercury would rise to the mid-eighties today, so Harris jerry-rigged a PVC with a cap and a hinge, mounted it to the truck and was coming down the 5 somewhere near West Blocton, 40 miles south of Birmingham, when his stomach started growling.

A young voice came through the speaker. "Mornin. Can I take ya orda?"

Harris, looking at all the pictures of the deep-fried goodness, said he wanted the griddled one with the maple syrup injected into the bun.

"Just the sanwich, or you wanna make it a meal?"

"Oh, what the heck, make it a meal."

The kid repeated the order before saying, "Which come to five dolla, forty-nine cent. Please pull around second winda."

Harris did, handing the money—exact change—to a twenty-something, his visor cocked sideways. The kid shoved the till shut, handed Harris a hot cup of coffee. "How many cream? How many suga?"

"I'm good."

The kid nodded, went to another register to take an eat-in order, simultaneously talking through his headset, telling the car behind Harris they didn't have any decaf at the moment, it would be a three minute wait. He then told the senior citizen on the other side of the counter to stick her chip in the slot before bouncing to the pick-up window, grabbing a sack and delivering it to Harris. "Thank ya, suh. Have a good day now."

Harris smiled, started to drive off when he saw a familiar face out of the corner of his eye. The Custer gal on the news, giving some speech in what looked like Spearfish. One of the ranches right there off County Road 75. Harris couldn't read the captions from this far, but when the camera cut to a closeup, he couldn't take his eyes off her, wondering if that brown hair was her natural color or if she dyed it. He stared until the car behind him honked and the kid in the visor asked would he pull forward.

Harris did. He grabbed his phone from the cup holder, dialed 411. The operator asked how she could direct his call.

"Rapid City Police Department."

The station dispatch answered. Harris asked for Detective Bates and they said he was out of the office, asking now if he would like to leave a message.

"This is Sheriff Weston Harris. Put me through to his cell. I gotta speak to him now."

It rang three times before Bates answered.

"Hey, this is Harris. You ever get any leads on that alleged prostitute found on the side of the road near Hisega?"

"The fuck are you talking about?" Bates said. "You got any idea what time it is?"

"Remember you sent that patrol officer to question a known pimp—"

"Yeah, why're you calling *me* about it?"

"Was it ever solved?"

"No."

"What about evidence? You get any fingerprints, DNA, anything from the scene?"

"Look man, it's fuckin two in the goddamn morning. Call me back at a normal time and I'll look into it."

Click.

Harris eased the Bronco into a space and ate the griddled sandwich in the restaurant because he knew there wouldn't be cell service once he was on the Cahaba. The sandwich wasn't as good as he hoped. It made his fingers swell.

At 10:30 his time, 8:30 Bates' time, he phoned the detective again. The mounted TV was still tuned to the news and a fresh set of anchors were playing the same footage from earlier.

Bates said, "We still got the crack pipe in evidence. Forensics identified three sets of fingerprints. Two of which we know who they belong to. And there was also a hair…"

"What kinda hair?"

"A single strand. Blonde."

"You test it?"

"Of course we did. Got a solid profile, but nothing in the system."

Harris sat there, the phone to his ear, looking at a brunette on screen, thinking she was a dead ringer for that Jane Doe on the side of the road.

About the Author

Brett Edwards is an actor and writer who has appeared in numerous films and television shows, including *American Sniper*, *The Longest Ride*, and *Narcos*. He has written and produced two screenplays that received awards at festivals around the country. Originally from Kentucky and now based in California, *Sacred Land* is his debut novel.

You can connect with me on:
🌐 https://www.sacredlandbook.com
f https://www.facebook.com/SacredLandNovel
✐ https://www.instagram.com/sacred_land_novel

Subscribe to my newsletter:
✉ https://www.sacredlandbook.com/contact

Also by Brett Edwards

Halfway There: A Short Comedy Series

See all 5 episodes on YouTube now!

Based on Brett Edwards' award-winning play, is about a struggling actor who is fired from a commercial and his agent in the same day, so he takes the ludicrous advice of his delusional, drug-abusing roommate before one last audition.

WINNER of the Silver-Remi Award (2018 WorldFest Houston)

NOMINATIONS

2018 North Hollywood Cinefest —Best Director (Madeline Puzzo) —Best Actor in a Short Film (Brett Edwards)

2017 Maverick Movie Awards —Best Lead Actor (Garikayi Mutambirwa) —Best Supporting Actor (Brett Edwards) —Best Director (Madeline Puzzo)

https://www.youtube.com/watch?v=oX2Bti1TAnw

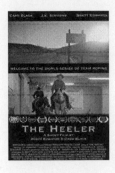

The Heeler: A Short Film

Ty Cooper is forced to find a new heeler when his partner (Academy Award Winner J.K. Simmons) is unable to compete in the world series of team roping.

WINNER of the 2014 Best Short Film at the Nevada International Film Festival

OFFICIAL SELECTION

2014 Sun Valley Film Festival, HollyShorts Film Festival, South Dakota Film Festival, Hill Country Film Festival

Streaming on YouTube now.